PARASITIC

An Apocalyptic-Horror Thriller

M.L. Banner

Toes in the Water Publishing, LLC

ISBN: 9781947510043 (eBook)

Version 1.04, May 2022

ISBN: 978-1-947510-04-3 (Paperback)

Version 1.03, March 2019

PARASITIC is an original work of fiction.

The characters and dialogs are the products of this author's vivid imagination.

Much of the science and the historical incidents described in this novel are based on reality, as are its warnings.

Prologue

Fifteen Years Ago

The dog came from out of nowhere, completely silent, rather than the usual vicious pooch announcing its terror long before it reached you. It crashed into her right side like a freight train. She only heard the briefest sound of the monster gulping one last bit of air before it struck.

When she hit the ground, she heard the animal grunt from their impact and then growl as it attempted to get a better grip on her side, so that it could set itself to ripping her flesh.

If she had any time to think about her situation, she would have probably panicked. This was where her training kicked in. Her gun was already unholstered, and so she quickly fired off a shot. But it was from the same side as the mutt. She missed. Quickly, she switched hands and shot once more from her left.

A long moment of quiet passed. Not more than maybe twenty heartbeats.

They both lay in a heap, but only she was panting.

Upon quick inspection, she concluded this was not your back-yard, shit-bird variety of pit bull; this was a pure-bred Vizsla: slick, muscular, and very powerful. The Bureau already knew that the dog's owner had bought a half-dozen over the years from a breeder in Jackson, about ten miles south.

Of course it never occurred to her superiors in the FBI, who put together this raid, that the dogs might be a threat, only their owner.

Well, they screwed the pooch on that one, she thought.

"Sitrep, people," blared her earpiece.

"Taggert here... Wren here... Anderson here..."

With some effort, TJ pushed herself onto her knees. She lifted her mangled shirt edge to inspect the wound. It looked pretty bad.

"Sitrep, Williams."

Her black FBI jacket came off—*damned thing was too hot anyway.* She pulled off her shirt with a grunt and groan, thankful she was wearing her sports bra and not one of the frilly Victoria's Secret-things Ted bought her. Folding it lengthwise until it was a long, thick strip of fabric, she wrapped it around her side, making sure both ends of the wound were covered enough. Holding the ends of the jacket arms, she spun it around, turning it into a cord, with most of it bunching up the middle. It too was placed over the wounded area. Finally, she tied the jacket's arms tight around her other side, cinching it down to hold the field dressing, and hopefully stem the flow of blood.

It would have to do until this was done.

"Williams, report," her earpiece hollered at her again.

"Williams here. Damned dog frickin' bit the shit out of me. Had to shoot it. I'm good to go. 10-76."

"Roger."

She should have called in 10-52, Ambulance Needed. But then she'd have to walk ten times as far back to their mobile base, and she really wanted to get this sonofabitch, especially after now learning he was training vicious dogs.

She drew her weapon again; it had been holstered while she'd rendered herself aid.

Each step forward elicited a painful grunt, and she could feel a warm trickle of blood drip down her backside.

Worse yet, she felt a building anxiety, giving way to a constant need to check her twenty for another crazed animal.

The ranch house was only a hundred yards away, and no doubt their perp would be looking out his window in her direction. So she had to approach it covertly, which was damned hard to do without much natural cover. With any luck, he'd think her gunshots were from a hunter, illegally shooting on the Yellowstone National Reserve property, contiguous to his. He had often called in complaints to Game and Fish about this.

The worst case scenario would be the guy coming out, guns blazing, and then they'd have another Waco on their hands. And that they did not want. The guy may have been a murderer, but they didn't want his dozen-member family hurt too. They were the reason TJ had to keep going.

It was because the kids hadn't been seen for several weeks, and all of them missed the first two weeks of the fall semester that a couple of deputies from the Jackson Sheriff Department were dispatched to check on the family. Upon arriving on the scene, there was a single panicked radio broadcast from one deputy. The dispatcher claimed the caller said only, "He's crazy." Nothing more. An hour later, the FBI stepped in as they were not coincidentally investigating two missing hikers from Prague, who were last seen wandering in the same direction as TJ was now.

She stopped to regain her breath, and to readjust her field-dressing, which was already coming loose. She was sweating like it was ninety out, when it wasn't much more than sixty. She pressed her palm to her bicep. Her skin felt cool. Do not go into shock, she told herself. As if one could coax oneself into not doing so.

She cinched her jacket-pressure-bandage even tighter, moaning at the pain, while she trudged forward the last few steps.

The moaning continued, but this time it wasn't her.

"This is Williams," she whispered. "I'm at the southwest corner of the corral fence-line, about fifteen yards from the home. I'm hearing some sort of... moaning. Going to investigate."

"Hold up Williams. Wait for your team."

The rest of her advance team reported in, but much farther away. She would be there long before the others, which meant no backup. Yet, if the moaning was from an injured family member or the hikers, waiting longer might end up killing one of them. To buttress her argument for moving forward, she was feeling queasy. It occurred to her, she'd have to finish this pretty quickly, before she passed out. The last thing she wanted to do is blow the whole operation passing out before they got 'em. She'd rather accept a verbal tongue lashing, if it meant they could catch this SOB.

Maybe I could claim delirium from the dog bite. It wasn't too far off, she thought.

She'd press forward, moving along the back fence line.

Within a minute, she heard the moaning sound again, only it was more of a groaning. It was coming from the dark opening of the barn, diagonally across from the corral.

TJ slipped in between the rough slats of the split-rail fence and yelped when she saw where she stepped. She thought for a moment it was another dog. But it wasn't.

Below her foot and against the fence lay a dead horse. Practically gutted. A dark stain circled the carcass; the blood had mostly seeped into the corral's soft dirt. There were multiple small round puncture wounds and deep gashes in its throat and sides, like it had been mauled by a wild animal.

Her head pivoted, searching around her twenty for the wild animal that did this. Her breathing accelerated, to the point of hyperventilating. The perp had more dogs. What if they were just as vicious as the one that attacked her? She felt a chill shoot across her spine.

TJ bent over to catch her breath. It was either the blood loss or her hyperventilating or both: her dizziness turned to double vision. At any moment, she felt certain she'd either panic or pass out. Touching the lower edge of the bunched-up shirt against her side, her fingers came away very wet and dark red. She was losing too much blood. She needed to call it. Losing any more blood, she'd surely lose consciousness, maybe even die.

A low growl, like a dull echo, pulled at her. Her head drew up, attempting to find the sound, and she instantly saw it.

Or rather him.

Their perp, Jim Tanner. Father of ten. Multi-millionaire, ranch owner. Perhaps even mass-murderer. Was the one growling. And running.

He was running toward her. In his hand, he brandished a metal rod, like a piece of rebar.

"Subject is running toward me, yelling," she warbled over their comms.

More like screeching, at her. He sounded and looked like some crazed wild animal. An insane thought hit her: maybe their perp, and not one of his dogs, mauled the horse.

"Mr. Tanner. FBI. Freeze!" she demanded, but it came out a weak croak. She raised her Glock 29. He was sighted in, with only the slightest of twitching. Good thing, there were at least two of him coming at her.

He kept coming, only faster.

"Mr. Tanner, I'll shoot you," she hollered. Her own voice sounded distant, like it was someone else's.

TJ dropped to her knee, not just to keep her gun hand steady: she was seeing three of everything now.

"Stop!"

He didn't.

She fired. Three times. One for each of him.

Then she tumbled to the ground, her strength leaving her.

"Subject down. Officer needs assistance," she whispered over her comms, and then passed out.

Present Day

Even though this incident had long since been paved over by years of other forgotten memories, the abject fear of attacking animals born from it clung to TJ's daily consciousness.

Only now did she consider that moment. Not for what she would have done differently, but for one important detail about that crazed dog, and equally crazed man. It only occurred to her on this day that the man they were going to try to arrest, the man she ended up shooting and killing, had one physical attribute that she had completely forgotten, until now.

Yet when the memory burst into her head like the pain she often felt from the physical scars to her right side, she knew it was important.

His eyes were blood red. Just like the animals they were seeing today.

Part II

PARASITIC

"He who fights with monsters should be careful lest he thereby become a monster."
Friedrich W. Nietzsche

DAY FIVE Cont...

... THE DAY I LOST MY WIFE.

THERE WAS SO MUCH WE DIDN'T UNDERSTAND AT THAT MOMENT.

FOR INSTANCE, IT WASN'T JUST THE ANIMALS WHO WENT CRAZY. THIS POINT SHOULD HAVE BEEN OBVIOUS TO ALL OF US. BUT BY THE TIME WE FIGURED IT OUT, IT WAS TOO LATE.

EVEN AS WE STARTED TO RELAX, OUR ONLY CONCERNS WERE FOR THE ANIMAL ATTACKS. AND THOSE, WE THOUGHT—IT WAS MORE LIKE HOPE—WERE POTENTIALLY EBBING. THAT'S WHEN PROVERBIAL HELL BROKE LOOSE ON OUR SHIP.

TJ AND I WERE BEING UPDATED BY THE SHIP'S STAFF CAPTAIN, JEAN PIERRE. THE INTREPID DID IN FACT HAVE SATELLITE. THEY HAD TOLD GUESTS OTHERWISE TO KEEP THEM IN THE DARK, SO THEY WOULDN'T PANIC—LIKE WE WERE DOING WHEN WE HEARD THE REST. THEY HAD BEEN MONITORING THE GLOBAL NEWS NETWORKS. IT WAS BAD: EUROPE AND PARTS OF ASIA HAD DEVOLVED INTO CHAOS, AND ANIMAL ATTACKS WERE SPREADING LIKE WILDFIRE OVER EVERY CONTINENT, EVEN IN NORTH AMERICA.

WE HAD WITNESSED SOME OF THIS FIRSTHAND ON OUR TRANSATLANTIC CRUISE: FIRST, AT MADRID, IT WAS A RABID-LIKE DOG; THEN, AT MALAGA, IT WAS THE BIRDS, FOLLOWED BY THE RATS; THEN, AT GIBRALTAR, THE MONKEYS; AND FINALLY, THE DOGS, BROUGHT ON BOARD BY SOME WELL-HEELED PASSENGERS, HAD GONE CRAZY TOO. ALL WERE SYMPTOMATIC: BLOOD-RED IRISES AND MOST HAD AN ABSOLUTE DESIRE TO KILL, EVEN WHEN MORTALLY INJURED. UNTIL THEN, WE HAD THOUGHT THE TROUBLE, LIKE THE VOLCANIC ERUPTIONS, HAD RUN ITS COURSE AND WOULD BE EVENTUALLY OVER. BUT THIS WAS BASED ON INCOMPLETE INFORMATION.

THE PET SPA'S VET FOUND HIS WILD BOARDERS AFTER THEY HAD GOTTEN LOOSE AND BELIEVED THEY WERE NO LONGER AGGRESSIVE. AND WHEN I RAN ACROSS A RED-EYED FERRET OUTSIDE OUR ROOM—THEY SUSPECTED IT WAS BROUGHT ON BOARD BY ONE OF THEIR CREW—IT WAS ALSO NOT AGGRESSIVE. BECAUSE OF THESE EXAMPLES, WE ALL HAD ASSUMED THAT THE AGGRESSIVE TRAITS OF THIS DISEASE WOULD PASS. WE DIDN'T KNOW BEING SYMPTOMATIC DIDN'T AUTOMATICALLY MEAN AGGRESSIVE IN EVERY CASE.

AND HELL, THROW IN A MONSTROUS ONE-HUNDRED-FIFTY-FOOT TSUNAMI IN THE MIDDLE OF ALL OF THIS, JUST TO DIVERT OUR ATTENTION FROM THE REAL PROBLEM. AND WHEN THE SUN PEEKED THROUGH THE VOLCANIC CLOUDS, WE WERE ALL READY TO FORGET THIS, AS WE WOULD WITH ANY BAD DREAM. BUT THAT WAS OUR NORMALCY BIAS... AND OUR IGNORANCE.

IT WAS THEN THAT THE BOOM WAS DROPPED ON US BY JEAN PIERRE.

MY WIFE TJ WAS PROBABLY THE TOUGHEST WOMAN I'D EVER MET, AND YET SHE WAS ABSOLUTELY PARALYZED BY A FEAR OF BEING ATTACKED BY AN ANIMAL. IT WAS UNDERSTANDABLE WHEN HER HEAD DROPPED DOWN IN

ANGUISH, AND A WELLSPRING OF TEARS FLOWED FROM HER FACE.

I TOO FELT GUT-SHOT. I HAD FEARED THIS VERY THING FROM THE MOMENT THE FIRST SIGNS OF THIS RAGE DISEASE (AS THE MEDIA WAS CALLING IT) SPRANG UP. AFTER ALL, I WROTE A DAMNED BOOK ABOUT SOME VERSION OF THIS MADNESS. OF COURSE, I HAD WRITTEN ABOUT MANY POTENTIAL APOCALYPTIC EVENTS. I NEVER REALLY EXPECTED ANY OF THEM TO COME TRUE. THIS ONE APPEARED TO BE WORSE THAN EVEN I HAD ENVISIONED: IT WASN'T TERRORISTS OR ANARCHISTS WHO HAD WEAPONIZED THE T-GONDII PARASITE, WHICH ALREADY INFECTED MOST MAMMALS AND REPROGRAMMED THEIR BEHAVIOR AGAINST US; IT WAS SOME BACTERIA FROM VOLCANOES THAT IGNITED THE T-GONDII PUPPET-MASTER TO PULL THE STRINGS OF ITS MAMMAL HOSTS AND SET THEM AGAINST US, EN MASSE.

AND AS BAD AS IT APPEARED IT WAS GOING TO GET, WITH MAMMALS OF EVERY STRIPE ATTACKING HUMANS EVERYWHERE, WE HAD NO IDEA THAT IT WAS ABOUT TO GET SO MUCH WORSE.

YOU SEE, IT WASN'T JUST THE ANIMALS, IT WAS THE HUMANS TOO.

THE REPORTS OF HUMAN ATTACKS SO FAR WERE INFREQUENT AND BLENDED IN WITH THE OTHER CHAOTIC STORIES AND WERE NOT RECOGNIZED AS A SIGN OF THE GREATER PROBLEM. AT THIS POINT, THE WORLD WAS RUNNING FOR THEIR LIVES FROM THE ANIMALS AND NATURAL DISASTERS, AND SO FEW HAD TIME TO ANALYZE THE DISEASE'S PROGRESSION LEADING TO ITS ULTIMATE HOSTS: HUMANS.

BY THEN, IT WAS TOO LATE.

OUR SHIP WAS IN FACT A PERFECT MICROCOSM OF THE T-GONDII'S EVOLUTIONARY PROGRESSION: FIRST ANIMALS WITH HIGHER BODY TEMPERATURES, THEN DOWN THE BODILY TEMPERATURE-SCALE, UNTIL FINALLY HUMANS WERE

AFFECTED. BUT WE DIDN'T KNOW ANY OF THAT YET. AND I'M GETTING WAY AHEAD OF MYSELF.

THE DAY THAT EVERYTHING FELL APART, THIS DAY IN FACT, STARTED WITH JEAN PIERRE'S SIGHTING OF A CLOUD OF BLACK BIRDS THAT WERE HEADED OUR WAY.

01

The Birds

It was like a gut punch.

TJ Williams had doubled over, grabbing her side right where the dog had gotten her years earlier. It almost felt like the dog had hit her full force once again, pushing all the air from her lungs.

But it wasn't the dog.

It was the piece of a missing memory. Something she had forgotten entirely. Until then.

Those damned red eyes!

"Are you alright, Hon?" Her husband Ted asked. He clasped a comforting hand onto her back and bent down beside her, no doubt thinking she was not dealing well with the future prospect of unending animal attacks. He wasn't altogether wrong.

She rose up and Ted matched her movements. His eyes poured out deep concern for her. She so wanted to alleviate his anxiety; to tell him "Yes, I'm fine." But she wasn't fine.

Her fingers reflexively brushed over her necklace. It was something she found herself doing constantly, even though she'd just received this anniversary gift from him. It was representative of his view of her, and in fact what she wanted to be: a fearless warrior. But that wasn't her at all. She was plagued with fear. And it was all because of that day.

Those dark images from the past, the ones she had been hiding from, all at once flooded her mind. That horrific moment in her life that had shaped her; that had molded her into the weak person she had become, so that now she practically hid from her own shadow.

Because of the pain that moment caused, she had long since repressed those images and their accompanying feelings of terror. Yet the terror always remained.

And somehow she'd forgotten that the dog's eyes were the color of blood?

And yet, as troubling as that was, it wasn't the gut punch. That came the moment Jean Pierre mentioned "people": that was when she remembered the man that she shot, the one who was about to attack her.

He had had red eyes too.

"As I was saying," Jean Pierre's voice had boomed over the stiff headwind which was whipping through the swing deck where the three of them had been standing. He had paused to get a better look at a black cloud off their starboard bow, getting closer. "It's spreading everywhere, to animals of every stripe—especially dog populations... and people..."

It was his people comment that was the key that unlocked the red-eye memory she'd buried.

She blinked back the pain to see Jean Pierre had pulled his binoculars away from his head to examine them, as if there was something wrong the eyepiece, or his own sight.

After a very long pause, he finished his thought, "...and people are getting attacked in larger numbers."

He paused again.

TJ's mind was a jumble. While Jean Pierre focused on the fast-approaching cloud, TJ thought more about what he actually said, not what she thought he was going to say.

Jean Pierre had kept his back to them the whole time while he peered through his binoculars at the building black cloud, delivering the bad news in large doses. He had told them that they'd been hopeful that the animal attacks had run their course, as their firsthand experience had demonstrated. But the reports coming from the outside world pointed to an escalation, not a cessation.

During this elongated break from Jean Pierre's delivery, TJ had looked past him to regard the growing cloud coming their way fast—anything to avoid considering what she remembered.

Far from a normal formation, it was in stark contrast to the blue sky, and it appeared headed right for their ship, almost course-correcting for their own movements.

Her anxiety burned in her gut, until it turned into fear.

"Now we've lost all communications with Gibraltar. We can only assume that... Oh merde!"

He lowered his binoculars and flashed a glance at them, his face and bald head paler than normal. Then he burst from his stance and dashed past them. In one motion, he opened the hatch and then leapt from the swing deck into the bridge.

TJ couldn't tell yet what he saw, not wearing her glasses, and so she glanced at Ted to confirm he couldn't either. But they could both guess. And with the same abruptness, they moved fast to the hatch opening, just as Jean Pierre made his announcement to the bridge crew.

"Attention everyone," the staff captain bellowed. "There is a giant flock of black birds headed right for our ship. I've been watching them the last few kilometers. My guess is they're coming from Funchal, Madeira. Sound the alarm. We need to warn the ship."

All but two of the crew moved toward the port side windows of the bridge to see for themselves.

Safety Officer Ágúst Helguson didn't hesitate after receiving the order from his superior. He turned aft and punched a big red button on the control panel behind him, which took up a large portion of the aft bridge wall. A light flashed on the panel and on all their functioning console screens, pulsing in sync with deafening horn blasts which began blaring outside and around the ship.

Officer of the Deck Jessica Mínervudóttir also remained at her post, eyes carefully monitoring the periphery of the ship from the bridge windows and the EDISC software on her console.

All of them waited for their staff captain's next command.

TJ glanced behind her, momentarily forgetting she was still outside. She moved quickly inside the bridge, not wanting anything to do with the crazy birds, which were now almost upon them. Ted held up momentarily, half in and half out of the swing-deck hatch, to gawk at the massive cloud of black dots descending from above. He stepped inside, pulling the hatch closed behind him, cutting off the piercing horn-sound from the bridge.

"Thank you," Jean Pierre said to him.

"What should I announce to the crew and guests?" Ágúst asked. He wasn't sure what to tell them, other than stating the obvious.

"Tell them to get inside ASAP."

Ágúst was already poised in front of the ship's intercom system microphone. He punched the transmit button. There was a crackle and squeak coming from the bridge's speakers. Ted imagined it was similar ship-wide, on all the public and cabin speakers outside of the bridge.

All heads turned to face the oncoming birds, now everywhere outside their port-side windows.

In anticipation of the question, Jean Pierre spoke in a hushed tone to Ted and TJ, "The general alarm stops when there is something transmitted over the ship's PA system."

"Attention! Attention, guests and crew. There is a large flock of black birds coming from our port side. We believe they are aggressive. Please move indoors quickly. You will be safe inside the ship. Attention. Please move inside the ship immediately. You are in danger outside." He let go of the transmit button and the horn blared again, everywhere except on the bridge, its head-hammering tone repeating over and over again.

The first wave of birds hit, just outside the bridge windows, pile-driving themselves into the outside speakers.

Deputy Security Officer Wasano Agarwal lifted his portable radio to his lips and called inaudibly to his security guards to get out to all the sun decks and make sure the guests were helped off the decks to safety.

Jean Pierre tapped away at his console screen, adeptly pulling up the camera views from several of the outside cameras focused on the Sun Deck one deck above them. Jessica did the same for hers and the other two functioning consoles. All the bridge crew, Ted and TJ turned their attention to the screens.

They all watched in horror.

At least two hundred guests were milling about in and around the pool and Jacuzzis. Many of them had wandered to the ship's port railings, presumably to get a better look at the birds, even before the announcement. Only a few were moving to the exits. None were moving fast. Some even appeared to be not moving at all. A few looked like they were vomiting.

"Can't they hear the alarm? Why the hell aren't they moving?" TJ whined.

Then almost everybody did.

They'd crowded around the consoles, each displaying four different views of the sun deck, but with little clarity. From the cameras' perspectives, it was just billowing plumes of black descending upon the entire ship. Each of them looked up at the bridge's windows to confirm what their screens were showing: the entire ship was enveloped by clouds of black birds. Some were pelting the ship, just outside of their view, their soft thuds unheard.

The open decks of the ship looked like an ant city that had been sprayed with pesticide: rapid movements, erratic convulsions, general panic, and even death.

They all gasped.

A large swath of the guests and crew were headed to the forward exits, but there were bottle-necks at each doorway. Hands swatted at birds; splashes of red were either seen or imagined—it was hard to tell.

"They're getting murdered out there," Ted yelled. He broke for the bridge exit.

"Ted," TJ yelped. "Where are you going?"

"I can't just stand here and watch." He opened the lone bridge exit.

"Sir?" Wasano pleaded to Jean Pierre.

"Yes, of course. Yes, we need to go. But OOD Jessica and SD Ágúst, you both need to remain on the bridge. We'll be in contact by radio.

"Aye, sir," Jessica snapped. Ágúst nodded, and then transmitted the announcement again, even though it felt superfluous now.

On the way out, Jean Pierre grabbed a radio for himself, and handed two more out to TJ and Second Officer Urban. "In case any of us get separated." He saw that Ted still had his. "Ted and TJ, we'll go aft, to the mid-ship Sun Deck exits. Wasano and Urban, update the captain—in case he hasn't heard the alarm in 8000—then head up to the forward Sun Deck exits."

"Aye, sir," Wasano and Urban responded in unison.

Jean Pierre and the Williams bounded out of the bridge and made their way aft through the Deck Eight port-side hallway.

Wasano and Urban followed behind them, stopping just off the bridge entrance, and pounded on cabin 8000's door. Urban closed the bridge exit, safely sealing the two lone officers inside.

"SD Ágúst?" Jessica called out, "Check your monitor... the mid-ship one, looking aft. Ahh, camera nine-fifteen."

"What am I looking fo..." Ágúst gasped. "I'm... Am I seeing this correctly?"

"I think so."

02

8000

Jörgen had pulled the edge of his hat forward so as to block out the remainder of the cabin's light from his closed eyes. But he'd been unsuccessful in his attempts to find sleep.

First he'd tried picturing the image hanging on the wall of his quarters: his wife Katrin beside him, their three fully-grown kids in front of them, and their four grandkids seated in front of them. When this didn't work, he'd tried to picture where Katrin and he would travel after his retirement next year. With the kids out of their home and no other responsibilities, they'd spoken endlessly about their plans to see so many new places; or take the time he'd never had to visit family and friends near their home in Lyngor, Norway; or to simply watch time slip by while sipping Udfa coffee with Katrin.

Yet with each tick of his watch, he had felt increasingly sure those dreams would never come. And neither would sleep.

Then his attention fell on the meeting he'd concluded moments ago. He had put off the conversation for as long as he could—or as Jean Pierre told him, he should stop beating around the tree: it was obvious that the outside world was devolving further into chaos and not likely getting better as they all had hoped. So he knew he had to tell his crew, starting with his number one, Jean Pierre, and then his first officers and many of his second officers. They all took the news as well as could be expected.

After it was done, and he had found himself alone in this suite, knowing Jean Pierre had the bridge, Jörgen figured this was his best chance to at least rest his frayed nerves, even if sleep wouldn't come.

That's when he contemplated several contradictions from the meeting: what his crew had reported with what Ted had told him about the red-eyed ferret and the airborne manifestations of the so-called Rage disease.

"It appears that many of the reported cases of illness are from food poisoning," Dr. Chettle told the group in his usual measured voice, while referring to the notes on his tablet. "We've had sixty-eight reported cases of this; some are in the temporary infirmary we set up on deck one. I suspect three times as many guests and a number of crew have been afflicted with some form of amoebic dysentery."

"How the hell did this happen?" Captain Jörgen demanded.

"Our new chef said he believes it was some dirty water that contaminated last night's dinner salads. He said it was a combination of being short-staffed, a few errors by newer staff, and, I quote 'a ferret that somehow got into the kitchen.'" Dr. Chettle lowered his tablet and scowled at their ship's vet and pet spa director, as if he were the cause of this embarrassing episode.

Jörgen glared his own discontent at his ship's sole doctor. He was angry about the doctor's feud with the vet as well as the food poisoning. But these were small concerns that he'd save for another day. His focus was on keeping his guests and crew healthy now, until they could figure out what to do when they arrived in the Bahamas in a few days. "Anything else we can do to mitigate this?"

"Other than the typical good hygiene—you know, washing hands—there's not a damned thing we can do but wait until this passes. The damage has been done. The good news is that it does not appear to be very serious, although it feels like it to everyone who's sick from it, and it's not contagious." Chettle usually preferred to overstate these kinds of things, sure that everyone he spoke to, including Jörgen, was clueless when it came to diseases. The doctor often grew short when answering similar questions again. So it was obvious the man was glad to have the floor in front of a larger audience.

"Well that is good. The last thing we need, after all that's happened, is another Legionnaire's Disease outbreak." Captain Jörgen consulted the next item on the checklist from his own tablet. "What about those in isolation from the dog bites?"

Chettle's attention was now drawn to two of the officers at their meeting, who looked ill, probably considering whether they needed to go to the infirmary.

"Doc?" the captain prodded.

"Sorry, sir. We had five crew members, including our vet Al..." Chettle paused to shoot another dismissive glower at Al—Jörgen had heard the doc didn't like Al because the man cleaned up after pets—before returning his attention to the captain. "...and four guests, who reported dog or rat bites. All but Al here and one guest remain in isolation. The guest refused. None of them show any symptoms similar to the animals, and other than mild infections and slight elevation in temperatures, they look fine."

"So," Jörgen now looked at Pet Spa Director Al, "was the Rage disease transmitted from one dog to the other by their bites?"

"That's our best guess, sir," Al answered. "We just don't have any way to test this. But our evidence is that one or more rats bit a toy poodle, who was already somewhat aggressive. Then the poodle turned rabid-like and bit the other dogs. Those dogs later became aggressive. It would seem that it is then spread by bodily fluids."

This was contrary to Ted's theory that it was something in the air.

"How long from bite to becoming aggressive?"

"The dogs appeared to become symptomatic within an hour or two after being bit."

"And what's the status with the dogs now?"

"They're still quarantined in the Pet Spa. And they're heavily sedated, so that I can continue to observe and run tests."

Chettle jumped in, obviously disliking Al taking over the floor from him. "If what Al says is correct, I'd suggest we release all our patients from isolation."

"That's fine, Doc. You have my approval."

Jörgen knew the next item, without looking again at his tablet. *Just give it to them. They can handle it,* he thought.

"The main reason why you, my top officers, are here is to tell you some bad news...The world as we all know it is changing for the worse. This Rage disease, as the media is calling it, is spreading like wildfire. In many of the main cities of Western Europe, and all of our prospective ports, and even our US home port in Florida, there are rampant animal attacks being reported. Many basic services have been disrupted. In other words, it is simply not safe for us to go ashore any time soon.

"We are not telling our passengers or any other crew about the outside world. Our hope is that this improves by the time we reach the Bahamas. Assuming it's safe, we'll port, resupply and then decide where we go from there.

"I need each of you, my most trusted officers, to work on keeping everyone's spirits high and to focus on the safety of our passengers and your fellow crew on board. Really, this is the safest place we could be at this time.

"We will continue to monitor the situation, and if anything changes, I'll report back to each of you.

"Remember, what's going on outside this ship is to be kept quiet. I don't even want you discussing it among yourselves, because I don't want others to become unnecessarily alarmed and increase their anxiety among everyone else, including our passengers. So mum's the word, and let's go take care of our passengers and continue to keep them feeling safe and comfortable.

"Do any of you have..."

The horn blared and Jörgen sprang from his seat, his captain's cap falling off in the process.

This was the general alarm. *What the hell is going on now?*

There was deep pounding on the door, followed by the high-pitched chime of the suite's doorbell.

A moment later, it clicked open, both Wasano and Urban bounding through. The horn, located just outside in the hallway, now blared so loudly it was almost impossible to hear anything else.

Wasano let go of the door, so that it clasped shut. "Sorry to interrupt sir, but—"

"—Why the alarm?" Captain Jörgen asked as he marched in their direction.

"A swarm of birds are attacking the passengers on our Sun Deck. We're trying to get everyone inside. The staff captain and the Williamses went aft to assist guests at the Solarium exits. The deck officer and I were headed to the forward exits."

Captain Jörgen pulled open the door again and yelled into the blare of the horn, "Let's go then."

They rushed the short way down the hallway, turned left into the hallway and immediately hit a wall of people..

03

Sun Deck

Most of the guests saw the birds before they heard them, pointing at the odd cloud formation and articulating their puzzlement: "What is that?" "Is that a cloud?" "Are those birds?" More fingers pointed and more bellies found the edge of the port-side railing on the pool-side Sun Deck and the open deck 10, above them. They all spoke in hushed tones, curious but not frightened. Not yet.

Not one guest, whether sucking on a zombie, basking in the sun, or sharing war stories about the previous night's tsunami, even considered asking the question that needed to be asked: Were these birds coming their way a threat? And yet, every guest had heard about or witnessed attacking birds firsthand.

Those guests and crew who bothered to take notice of the swarm of birds headed right at them still chose naive ambivalence over learned logic. And many were about to pay a stiff price for their chosen ignorance.

Even when it became obvious that the frenzied flock of birds was about to descend upon them, their reactions—trained from years of normalcy—were more of shock or surprise than of fear.

It was only when the birds struck that full-out panic gripped the majority of the Sun Deck's passengers and crew members.

Frau Wankmüller's reaction was similar to most. She marveled at what she first thought was a hail storm, though she had never seen hail stones as large or black as these before. She watched them violently collide with deck chairs, loungers, railings, and people. When the dark hail squawked and screeched, she still held firm to her lounger, not wanting to mess up the pleasant buzz she felt from the uncountable number of rum drinks she'd consumed. She only reacted to the bird melee after one buried itself into her leg. At first she was jolted by the impact, but immediately discounted the attack to her fuzzy vision playing tricks on her brain. And when the offending fowl yanked out something that looked vitally important to her wellbeing from the newly formed bloody hole in her appendage; that's when she finally screamed.

Besides now flailing, the only other resistance her addled brain could come up with was to toss her empty drink glass at it. Missing the bird completely, the decorative glass connected with and shattered off of the elbow of a fellow passenger who was busy battling beasts of his own on the deck flooring in front of her. Before Frau Wankmüller could scream again, she was knocked out cold, when another bird hit her in the back of the head with such force that it broke its own neck against hers. She flopped forward and then back into her lounger unconscious. Now that her body was still, it was too much for other nearby birds to resist. Within seconds, a mass of black was feasting on the soft flesh of her eyes, neck, and stomach.

Like several passengers, her daughter hid underneath the lounger beside her, gazing wildly at the birds as they made a meal out of her mother above her.

The blaring ship horns only made matters worse, as no one could hear anything above them or the pandemonium topside.

Only the birds seemed to give the horns any notice, as dozens pelted them like kamikazes giving their lives for some greater bird cause.

A few passengers had the good sense to attempt to make a run for one of the entrances inside the ship. Those close to the entryways were also being coaxed inside by crew members and fellow passengers. But just like when a plane crashes or a ship is sinking, most passengers blindly ran forward, rather than first looking to find the best route. Illogic born from panic drove most folks forward to a cluster that had collected before the entrances, where many had stumbled or stopped to fight off their attackers.

Inside, large crowds had developed behind the forward stairwell entrances and the deck-to-ceiling glass walls surrounding it and the Windjammer cafe on both sides. With the first wave of the bird attack, before those outside thought to find safety inside, those already inside seemed to understand that it was not good to let the birds in, so they had shut the big sliding doors. Even the crew members, whose job it was to open doors for passengers who needed the help, were pushed aside by those who sealed the openings and resisted every attempt to open them back up. When the occasional bird bounced off one of the glass panes, those closest yelped in surprise and tried to step back, but instead were pushed more forward by the growing swell of gawkers behind them.

The crowd inside stood gaping at the onslaught outside, feeling safe behind the glass enclosures.

With each passing second the hordes of people inside grew, fed by more passengers streaming from upper and lower decks. Most were coming to the Sun Deck to catch some sun or get some food at the cafe, oblivious to any problems until the general alarm sounded. Now they collected en masse and gawked.

Crew members from inside the ship attempted to get outside and help. But they couldn't get by the swelling crowds, protected by the closed doors. And instead of being fearful, they pushed and shoved forward to the glass to take in the amazing spectacle outside.

As the assemblages collected and grew, the swell pressed against those up front, restricting their movements and making it impossible for anyone outside to come in, even if the doors were open. Passengers outside pleaded with those inside to let them in.

Even with what was going on outside, those inside felt protected by the heavy glass keeping them separated from the onslaught.

A screaming bikini-clad woman came out of nowhere, as if she just materialized from the darkening murk outside. She banged hard into the port-side window-wall. Several of the crowd collected behind the window shrieked and then screamed when they saw the woman was covered in an undulating mass of black, pecking away at her face and exposed body parts, now raw and bleeding.

Other outside passengers followed, some covered with birds, others not. All banged on the doors and windows, demanding entry. But the crowds behind the glass walls held firm, unable to move away from the horror.

Holding back the mad birds from the mid-ship stairwell was a two-story observation glass wall. Before the tsunami, its floor-to-ceiling windows bathed the stairwell in light. Now, a large eight-foot-wide by ten-foot-high section, broken from the tsunami wave, was filled with thin plywood, a temporary fix this morning by the crew, with the intent of replacing the broken windows either in Nassau (if they were available) or more likely upon return to their home port in Miami. Other than restricting the passengers' view out, they would have been solid enough for the occasional children's hand or gust of wind. They were certainly not intended to hold back panicked passengers.

Because none of the inside gawkers could see through the plywood paneling, there were only a few behind it and therefore nothing to buttress the thin material against the immense pressure being brought to it from the other side. Outside, a mad crush of passengers, insane with fear, intuitively sensed the wood wall's weakness. They beat and pushed against it. When their force was far more than the temporary wall could hold, it shattered inward. With a way inside, the outside mass of people poured in. And so did many of the black birds.

The inside crowd joined in the panic, now pushing the other way. They flooded the stairwells, the elevators, and the restaurant entrances. All attempted to get away from the oncoming threats.

Passengers trampled fellow passengers, while the inside din of screaming grew to such ear-splitting loudness, it surpassed the decibel levels of the ship's blaring horns. All of this noise and movement attracted still more birds inside.

At some point during the rampage of birds, something changed. Amongst the panicked crowds many passengers and a few crew members started attacking each other.

04

Boris

Before the Sun Deck's insanity started, Boris Thompson and his wife Penny did mostly what they were told: they soaked up the sunshine by the pool. The captain had directed them and everyone else on the ship to do this in his morning address. Yet the ship's doctor told Boris to remain in the infirmary because of the dog bites he'd received. Supposedly, they wanted to "observe" him. Choosing which command he'd follow was easy: he wasn't about to miss the first sunny day of the cruise. Besides, as far as Boris was concerned, a ship's captain had a higher rank than the ship's doctor, who had earlier annoyed Boris with comments about his weight and abnormally low body temperature.

Each time he thought of the doctor and that damned little dog, he reflexively scratched around one of the six bandages covering his "superficial wounds" made by the insane dog. He felt lucky not to have been hurt worse and was still pissed at the doctor for not believing that it was a toy poodle. If he were making it up, he'd have said it was a Great Dane or a German Shepherd, something much more macho than a blooming poodle. Still, thoughts of the attack terrified him.

Boris glanced around the deck, trying to remain on guard if the evil little pup were to show up again. He just didn't believe they'd caught 'im.

"You keep scratching at that, it's going to start bleeding again," Penny droned on; at the same time she was scratching at a raw part of her belly that had formed at the top edge of her bikini bottoms, already stretched to their limits. He had warned her that the damned thing was not her size.

"Bloody hell, woman," he snapped at her.

She busied herself with her second rum drink, sucking away its final frothy remnants.

Boris remained calm, reminding himself that it was their anniversary. He was attempting to make every effort not to say anything cross to his wife during this momentous celebration. "Sorry love. It's just the damned things are itchy as hell." It still annoyed him that first the doctor was on his fanny about his wounds, and now so was Penny. He bit his lip, hating that every inch of his body felt anxious.

Something brushed against his elbow.

This startled him so much, he jolted his arm forward and away, knocking his own full drink glass onto the exo-skeletal leg brace protecting his knee. It catapulted its flavorful contents all over his other leg, the chair and then onto the rubberized decking of the jogging track before them. He pivoted at the same time to prepare himself for what he was sure was the attacking mad poodle's next assault. Boris' opposing arm cocked back, ready to unleash his balled-up fist on the red eyed devil before it could take a seventh chunk out of him.

Directly in front of Boris, a mere moment before he'd administer his pummeling, was the bum of an elderly man. The man's rear thrust upwards and farther toward him, now bumping up against his shoulder. The old man's only sounds were the squeaks of his chair.

"Now look what you did," trumpeted an old woman's voice, raspy and condescending, "you made that man spill his drink."

Boris couldn't tell where this disconnected voice was coming from because the backside of the man's knickers, now thrust into his face, filled up his whole field of vision.

The offending backside spun around, pivoting on furry slippers, and then Boris could see daylight once again.

"Damned ship put our chairs too close together," the old man croaked back to his wife and then faced Boris, a grimace etched into a swarthy mug, ancient and wrinkled like a bed-sheet at dusk. "Sorry son." He scowled at the reddish-brown liquid splashed everywhere and then back to Boris. "Can I buy you another... whatever *that* was?"

Boris wanted to be angry, but this man couldn't have weighed more than forty kilos, and seemed genuinely embarrassed by his bump. He stood patiently waiting for an answer, stooped over, loose skin waggling in the breeze.

"Are you buying the man a drink?" demanded his equally stooped-over wife, impatiently waiting for her husband to finish up with her chair.

The elderly man ignored her, a grin forming. It was a curiously happy look that said, *That's just my old woman. You'll understand this, if you make it to my age.*

Boris liked this old guy instantly, and now he wanted to buy him a drink, not the other way around.

"It's nothing, sir," Boris said loudly, so that the old man's wife could hear. "I'm just a little jumpy and I'm a bloody klutz. Can I get drinks for yah? We have one of those all you can drink packages, so it costs us nothing."

The old man wanted to say no, but then scratched his cheek, more of a habit than his attempting to dispense with an itch. The deep fissures of his face moved around his burrowing fingers. Boris could tell the old guy was programmed to react with a "no!" Probably pride more than desire. But the man continued his hesitation, obviously wanting one.

To make the old man's decision easier, Boris pushed himself up and out of the clutches of his lounger, ignoring the sticky liquid coating his left leg and his right leg's inability to cooperate. "Come on, sir. Let me get you and your wife a drink. Our treat. Tell me what you're both drinking. We're having the ship's special: some tasty rum drink called a zombie."

The man's wrinkle lines went vertical, and a grin now covered his whole face. "Mercy no. We're whiskey folks. Both my wife and me. Thank you, we'd love to take you up on your offer. I'm David Cohen." David thrust out his withered hand, gold Rolex dangling off his wrist.

Boris returned the shake and noticed immediately David's forearm had a series of numbers stenciled on it: A-18523. It was almost unreadable, but he knew immediately what it meant: David had spent time in the Auschwitz concentration camp. Boris and Penny had just visited that horrible place last year and it made such an impact on Boris, he remembered everything. Boris quickly averted his eyes from David's, feeling guilty for staring at the tattoo, and more so for guessing what it meant. "I'm Boris, Boris Thompson, and my wife Penelope."

Penny waved with one hand, her other clutching her drink glass, her lips glued to its straw.

"Evie—hi." David's wife waved back.

"Very pleased to meet you, sir. I mean, David."

"Pleasure's all mine, Boris. And sorry again about the chair."

"It's just like the airlines, where they pack us in like sardines—"

"—Don't forget mine, Boris," Penny interrupted, holding out her empty as proof.

Boris just smiled and began his waddle toward the bar, the temporary brace on his injured leg squeaking. He had to move around several people, who seemed to be slowly milling around, pointing out to the sea, as if they saw something important.

He ignored them, focusing on not falling on his face again and fulfilling the first half of his mission: get Penny's drink and one whiskey for David's wife. Penny and he had the bar package, which allowed them to drink as many alcoholic drinks as they wanted, only one at a time. But the pool-side bartender—he had forgotten the man's name already—took pity on the hobbled Brit, and allowed him to carry two at a time, as long as both Seapasses were swiped. Boris wasn't too sure if the bartender would allow him to get two and immediately fill another order for two more, so that he could get all four of them drinks. He'd worry about that after he returned to get David and his drinks.

"Hi Boris, back for another round?" asked the slight man from the Philippians. Doe was his name—he just remembered.

Boris was about to belt out his order to Doe when the ship's horn, directly above their foreheads, blared so loud Boris thought his head would explode.

Doe too seemed jolted from the horn sound. But then Boris watched the bartender's face go from confused to shock and then something more: it looked like fear.

Boris twisted around and glanced at the pool below them on deck 9, and then the upper deck where they were, but he didn't see anything that would warrant concern.

All at once the outside turned dark from a thick cloud that passed over them.

Then it fell down upon them, like it had lost the ability to stay up in the air.

The upper sun deck and lower pool deck looked like they were holding a giant rugby scrum, involving the whole population of the ship. Most were either running or flailing away at the enveloping cloud. An ear-piercing cacophony of horn blaring, squawking and screaming filled the air.

A grunt and scream beside him caused Boris to twist back, where he saw Doe fighting with two black birds.

The cloud was birds!

Doe howled again, this time from pain, as one of the black birds ripped at his cheek.

Penny! Boris thought. She was in danger from these birds.

He spun too quickly, his braced knee not moving the way his brain thought it should, and he flopped hard onto the decking.

In front of Boris, also on the deck, a woman covered her face, curled into the fetal position, as birds mercilessly pummeled at her head and arms with their beaks, bringing up blood with each head-plunge.

Boris got up onto his knees and spotted a wadded-up beach towel beside him. He snatched it up and heaved it at the birds, connecting with one. Two others fluttered above, squawked at her, and then continued their assault.

Boris pulled himself all the way up using the fixed bar stool, grabbed a dirty plate left on the bar, stumbled over to the woman, leaned over her and swatted at the twin fowls, connecting so hard the plate broke in two. One broken piece and the two birds thumped off a railing a meter away.

Boris stood erect and fixed his sights back on his Penny. She was so far way. He clutched the large plate piece harder, brandishing its ragged edge outward, ready to use it to chop and slice at anything that stood in his way. He hobbled forward toward his wife, periodically swinging at one bird at a time. He'd get to his Penny, not fall in the process, and kill as many of these damned red-eyed monsters as he could.

Penny wondered what all the commotion was about in front of her and below her on the Sun Deck. But she didn't wonder enough to task herself with looking up. She was too focused on her book and her drink. When the ship's horns blared and she was jolted by a bird landing in her lap, she looked up. The lap bird flapped its wings in a frenzy, like it forgot how to fly. Then it screeched at her and tried to right itself, glaring its bright-red eyes at her.

Even in her slow to react state, Penny sensed its evil intentions. She belted out a scream and swatted at the bird with the back of her book hand. When another hit her in the shoulder, her screams grew several octaves louder. She gave up swatting, and instead covered her head and closed her eyes when it had reared back and was about to go for her face. She waited for the pain. She heard a loud squawk and then a dull thump, but felt nothing more. She quickly flashed her eyes open, catching a glimpse of the offending bird sailing end-over-end over the railing down onto the next deck and into the pool. Then she felt pain.

She glanced down at the one on her lap, which had dug its talons into her leg, and caught the dark arc of something flashing by her, connecting with this bird, knocking it away.

Casting a shadow over her was their new friend David. His hand was out, the other clutching a thick hardback book, newly coated in blood and feathers.

"Follow me. We're going inside," he demanded.

She flashed him a look of confusion, as he quickly withdrew his hand, gripped his book with both hands and yelled, "Duck!" He swung at her head just as she threw herself to the decking.

David then dropped to the deck himself and grabbed something from a tray before pushing himself back up.

"Make a soft fist," he commanded above her, his voice no longer raspy or frail.

When she glared at him with more confusion, he bellowed once again, "Stick out your hand and make a soft fist. Now."

She thrust out her arm, wrist all floppy-like. She turned her head away from him, to check out a woman screaming directly behind her and felt something being wedged onto her hand. "Wha—"

"Now tighten your fist, like you want to punch something," David explained. His voice was calm, but still loud enough to be heard over the craziness going on around them.

She saw it was a heavy drink tumbler, not like the decorative glasses used for her rum drink. She complied, feeling the glass around her fist tighten.

"When you see one of those birds, punch at it with your new fist. Now let's go." He tugged on her elbow, intending to lead her toward his wife, who had sought protection under a lounger.

A bird hit beside Penny's feet. At first she yelped and pulled away from David's grip. But then she felt the weight on her fist, cocked her left arm and drove her heavy fist at the bird, pulverizing it into the decking. Pulling it away, she marveled at the glass, now colored red. "I'm like the bloody Iron Fist," she proclaimed.

"Oy!" Boris yelled from behind Penny.

She smiled at him and proudly showed off her blood-soaked glass fist.

Boris tossed a blue-striped towel over her head and then yelled, "David. For Evie." And he tossed him the other.

David snatched it from the air, tugged Evie out from under the lounger and laid the towel over her head, pulling her behind him. As they moved in front of Boris and Penny, David hollered, "We're going aft, toward the mid-ship entrances; the traffic's lighter there."

Boris pushed his wife forward, and he took the rear of their human conga line to safety.

Every once in a while, when they'd slow or stop to work their way around people, Penny would punch at the air yelling something like, "I am the immortal Iron Fist."

Boris couldn't help but smile at this, as he was picturing himself as a cricket batsman—the best on the planet—each time he'd take a giant swing at one of the birds.

Another run for the batsman.

The oddest part of their mad journey across and around the jogging track to their exit to safety was the fact that none of the birds seemed to bother Boris. They swarmed most everyone he saw who was moving.

What he couldn't see because he was too focused on continuing their track was that he wasn't the only one untouched by the birds: others, some hiding, some running, some just sitting in shock, were also completely ignored by the birds.

05

Wasano

Wasano Agarwal halted at the turn of the railing of the half-deck stairwell, unable to move any farther through the swarm of passengers. He may have been Intrepid's new Director of Security—he became senior director when Robert Spillman was gutted yesterday—but he didn't feel like it. He'd already lost sight of his captain.

Wasano craned his neck forward, attempting to catch a glimpse of Captain Jörgen, but it was impossible to see past where he'd turned from the half-deck and somehow slipped through the throng and up the stairwell toward the next deck. Wasano, on the other hand, hit a wall of people attempting to push down the blocked stairwell. This crushing mass oscillated like agitated cockroaches, trying to get out of the light. He could barely move, much less get forward.

"What do you see, sir?" Wasano yelled out, doing his best to project his voice over the alarmed passengers and a few crew. Some of them were screaming, attempting to push down the stairs to get away from the sun deck and what he imagined must be awful outside. Some were bloody, but thankfully those passengers appeared to be only slightly injured. He was more worried about the majority, who were in some form of shock, their faces drawn and pale. A few were even non-responsive and looked like they might fall over. The crowd appeared to hold them up and shove them along. Other than these zombie-like passengers, everyone seemed to be infected by some form of panic. He knew he was. But it was the panic-filled screams that brought him back.

They reminded him of the Express train platform in Mumbai, and his father.

Amit Agarwal was a second generation coolie, and Wasano was destined to follow in his footsteps. After school, Wasano would help his father, to earn a little money for himself and his family, but to also learn from Amit, so that he could become just like him. Wasano even had his own license, which was required of all coolies. And he proudly wore the uniform: bright red shirt and yellow turban. Porting heavy bags for passengers from one train platform to the next was back-wrecking and neck-breaking work: most bags were carried on their heads. Wasano was always smaller compared to his friends and other coolies, so he became determined to make himself stronger and to work harder, just like his father. It was all planned out for him, until his father died.

That day was a particularly busy one, with passengers crowding Amit's platform, not unlike this mid-deck. Wasano struggled with half of one passenger's load; his father, farther out front, had the remainder. Then something happened. A ruckus in the crowd caused people to rush, with little room to do this. Amit attempted to move along the edge, but the stammering crowds pushed him and his load pulled him over. He tumbled onto the tracks. Wasano dropped his bags and tried to make a dash for Amit, but he couldn't get past the crush of people, who all seemed to be going the other direction. He yelled his father's name, as the Tejas Express arrived.

Even over the screeching of the train's brakes, he heard his father scream.

The inhuman screeching sounds, followed human screams, were in front of Wasano now.

Somehow, he had gained a little ground on the mid-deck by inching forward, and he could actually see the stairwell open up to the next deck. He could also see the source of both the screeching and everyone's panic. In response to his captain, whose head he could barely see, and to Urban, who was behind him, he hollered, "I see the birds!"

Deck Officer Urban Patel had been following Wasano closely. He too must have given up moving against what felt like a stampede of sheep.

At the start of the half-deck, just ahead of them, a large man tripped over his own feet and tumbled forward, taking down a half-dozen others in front of him. Still others, attempting to hold up, were driven forward by the swelling horde behind them, causing even more to tumble on top of the now-writhing pile.

"People! Please slow down. You're safe now," Wasano yelled, hands held up. He didn't believe it though, and instead he and Urban tried to move through the crowd and to help up those who had fallen.

"Please folks, don't panic," the captain bellowed above them, still mostly out of sight. And then, "Wasano, I need your flashlight."

Wasano found an opening in the crowd that formed where the pile of toppled people stopped and the others still on their feet had continued downward around them. At the inside rail, he slipped around the edge where it moved up the stairwell. Now he could see Captain Jörgen reaching down to him. Wasano slid the large Maglite out of his belt loop and stretched it out over several bobbing heads, until Jörgen snatched it from him and plowed back through the bottlenecked crowd. They were milling on and above the stairs, twisting and turning to look back at where they had come from. Jörgen then began swinging at any bird within reach of his new weapon.

Wasano gazed at the hordes still frantically attempting to move as far away from the Sun Deck as possible. They pushed forward, only gaining room when those at the edges of the pile toppled over into it. They still looked either panicked or forlorn, but some of the faces were twisted with anger, spitting out profanity-laced commands demanding others move.

The pile of people continued to grow, with many flailing around, desperately trying to get loose of the others. Some were clawing and kicking, and hurting others in the process.

Wasano was always amazed at how illogical people became when they panicked. He felt the panic swell that day in Mumbai, when others seemed to be pulled into the well and tumbled into the tracks right after his father. If the people had remained calm, no one would have needed to get hurt, not the least of which his father. If they had just done what they were supposed to. Like these people.

He saw a woman at the top of the pile and he reached down and helped her onto her feet.

Urban worked his way through another opening, over to the other side of the large half-deck separating the two stairwells. Urban lunged for a large man covered in blood in a vain attempt to help pull him up. But when he grabbed the panic stricken man's arm, the man clawed him with his other hand, gouging bloody nail marks across his forearm. Urban let go, reared up and clutched his arm, to stem a trickle of red starting flow. "Dammit, man. People, settle down," he demanded.

Seeing that this was getting worse by the second, Wasano pulled guests up and out of the pile more aggressively now. He was worried there would be more serious injuries if they didn't mitigate this immediately.

Another crew member arrived, and started to help them pull people from the top of the pile collecting on the half-deck.

With more room up and down the stairs, and along the railings, passengers began to flow around the obstruction at the half-deck landing. They processed down the stairs, relieving some of the tension against the human barricade, which also appeared to thin. This had a calming effect on everyone, even with the screeching and screaming above.

Then something happened.

It was as if a panic switch was flipped on once again, but elevated to a nonsensical level.

A surge in the middle of those still on the stairs pushed out hard, causing more to flop back into the pile. The screams started up again, loud and piercing. They were panicking again. Many turned and ran back up or tried to shove their way by the pile and continue down. More people fell, some tumbling down the stairs. Others were stepping on top of those in the pile.

At least a couple of people in the pile—now numbering thirty or more—yelled animal-like screeches, and more were flailing, causing more harm to those around them.

Urban was fighting with the same large man who had scratched him. Now this man appeared to focus all of his anger on Urban, as if he were the cause of this problem. The man must have become insane, because he ignored an open compound fracture to his own forearm: it was bent at an odd angle. When the large man lunged for him, Urban was careful not to touch the man's broken radius, shooting straight up out of his skin like a flagpole. Instead, he tried to block the man's shoulder, but he missed and fell forward into the man. The crazed man's head hit Urban's neck and then something ratcheted down hard onto his scruff and ripped. It was Urban's turn to panic. He yelped when he saw the large man pull away, face crazy, bloody mouth full of organic tissue—his tissue. The large man's eyes were a crimson fury.

06

No Help

The crush of people was almost overwhelming.

Ted focused on Jean Pierre's back as the three of them swam up the mid-ship stairwell against the sea of humanity racing past them. Equally reassuring was knowing TJ was behind him, her vise-like grip on his shoulder to keep her from getting separated.

He had definitely not thought through this action, like he normally did with anything he did. Had he thought about the prospect of rushing out to face thousands of bloodthirsty birds to save some people, especially after seeing their panic firsthand, he probably would have chickened out of the whole thing. But everything was set into motion.

Focus on Jean Pierre, he told himself.

They halted at deck 9.

Jean Pierre snapped his head from side to side, scanning the flood of people frantically milling past them.

Ted eyed the doorways leading outside to the pool and Jacuzzis. They were clogged with people stopped by the doors from streaming inside, and others holding up just inside the doors, waiting to continue up and down the stairs. A good number were going into the Solarium's two entrances, just off both sides of the stairwells. This made sense to Ted because the Solarium was a separately enclosed giant atrium, with a large indoor pool and spa as its centerpiece, surrounded by tables and chairs, and a small restaurant completely forward, just above the bridge. It had two smaller doorways which could easily be sealed, whereas the entry/exits leading outside from the stairwell in between were large sliders and he heard one radio report that at least one of these leading to the Forward stairwell and elevators were stuck open. There was no way to go against the crowds, and no way to go outside, at least until they thinned.

Obviously, Jean Pierre was thinking the same thing, because he led them through the throng of people and into Solarium's starboard side entrance. It seemed like a good strategy, as they could close off the Solarium from the birds and help those people first, before then moving out to the pool decks when they cleared out.

Upon entry to the Solarium, Ted was struck with the sheer number of people there. It appeared that at least half the passengers from the pool deck and sun deck above were now here. Cruise ships and their schedules were designed in such a way that passengers were segregated—of course they never knew it—so as to not congregate too many in one place at one time. Only during muster drills at the beginning of a cruise did you get the full sense of how many people were on the ship at one time. But musters were well organized. This was chaos.

With so many panicked people clustered into one area, even one with a two-story windowed-atrium, the echoing din was almost deafening. And a few of the crazed birds had found their way inside as well, continuing their relentless assault. Shrieks from passengers marked their location.

Jean Pierre hopped off to the left, in the direction of one of the screams, while Ted felt drawn toward another.

Ted felt a tap against his back and realized it was TJ. He had been so intently focused, he didn't remember her letting go of his shoulder. She handed him one of two serving trays she had collected from an abandoned cart they'd passed. He was only momentarily unsure why, and then understood: she was intending for him to use it as a weapon.

He tossed a quick glance at her, first catching the glint of her Orion the Warrior necklace he had given her for their anniversary—was that only yesterday? They needed her warrior side right now. He then found her eyes: piercing blue, intently fixed on their target up ahead. Ted couldn't help but flash a smile at how well she was handling the prospect of dealing with more wild animals. Only moments earlier, up on the bridge, she seemed overwhelmed with the news and seeing the incoming birds. Her FBI training must have kicked in, and she somehow pushed aside her abject fear of animals. It was like something in her had changed and the fears that had possessed his wife no longer had control over her.

She stood resolutely, wearing her body-hugging running outfit. A Nike swish on the hip of her compression shorts confirmed her body language: "Let's do it!"

A man and woman screamed beside him, and Ted turned that way. A black bird had clawed its way into the woman's hair, screeching and pecking at her head, clawing its way for her eyes—*they seemed to be always going for the eyes.* Her husband or boyfriend attempted to dislodge the bird from her, reaching up to grab it, or swat at it, in an attempt to get it away from her. But he was too slow: with each swipe the bird got him, drawing blood and profanities from the man.

Ted lunged forward, tray clutched and drawn back.

"Watch out!" Ted yelled at them, but realized that was a dumb command, because he really wanted them to duck. The man seemed to understand his Ted-speak by ducking, just as Ted swung. Ted's tray connected with a thunk, and the bird shot outward, spinning in the air and then splashing into the pool.

The man remained crouched low, just behind and below the woman, which was good, because she collapsed into his arms, as if she lost all strength to stand. Either her injuries were greater than they appeared, or she had just fainted. The man shot a glance up to Ted. He didn't verbalize his thanks, but his face said it.

A scream behind Ted, pulled him away from his momentary feeling of triumph. He spun around, expecting TJ to be right there, but she wasn't. Farther away than he expected, he saw two women entangled... struggling.

One of them was TJ.

He dashed in their direction.

Clawing at TJ was a rather large, pale woman in a pastel-colored onesie. A small older man was cowering under a table, eyes dinner-dish wide. TJ was barely holding the pastel woman back as the two rolled on the wet decking. Partially out of shock, but also because he couldn't see a way into the scuffle, Ted stood before both of them, hesitating, with arms drawn back; a home-run slugger, about to rip the cover off the baseball, if he were just given the right pitch. Then he saw his opportunity.

TJ flipped the pastel woman around and held the woman above her. For a moment, it almost looked to Ted like Pastel Woman was trying to get away from TJ. Just a moment's hesitation, and in that moment, upon seeing Ted Pastel Woman squealed her frustration at him, just before he silenced her.

He released his swing, swatting the woman's forehead with the flat end of the tray. She buffeted back, momentarily confused as TJ slid out from under the rotund woman. Then Pastel Woman snarled again at Ted, her face twisted and bloody. He momentarily wondered if he had caused this, but saw flecks of organic material around her mouth. Her skin was pale and sickly, as if she had a really bad fever. Her movements were erratic, like a confused animal; her guttural grunts, like some hellish beast and not the sounds he would have expected from an older woman; her eyes were shiny red and wild with insanity: they were the same eyes as the dog, as the birds, as the rats, and as the ferret.

The infection had crossed over to people.

"Holy shit," he mumbled.

Pastel Woman sprang up on her feet and lunged for Ted, knocking him down. The woman grabbed him with such force, he would have thought her to be a male body-builder not a flabby woman who was older than him and most probably hadn't even seen the outside of a gym in decades. He could feel the putrid warmth of her breath on his neck, and he thought for a flash this might be it. She was about to get him.

Then he heard a deep thwack and the woman released her grip, and her weight tumbled off him. His wife's voice trumpeted, strong and absolute as she stated, "Get your hands off my husband, bitch!"

She must have swung her tray edge-first, connecting hard across Pastel Woman's face, because that woman lay in a heap, unconscious.

Ted glanced up at his wife. TJ stood triumphantly above him, hand thrust out. She was breathing heavily, her face still intense, but mostly unreadable. At some point she'd put her sunglasses on. Then her lips curled and a grin formed. He accepted her hand and she pulled him up easily.

He quickly cast his gaze upon the Solarium's convulsing crowds.

Only then was it obvious to him: close to a dozen people—passengers and crew—were attacking other passengers and crew inside the atrium.

"It's crossed over to the people," he yelped. "We need to get out of here."

07

Infirmary

A crewman struggled to carry an unconscious woman who wore shorts and a t-shirt coated in splashes of red. A blood-soaked beach towel was strapped around her calf with a man's belt. "Where can I put her?" bellowed the crewman.

Dr. Chettle pointed to a corner of the room, where there was an open spot on the floor. Its occupant had been released a few minutes ago. He watched the crew member lay the woman down and one of his volunteers, charged with triaging the incoming patients, quickly checked the woman's vitals. The volunteer peeked under the injured woman's makeshift bandage, pulled out a red marker and drew a single red line across her forehead: her injuries were life-threatening, but they could probably save her. At least it wasn't a black marker, which would have meant death was eminent.

He'd had two patients with the black marks of death in the last few minutes. He didn't want any more.

The day, like the patients coming to the ship's ad hoc infirmary, had quickly gone from green (minor injuries) and mostly food poisoning illnesses, to yellow (non-life threatening injuries) from bird attacks, to red and black because of the more serious and yet very odd injuries.

He moved over to the newly-delivered bloodied woman in the corner and examined the loose red bandage wrapped around her leg. His nurse, Chloe Barton, joined him on the other side of the injured woman, having just finished suturing one of the many bird-bite wounds they had had in the last few minutes.

"What do you need for this one, Doctor?" she asked.

He glanced up from his patient to find Barton already slipping the cuff of their electronic sphygmomanometer around the woman's forearm, obviously taking a cue from the woman's red designation. Chettle's view of Barton's abilities and usefulness had grown exponentially in the last 24 hours. She'd been an enormous help to him and the injured. It was like she'd taken a common sense pill: pressure seemed to forge her into one of the better nurses he'd worked with over the years. Perhaps she needed a hectic atmosphere, like an ER. When this whole mess settled down—if it settled down—he'd recommend that she work in an ER, rather than the day-to-day boredom of dealing with the cuts and bruises of stupid or drunk passengers on a cruise ship. Her talents were needed in an ER setting. But at this moment, he was very glad to have her here.

"I don't know, I was just..." Dr. Chettle halted and glared at the exposed wound, a fresh stream of blood pooling around its edges. "We're dealing with human bites now." He looked at Barton, almost to confirm what was an obvious but still unbelievable fact: this was the fourth human-bite case they'd witnessed in the last half-hour.

He looked around for the crewman who brought the woman in, wanting to find out what happened. But the man had already left. Chettle had only picked up a few dribbles about the pandemonium up on the pool and sun decks. And based on the injuries, as crazy as it sounded, he could at least explain the bird-bites. When the human bite cases started to appear, he had no explanation. Human bites were almost always reactionary, a means of defense.

He'd only seen offensive attacks such as these in drug abuse cases. If there was only one case on the ship, perhaps he could explain it. But four? He needed to find out what was going on. He caught another crew member steadying a new incoming patient, this time an older man, but with a similar looking bloodied arm. The old man weakly held a red towel against his wound.

Chettle turned to his nurse. "Completely clean, suture, and dress the wound"—he paused to consider all the cases—"and make sure there are no other wounds. I'll be right back." He stood up and turned away from the injured woman and Barton, who was already removing the towel from the wound, while clutching a bottle of Hydrogen Peroxide.

"Hey you," Chettle bellowed to the crewman across the room. "What's happening up there?"

The crewman's eyes darted to him and around the room. Right away, it was obvious he was both scared and confused.

"It's okay. You're safe here. Now please tell me what's going on topside?"

The man looked down and up again. "Ahh, they're attacking each other?"

"Who? Who's attacking?"

"The people."

"How..." Chettle turned his attention everywhere around the room and yet nowhere. His eyes fell upon the spots of two of his earlier patients who had been feeling really sick from the same food poisoning that hit maybe forty percent of the ship's passengers and similar numbers of crew. Both patients were confused and one was drooling and almost unresponsive: the one with the

Hawaiian shirt, who was no longer in his bunk. Three different types of incidents: food poisoning, then animal bites, and now human bites. All, within days of each other and all seemingly unrelated. And yet something in his gut told him they were, even though that didn't make a lick of sense.

"Hey Doctor. Can my brother go now?" hollered a hulking German man, two beds down. Chettle stepped over to the bed, where another much skinnier German, bare-chested with a blanket around his shoulders was sitting up, alert. The beefier version of the man—if Chettle remembered right, they were brothers—was standing beside him. The beefy one gazed at the doctor with scornful eyes. He was the one who asked the question.

Chettle flipped through his charts, searching for the bed number. Franz Litz and his brother Hans. Franz was bitten by a dog. He supposedly tried to pull away a crazed dog that was attacking another passenger and was bitten in the process. Franz had been disoriented for a few hours, but seemed alert now. They'd long since cleaned and dressed his wound. Chettle knew he'd need more bed space, especially now. So there appeared to be no reason to hold this man. "Yes, you both can go. But—" Chettle stopped mid-sentence, his head drawn to the other side of the infirmary, where there was a flutter of colorful movement.

"Great!" exclaimed Hans. He yanked at his brother's arm, pulling Franz out of his makeshift bed. "Let's get out of here and go to the pool to take in beer and bikinis..." his voice faded off as both brothers gazed at the flash of commotion away from them.

The man in the bright Hawaiian shirt, who had earlier left his bunk, was now stooped over another patient—a woman who Chettle had sedated after multiple bird bites and who was finally resting. She was now screaming in a perfect soprano pitch. Hawaiian Shirt almost appeared to be growling back at the woman, and the woman was pushing at him and kicking, trying to keep Hawaiian Shirt away.

Chettle started after Hawaiian Shirt, not sure what he would do, but knowing he had to intervene in some way. "Hey," he yelled at the man. "What are you doing?"

Hawaiian Shirt hesitated and was kicked to the ground by the screaming woman, but he immediately pushed himself up from the floor and leapt at the kicking woman, who had wiggled out of her bed and was now trying to stand. Her voice broke into an even higher pitch, if that was possible.

Chettle reached the man, who was chomping his teeth like some comedy routine where he was mimicking a Great White chowing down on a lowly fish.

Just as Chettle reached Hawaiian Shirt, the man's chomping teeth found the flailing woman's hand, clasping down on it like a vise, cracking tendons and bones. Her screech reached glass-breaking levels when Chettle tugged at the man's Tommy Bahama, pulling the woman his way too.

Hans' face turned from scowl to shock upon seeing the same thing Franz had: the bloke in the colorful shirt had turned his chomping-act onto the doctor.

Franz had felt wobbly at first when his brother had so abruptly pulled him out of bed. He was alert now and standing upright. And although he felt plenty warm now, he pulled the blanket he'd been wearing more firmly around his shoulders and gazed at the scene.

The threesome of the doctor, the injured woman and the colored shirt guy all struggled on the floor; the doctor was now the one doing the yelling; there was so much blood.

Another scuffle occurred right beside them. An oriental crew member appeared to be fighting with another patient, and both were flailing around on the floor. The oriental was pounding the patient's face with balled-up hands, like a machine whose only purpose was to pummel objects: a machine that was screaming... *no, screeching*, like an animal. *"Was zur Hölle?"* Franz yipped (What the hell?).

"Der Mist. The Americans call it a 'shit-storm,' little brother. Let's go."

Franz could see the woman who had been bitten on her hand—it looked bent at a funny angle—was now pounding with her other hand on the crazy guy with the colorful shirt, who was busy trying to chomp down on the doctor's neck. "But... but shouldn't we help?"

He didn't look up at Hans, totally transfixed by what he saw.

The infirmary's noises had now grown ear-splitting, as most of the room's occupants or visitors were rushing in panicked dashes for one of the two exits.

"That *Drecksau* (dirty pig)?" Hans said about the doctor. "No, we go now."

Franz felt his big brother yank his arm back and pull him toward the closest exit. He did nothing to resist, while his arm was nearly dislocated in Hans' anxiousness to get them out of there.

The whole time, Franz watched the "shit show." He caught another glimpse of the colorful-shirt guy's mouth finding the doctor's jugular, sending a geyser of blood in the air.

But what drew Franz' gaze, just before he exited the infirmary, what made him shiver from a growing cold inside of him, as he glanced at each of the multiple scuffles involving people screaming, growling and attacking, were the evil red eyes of the crazy-looking ones.

08

Flavio

Flavio Petrovich was awakened by a rattle and crash. He lifted his head slightly, eyes ratcheted open, scanning his cabin. Not that he could see anything, his cabin was pitch-black. Even if he had left his lights on—he remembered turning them off—he wouldn't expect to see anyone or anything because he didn't share his cabin with another crewmate. That meant the noise had to have been made by some other damned rude person outside his cabin. Another crash and a heavy bang against his door set Flavio on a boil. He couldn't get a moment's rest. It wasn't bad enough that he had to deal with all of the stupid crew members, and the obnoxious German guests, and then the crazy red-eyed rats, but now his fellow crew wouldn't let him sleep.

Why can't they leave me alone, in peace?

"Is that too much to ask?" he bellowed at the murk.

His fingers fumbled through the darkness, finally finding and flipping his phone around to see the time. It was 13:42. He'd only slept three hours. Now he was really pissed. He was going to give this person an ear-full.

Flavio tossed back the covers, slid his feet into his slippers and marched over to the door of his cabin. Admittedly, he was glad to have one of the few private cabins for non-officer crew members, because of his seniority with Regal European. Although he always felt it was their way to try and placate him, instead of paying him a higher wage. He slapped the handle, twisted it violently, and threw open the door.

Inside the doorway, he held up and froze.

As this was a deck three, crew-only hallway at the far aft of the ship connecting mostly officer's cabins to other crew areas, the last thing he expected to see was trash. But right in front of his door was an overturned cart, just like the ones used by room attendants to clean up rooms. Half of the contents of a bag of trash attached to the back of the cart was spilled across the orange-carpeted floor. A crushed tampon box stood up like a sign-post of all that was wrong, right before his slippered feet.

"Vat da holy hell is this?" he blared to no one.

A scream to his right.

He turned to see a running room attendant, gaping mouth hanging, in full stride bounding over the cart and the trash, as if it wasn't his place to deal with this. He probably was the one who made the mess.

Flavio was about to yell at the man's back, before he was out of earshot, when he heard another scream… more like an animalistic screech.

Again, Flavio turned to face the noisemaker: it was another crew member running right at him. He wore a black jumpsuit and roared like a tiger whose cubs were poached. The man looked as angry as Flavio felt. More. *Perhaps you should have picked up the trash,* Flavio wanted to instruct the attendant, who was probably out of the hallway by now.

The jumpsuited-crewmember didn't belong here though: his uniform indicated he worked in the engine room, and he certainly didn't have a cabin in this hallway. Jumpsuit Man attempted to run by Flavio, dead-set on the attendant, and didn't seem to notice Flavio, much less the large obstruction in the hallway. Instead of jumping over it like the attendant, he plowed through it, without any success. Jumpsuit tripped and fell hard, face first. There was a crack that Flavio knew all too well: the man had broken a bone.

"Whoa—whoa there, crazy man. Settle down," Flavio instructed as he took a step into the hallway.

Jumpsuit didn't "settle." He convulsed and flailed, no doubt causing more harm to whatever part of his body he broke.

Flavio stepped closer to the man. "Are you crazy?"

Jumpsuit twisted back to glare his anger at Flavio. The man's eyes were a fire-like red and he had a deep gash in his cheek that seeped blood. Jumpsuit's arms were thrashing in the air and against the carpet: a cross between trying to get traction and a temper tantrum, but the man's brain couldn't decide which, so he did both without any control.

A couple of years ago, the crew members like Flavio who dealt directly with guests were given a security seminar on what happened when someone was shot with a stun gun. Some of the security guards were getting them. Corporate said they were non-lethal and wanted to show the crew. One of the old-timers, Eddie, who worked with Flavio in the MDR, volunteered, acting as if there were nothing to it. When Eddie was hit by the electrodes, or whatever they were called, he convulsed violently on the floor just like Jumpsuit Man. Unfortunately for Eddie, no one knew about his heart condition. He died, along with the stun gun program.

Jumpsuit finally gained a little traction on the garbage, squishing beneath his feet liquids, soaps, creams, and other unmentionables, all disgusting discards from people's trash.

Flavio reflexively took a step back toward his room, thinking it was a safer place to be than in this hallway, with this convulsing freak.

Jumpsuit found his footing, although one foot wasn't working too well: it was bent at an odd angle.

Flavio could have sworn he heard a grinding sound and imagined bones upon other bones, breaking and grinding inside the man's mangled ankle. But Jumpsuit ignored what had to be excruciating pain. It was as if the man no longer felt pain, or he felt it and just didn't care. Then again, maybe he did feel the pain, because Jumpsuit brayed an unearthly sound which was a mix of a tormented scream and a vengeful battle cry. Flavio had heard both before, but in a much different theater.

Flavio stutter-stepped backwards when he realized Jumpsuit was somehow moving toward him fast on his broken ankle.

Flavio's heel slid—*on the damned tampon box*—and he started to fall backwards into his room. At that moment, for perhaps the only time, Flavio wished he had had a roommate, because there was no one there to help him. He looked up, just as Jumpsuit landed on top of him.

09

Deck Eight Falls

Just outside of cabin number 8531, a nearly naked woman, known to a few on the *Intrepid* as the woman who liked to marry and then murder her husbands, and to the rest as simply Eloise—*this was before she was purged*—straddled a man in black overalls and plunged her digits into the man's eye sockets, burying two of them up to her first knuckle. Her forefinger, already chewed off at the second knuckle, pressed into the man's temple, generating pain for her, and more anger. Eloise palmed the man's head like a bowling ball, screeched an anguished cry, and drove her mouth into the man's cheek. As she bit down and pulled back, enough skin, muscle and tendons ripped free to expose the man's teeth. After she chewed on his raw tissue, the man who'd just been promoted to mechanic bellowed a final howl before Eloise tore into his throat to silence him for good.

An alarm blared an ear-rattling tone, drawing Eloise's attention. She glared a serpent-like gaze at the speaker with headlamp-like anger and howled at it in reply; her newfound food burst out of her mouth.

She sprang up, intending to attack the speaker with equal abandon, when a rotund man from cabin 8520 brushed past her, his terrycloth bathrobe and black boxers fluttering as he dashed down the hallway.

Eloise brayed at the man's back, a guttural scorn for disrupting her focus. Bathrobe Man raced forward, unabated down their starboard-side hall, toward movement a couple of dozen cabins away. She cast her eyes back down at the man in the black overalls below her, holding her gaze on the dying man.

The decimated mechanic would never get a chance to tell his wife that he would have been bringing home more money for his family because of his promotion. Instead, he lay in a growing pool of red, gurgling, shallowing puffs of air bubbling out his newly enlarged mouth and opening in his throat. His eyes were now growing bowls of crimson, their soupy liquid pouring over its corners like tears down his face. Finally, his last breath—barely half a puff.

Eloise turned back to the speaker, no longer blaring horn sounds, but the voice of a man commanding them to do something she didn't understand. She spun back to glare at Bathrobe Man, who had tackled a couple of German tourists running the other way. The trio thrashed and wailed together. This drew Eloise's interest. She responded with an anticipatory snarl and leapt off the dead mechanic, dashing toward the rising din of screams.

Asap jumped again at the screeching sound, somewhere close, out in the hallway. Between the crazed dogs and rampaging monkey earlier, his skin crawled with each new sound that didn't normally belong on a cruise ship. To make matters worse, he was way behind on his duties. He needed to stop being so damned jumpy and focus on getting all of his port-side rooms cleaned. He had maybe half his normal time to get his rooms clean because he spent so much time consoling his roommates over the death of Catur. It was still weird to think that someone he knew got killed on this ship.

Yacobus and Jaga were more affected by their roomie's death than him. Asap figured Catur probably did something stupid to get himself killed by that monkey. He would miss him, at some point. But he wouldn't mourn him. This thought felt... foreign, like it wasn't his own. He used to be more caring. Now it just didn't seem to matter.

He fumbled with his key card, almost dropping it. The lock clicked open, but Asap didn't move. His eyes found the green sticker, confirming what he had thought he'd forgotten to check. The green-stickered rooms were the ones cleared by the crew hours ago. And as his roomies reminded him, it was a non-green room that supposedly contained the crazy monkey that had leapt out and killed Catur. All of Asap's rooms now had the distinctive green stickers on them. So they were clear of any crazy monkeys. Further, he should have been lucky as all of his cabins should have been empty, since all passengers were supposedly topside, enjoying the pools. Of course, he wasn't that lucky.

Several of his guests were ill from something they ate, and some were in their beds or in the bathroom, puking toenails; often they missed their toilets, which meant he'd have to clean it up. But as much as that annoyed him, what was most disconcerting were the others.

Some of his passengers were in a weird state, like a drunken daze. They were either confused, babbled some gibberish, or they were completely out of it. He could slap them and they'd do nothing. The weird ones were now taking up two out of every three of his cabins.

He knocked again on the cabin door in front of him and listened. *This was taking too damned long and he didn't want to see another one of those weird ones!*

The only consolation was that he couldn't clean the rooms the passengers were in. So other than a little puke, he didn't have to do much more with these. He'd freshened up their towels and let them be. With each cabin door he closed, he was one step closer to being done with his mid-day duties. That's at least how he should have felt. But really he thought he'd never finish. And that pissed him off.

"Better to be pissed off than pissed on," Catur used to say. Thinking of this incensed him even more. Asap felt his anger reach a boiling point, to the point of it becoming overwhelming. He couldn't remember feeling uncontrollable rage before, like he was feeling now.

And with each room, his rage grew, now manifesting itself in a desire to commit violence to whomever was behind this door, if only because they didn't answer him. More than wanting to tell his needy guests to stuff their requests for more towels, or tissue, or lattes down their fat traps, he now wanted to rip their sniveling throats out or break things over their heads.

When an image of what this might look like came to mind, Asap was taken aback. He was always frustrated by others, but he rarely thought of violence as a response. Now that was all he felt: an absolute need to commit violence.

His shock slowly bled into a feeling of empowerment. It was as if he was no longer a pawn of this ship and its owners, and the guests he had to incessantly coddle. He felt like he could finally stand up for his rights. He could finally do something about the injustices constantly poured out on him.

His fists were balled up, waiting to pounce on something, but he couldn't remember what. That was something else going on recently inside his head, and it too bothered him.

He was forgetting things. Lots of things. And he never forgot things before. This was just another example.

He stood in front of this cabin door, and tried to remember why he was in front of this one... He also couldn't remember if he had one more cabin or two to finish after this? Then, was he going to report all of his sick rooms to Chettle, or just let them die? He was leaning toward the latter: if they were dead, he didn't have to service their rooms again.

Oh God, what's going on?

He glanced at the door, and then the placard that told him the cabin number. You're on Deck Eight, he mentally yelled at himself, momentarily wondering this because he wasn't sure.

What was I supposed to do next?

The door rattled, almost in answer.

He violently pushed in the heavy door, as if it were the reason for his memory lapses. It clanged off someone standing behind it.

What an idiot to be standing behind the door.

He remembered the cabin belonged to a single man—Asap couldn't remember the man's name anymore—who stumbled back a little from the impact. The man glared at Asap, his eyes full of fury. Then he screamed a jumble of unintelligible words and ran through the doorway, knocking Asap down. Then the man dashed down the hallway.

As Asap prepared to push himself back up, he realized that there was lots of screaming and other noises everywhere, including much door rattling.

He righted himself and watched with fascination as a guard ran his way. Asap started to move out of the guard's way, so the man would have easy passage, but then stopped. He had as much right to the hallway as this guard did. So Asap stood his ground, facing the guard head-on.

The guard ignored Asap and punched past him, almost knocking Asap down again. The guard was grunting and groaning and seemed fixated on the loud voices he heard coming from within the bridge, just out of sight at the end of the hall.

That's it. I'm done with my work!

Asap was now standing before another cabin door, feeling his anger grow even more, but part of him knew he needed to figure out what was going on. Something bad was happening around him and maybe even to him. He could feel he was different inside, but he didn't want to think about it.

The cabin's door was ajar, kept open still with the life-preserver wedged in it, as was advised by the staff captain last night. That meant this cabin was empty: perhaps its occupants—again, their German names escaped him—were in the infirmary or topside on one of the decks. He could only hope.

There was a scream (he guessed) from inside the bridge. The voice sounded familiar. It was Jessica Something, the real pretty bridge officer so many of his male crewmates spoke of when they were talking about female crew they'd like to have sex with. He then heard some sort of struggle.

Asap decided to take himself out of this. He kicked the life-preserver out of the door and shut it behind him. Bent over and out of breath—*why am I breathing so heavily*—he looked up, saw himself in a mirror and gasped.

He took great pride in keeping his complexion perfect by using the right soaps, rinses and conditioners. And he kept his hair carefully groomed. The man that looked back at him was pale, almost to the point of death. His hair was standing up and out in all sorts of directions. "And my eyes," he whimpered.

There was a grunt on the other side of the cabin.

Asap turned and for the first time saw he wasn't alone.

A thick German, face covered in blood, eyes matching the rest of him, stood over the lifeless body of what Asap guessed was the German's wife.

The German man screeched a horrible-sounding cry.

Asap screeched back.

10

Bridge Troubles

"Be OOD for a moment, would you?" Jessica asked. "I need to use the head."

"Sure," said Ágúst, her only other bridge mate, and the ship's Safety Director. He then grinned wildly. "But don't be gone too long, or I may steer us to Barbados."

"Maybe I'll take my time then," she said, loosely manufacturing a smile as she dashed through the door closest to her.

The smile immediately slid off her face once she closed the door to the bridge's only bathroom. She stared at the light pouring in from the gap below the door. It was far from an air-tight hatch; this was just an area built into the bridge for the officers' convenience. Being only separated by thin materials off the bridge, it offered little protection to life's need for private moments like this one. But there was only one head for the entire bridge crew, set up so they could remain on a secured bridge until their shift ended. A slight convulsion jolted her.

With her head drooped, she let her slacks slide down to her ankles and waddled over to the toilet, attempting to muffle the sobs breaking free from her palm. When seated, she held her phone up to her face and gazed at its screensaver: a selfie with her husband and child, taken five months ago, just before she boarded the *Intrepid* to start her most recent ten-month contract. It felt so long ago. Much too long. A few of her tears splashed the screen, but she didn't wipe them away. She continued to stare at the glistening picture, willing it to come to life in her mind.

There had been no word from them since they'd left Malaga. Were they alive, and if so were they still at home? She had no idea. Meantime, there had been no emails or texts from them either. And the two times she tried to call them, a computerized voice told her the circuits in Reykjavik were busy.

She kissed the screen, clicked it off, and flushed the toilet. After splashing some water on her face she opened the door back onto the bridge. She pushed the pain deep down. Immediately, she was alerted to an alarm coming from her console, bringing her back from her momentary respite with her family. It was a navigation alarm she had set for herself: a reminder to reset their coordinates.

To stay on the path somewhat cleared of volcanic ash carried by the jet-stream, as the captain requested, she had to get creative with her navigation. The captain's plan made sense, as he'd felt sure that getting out of the ash clouds was paramount to mitigating their exposure to whatever was infecting most of the animals.

Her solution was a course that required corrections. First, they'd set in their coordinates to Sao Miguel in the Azores. This took them into the middle of the jet-stream's cone, with volcanic clouds to the north and the south of it. Once in the middle of the area free of the clouds, she could set a straight heading to Nassau, Bahamas, their next port. They were now in the center of this area.

She'd also calculated that this was the most fuel-efficient point to reset their coordinates. And efficiently using their fuel was important to corporate's bean counters.

At this point, all she needed to do was enter the new headings and then tell the ship's computers to follow the new coordinates. She set the alarm because if she forgot, and they didn't correct their path, they'd ultimately crash into their current set destination of the Azores in a couple of hours. Not that she would have forgotten.

"My turn," Ágúst announced, practically running to the head. He'd had an upset stomach all day, but didn't want to leave his post, especially in light of all that was going on. Unfortunately for him, he had the same stomach bug afflicting many others, from what was believed to be accidental food poisoning by their British chef. He should have told the captain and have been relieved by someone else. But she understood his dedication. It was one of the many reasons she liked working with Ágúst.

Jessica nodded at him as he breezed past her, and she moved to her console, pulling up the coordinates she had worked out. Just two more key strokes to get the Intrepid pointed in a more south-by-southwesterly heading. But before she executed the new commands, as always she would recheck her numbers and make sure they were absolutely correct.

Another alarm rang out, making her jump. But this alarm was more like a buzz. And then she understood it was just the intercom. She glanced at the door to the head, hearing Ágúst puke again through the paper-thin door. *There can't be anything left inside the poor guy,* she thought. She'd have to deal with the intercom first, then her calculations. She had plenty of time.

As she made her way to the hatch, one of the many ship's rules sprang into her brain: it was the one where the OOD always had to have their eyes on the console and their bow. Because she was the ship's OOD at this moment, she was breaking that rule by answering the door.

The intercom chimed again, and this time she heard a voice. "Help! Please! They're coming to get me."

"Who is this?" she hollered into the box that was fixed a few inches above her mouth, forcing her to stretch up to the box. She had projected her voice loud enough so that Ágúst could hear what was happening as well, and hopefully finish his episode.

"This is Second Officer Brian Murphy. Please let me in. They're attacking us."

That was all she needed. She saw what was going on outside through their screens. She put her body into the locking latch, clicking it home, and then tugged on the hatch. The Second Officer was obviously helping, because it became instantly light.

When it flopped open, Brian rushed in and brushed past her before he turned and puffed out, "Oh thank God. I thought I was done for." He bent over, holding himself up at his knees, not looking up while he collected needed air in short breaths.

While he did, he gazed at her. The fear hadn't left his face, but he looked like he was starting to feel safe. Then his face twisted up and he yelled, "Close it. They're here."

Jessica turned away from Brian and flashed a look into the doorway. It was filled with a guard, who barreled through the hatch and crashed into her, knocking her onto the deck.

11

Flavio

Flavio was beyond upset: Jumpsuit Man had piled on top of him and was attacking him for reasons he didn't know; his sleep was interrupted; and to top it off, he had another splitting headache.

He tried to push Jumpsuit Man off him, but the crazy guy kept thrashing, and something so strange... It appeared as if the man was trying to bite him. Why would someone from engineering try to bite him? The man was obviously insane, but why the biting?

Flavio braced himself and then when Jumpsuit Man lifted up to get a better angle of attack, Flavio placed a foot under the man's stomach and shoved with all his might, sending Jumpsuit across the room with a crash.

Flavio fixed his gaze in that direction, but he could barely see the man, because his cabin lights were still off. The only available light was coming from the hallway, through his open door. He was thankful that he'd taken the spring off the door, or it would have shut off all light.

He had heard the man's head hit the floor and the opposite wall hard, and now the man was spasmodically flailing around, just as he was before in the hallway, trying to right himself. Flavio could also feel the crazy guy glaring his weird red eyes at him. He couldn't see the man's eyes, but he could feel them. He knew the man was going to attack again.

Flavio had enough of this shit. He spun around and reached up above his desk, snatching from the wall his employee of the year award that he'd received for saving a guest from drowning. It was a useless piece of wood and a thin piece of metal, which only graced his wall for that occasion where a senior officer might visit his room, though that had never happened. It served no other purpose, but it did have some heft to it.

Flavio spun around, just as Jumpsuit was coming at him. Extending his arms back, while clutching the award, Flavio swung just before the man was upon him, connecting directly with the man's head. The award split in two, just like he suspected the man's head did as well. The man now lay in a heap beside his bed, the hallway light illuminating enough for him to see blood trickling out of a good-sized gash to his forehead. He was unconscious but not dead because Flavio could also see the man's chest rising and falling rapidly.

Flavio squeezed his eyes shut, a weak attempt to push away his migraine. Then he opened them back up and huffed a huge sigh, glaring scorn at the unconscious man bleeding on his floor. Another annoyance he didn't want.

And who would clean up the blood?

Flavio popped up, stepped over to his bed and flipped the light switch on, while keeping his gaze on the man. He humphed at the growing pool of blood being soaked up by his carpet. That was not going to come out easily.

He glared at the man, trying to decide what to do with him, and then made up his mind. He needed answers, which meant waking the guy while he still could.

He yanked off a pillow case from one of his six pillows—he needed many pillows to help him sleep. Then from a drawer, he pulled out some paracord, and using one of his many knives, he cut off two separate two-foot sections. Grabbing Jumpsuit's legs but avoiding the man's broken foot—he didn't want to wake him yet—he gave a hard tug. Then, with the precision of an American cowboy roping a steer at a rodeo, Flavio hog-tied the man's legs and then his arms. The pillow case slipped over the man's head was a final measure: he did not care to see the man's eyes until he had to.

He stood up and padded over to his open cabin door, but hung in the doorway. He poked his head out into the hallway, for one final confirmation of what he thought he had seen: that it wasn't some sort of weird flashback to his time in the army. With the headaches often came flashbacks of that day the Russians invaded his beloved country. But there was no time for this.

The overturned cart was still there, along with the garbage strewn in the hall. And although he could hear a commotion in the distance, out of sight, he didn't see any more crazy people.

Then he heard it.

It was the same angry bray he'd heard from the crazy man on his floor. Something had happened. It wasn't just this one crazy man; others were crazy. He knew it wasn't just the crazy rats and dogs; this was bigger. But was it the whole ship or just his area here? He needed to find out more, and find out if the captain was still in control of his ship.

His migraine crashed an agonizing drum-beat inside his head, as if to answer him. "Have you forgotten about me?" No, I have not, he thought, while rubbing his temples. It would be so easy to cast Jumpsuit out of his door, close himself in and go back to sleep. Whatever was going on was going to continue with or without him. Especially if some plague of craziness had struck the ship.

But his captain and the officers, even if they were talking heads for the corporation that owned his ship, might need his help. It's not like their two-bit security officers knew anything about fighting: they were overseen by a washed-up American cop. This was his ship and his people, and if he didn't do something about what was going on, then who would?

For just a moment, he allowed himself to think about the family he'd lost in the war. When the Russian troops invaded, it would have been easier to have given in to them. To lock his doors, ignore his superior's call to report to his regiment, and instead go about being the man of his household, protecting his momma and younger brothers and sister, like he had since his father had died. But just as he felt the calling now to right a wrong that was going on, he knew he had to stand up against this regime. If he didn't, who would? Turned out it didn't matter, as the rest of his adopted Ukrainian Army folded over like wet towels. And the bombing and crossfire of their short, one-sided battles ended up killing his family. If he was there when it happened, he'd have been killed too. And a big part of him felt like he should have been there to protect them. At least, unlike so many of his countrymen, he stood up for what was right. And he would do it now as well.

His migraine would have to wait, as it always did.

Flavio slammed his cabin door, grabbed a bottled water from his mini-refrigerator and knelt before the silent man. Whisking the pillow case off his head, he splashed some water on the man's face and watched him spring to life. Instantly, the man became crazy again; red eyes drilled into Flavio with fury, mouth screeching animalistic brays. He was crazy all right. Flavio knew what he had to do.

He slipped the pillow case back over the man's head, causing him to thrash even more. Folding the top of his own digits toward his palm, and stiffening his hand and wrist, Flavio waited and at the right moment, chopped with the side of his stiff hand just below the man's ear, making him quiet again.

Time to go to war again, but this time against an unknown enemy. Regardless, he would have to dress appropriately.

A rudimentary plan started to form in his mind, while he slipped on his camouflage pants and long-sleeved olive shirt and laced up his boots. He'd get to deck 8 and the monitor room. There, he could communicate with all the parts of the ship, so he knew better what he was up against.

He remembered Jumpsuit's chomping mouth and attempts to bite him in the neck and thought he'd add extra protection. He tied a heavy scarf around his neck and pulled out his leather work gloves to protect his hands. Last, he pulled out his two carbon Moriknives, with plastic sheaths, and slipped one on each side.

A thought occurred to him and so he considered it, nodding acceptance and stepping to his closet to get what he knew was perfect for this mission. He had found a giant wrench, left on I-95 a year ago. It was almost two feet long and was heavy. It was the perfect blunt weapon, he thought as he glanced at Jumpsuit, lying in silence, chest still heaving.

Slipping each glove on, he lifted the wrench-weapon and threw open his door and rushed into the hallway. Checking both ways, Flavio dashed forward, turned a corner and headed toward the nearest crew elevator.

If Jumpsuit had been conscious, the crazy-man would have heard the *thump-thump-thump* of boots double-timing away, followed by an animal-like screech, then immediately by the *thwack* of Flavio's wrench-weapon striking something soft, followed by the *thump-thump-thump* of his boots, as Flavio headed into his next battle.

12

Deep

Whaudeep Reddy of India, or "Deep" as his Regal European name tag declared, stared in stunned silence at the monitor room's screens. It was like watching a T.D. Bonaventure horror movie in HD. Only this was real, and it was live.

Deep was so fixated on the monitor room's screens, he didn't even blink once as he moved his focus from one screen to the next, holding his gaze just long enough to see each camera's passing three-second image. Then it moved onto the next camera view. Each of the nine screens displayed one scene or another of the same type of rolling images. All revealed the ship in complete chaos.

The firsthand experience with the monkey attack was beyond scary. This was worse. Ironically that was the reason Deep was here: Fish was so freaked out by almost getting eaten by the monkey during their card game in the Living Room, Deep had volunteered to take his shift. This shift.

And what a shift it was. First he watched birds attack the guests and crew. At that moment, it was the most bizarre thing he'd ever seen. He did nothing of course; what could he do? So he just watched helplessly as passengers and crew were running for the exits, or beating back the assaulting birds with whatever they could get their hands on.

Even on the little screens, he could see the blood, and the terror on their faces. But that was nothing compared to the next wave.

It had come out of nowhere. The first indication was odd but still explainable: a couple of passengers rolling around the deck and he assumed they were simply trying to get up and release themselves from their entanglement, or they were fighting a bird attack in an uncoordinated fashion. But that was all he could gather during the camera's three-second glimpse, before it cut away to the next camera view.

Then Deep caught another similar scene on a screen showing the mid-ship, starboard deck 5 cabins. There were two passengers also on the floor. But one was on top of the other whaling on him with his fingers extended like little knives, rather than fists, as Deep would have expected in a fight. He thought knives, because he could have sworn in the three-second vignette he'd seen, blood coating each of the assaulting man's digits. Then that camera cut away again.

Within minutes, most camera views showed either passengers or crew running in a panic, or in a fight with one another. It was impossible to make heads or tails of what was going on though, because the view of each of the ship's 460 cameras continually changed every three seconds, like 460 irritated eyelids blinking back what they didn't want to see. And then each fluttered, revealing the next three-second scene. All nine of his screens blinked from scene to scene at a dizzying pace, but none of the vignettes provided enough information to really know what was going on. Deep had had enough.

He typed a command to show the continual streams of several specific cameras. He called up cameras, 28, 57,

98, and on the same deck 99, 247, 394 and 395, 421, and finally 422. This gave him the uninterrupted views of the areas he had seen the most activity around the ship, just before and after the bird attacks.

His jaw fell open.

Each of the cameras he had chosen showed the same thing: scores of people had gone crazy like the birds and the dogs, and were now attacking other people.

A scene in the Solarium told him the whole unbelievable story. A very large woman in a multi-colored dress had been bent over heaving the contents of a recent meal. Deep was watching her, because she was right in the center of the camera's view and at least two other people who appeared to be overcome by this crazy-disease ran right past her.

Why were the crazy people attacking other people who were running away, but ignoring this big target that wasn't moving? It made no sense to Deep, and so he watched.

Then Deep was surprised to catch the streaming video of that very pretty blonde with the pony-tail, dressed in her tight running outfit. Her author-husband was in front of her. They stepped quickly by the big sickly woman; the husband—he couldn't remember their names—seemed to be fixated on helping someone on the ground, just out of the camera's view.

Deep watched the blonde pass by the sickly woman, and like a switch had been flipped, the sickly woman sprang up and attacked the blonde. *Or was the sickly woman attempting to attack the husband, but the blonde was in the way, and the two got entangled?*

There was a loud thump on the door, which made Deep shudder.

He cocked his head over, while remaining seated, and saw a pale-looking crew member in the small window inset in the door. The crew member glared at him with strange red eyes, like they were bloodshot from a three-day straight shift, but even redder.

The crew member opened his mouth, like he was intending to mouth words, knowing Deep couldn't hear anything through the heavy door. Instead, the mouth of the pale man opened wider, and then wider still.

Deep turned his shoulders, fully intending to run the other way and hide. It was so creepy, his skin crawled.

But then Deep remembered that that door was as solid as they came. It was a specially reinforced hatch meant to secure the monitor room and its recordings from terrorists. Part of some of the upgrades during its time in dry-dock.

He sat up straight, feeling safer now that he had thought through his position.

The pale crew member seemed fixated on Deep, mouth stuck open, a line of spittle growing off his chin. Then the crew member's head spun, like he heard something. His mouth closed and he moved away from the window, out of sight.

Deep glanced again at his main screen—his mind processing what he just witnessed firsthand—desperately wanting to see what was happening to the pretty blonde. She was holding the sickly-looking woman—who wasn't acting very sickly now—back, and having some difficulty because the larger woman was flailing around so much. The larger women appeared to be trying to bite the blonde. For a moment, Deep thought that the blonde wasn't fighting the larger woman, but holding onto her. Then the blonde's author-husband bashed the large woman in the head with a serving tray.

Deep wanted to watch what happened next, but another camera caught his attention. It was one of the bridge. There were only two officers there: Jessica, from Iceland and the most beautiful of all blondes on their ship, and their safety director, Mr. Helguson. Deep watched Jessica open up the hatch and a second officer he didn't recognize rushed through the opening and was frantically telling Jessica something.

"Dammit! I wish I could hear what you're saying!" Deep spat at the screen.

While Jessica was focused on the other officer, someone rushed through the hatch—she didn't close it—and ran into Jessica. It was one of those crazy people.

Deep rose from his rollered-seat abruptly, sending it across the span of the small room and crashing into the other wall.

"I can't help you, Jessica."

13

Bridge

At first Jessica was only startled, thinking it must have been some sort of mistake: this man didn't mean to run into her. But just as suddenly as she was slammed into the bridge flooring, she knew she was now fighting for her life.

The man on top of her seemed enraged to the point of being crazy, and she desperately tried to push him back, her hands clasping around and then slipping off his sweaty upper-arms. His mouth chomped at the air in an exaggerated way.

He's trying to bite me.

His mouth moved closer, and she exhaled a brief scream; she'd forgotten to breathe, holding it much too long, and then she tried to gulp back needed air.

This seemed to stir up the crazy man even more, his mouth chomping rapidly in anticipation of reaching her. A wad of his saliva plopped onto her neck, right below her Adam's apple.

The crazy person was telegraphing his next target.

She was equally disgusted and petrified at the same time. And yet she was able to react to his movements, mostly keeping him at bay.

Fatigue was already bearing down on her, aiding the crazy's unending assault. If this battle persisted much longer, she suspected she'd lose, even though the slight man didn't weigh any more than she did.

He was so close the heat from his putrid breath felt scorching.

She turned away, seeking help from Brian Murphy, the second officer who entered their bridge with this crazy person in tow. But Brian was cowering behind a console. He stared wildly at her and the crazy man on top of her.

"Help me!" she begged. However, expelling the air to say this only gave the crazy man more ground. And she knew she couldn't hold on much longer.

Her words seemed to shake Brian from his moorings. Maybe it was the man's ingrained chauvinism or maybe he forgot himself. She didn't care; she was just glad that he seemed to be heading her way, though way too slow. She knew she only had a little fight left in her.

She couldn't look at the crazy, who kept chomping his mouth and teeth, like she was some piece of meat. She was used to being treated this way among the men in her profession, but it was always figuratively, not literally. *This was insane.* "Help!" she bellowed again.

Brian disappeared and then reappeared, now holding up a model of the Intrepid, a to-scale rendering of the ship. He held the model back and then arced it around in an attempt to knock Crazy Man off her. But he was too high and he didn't have a good grip on the ship model.

It connected and then bounced off Crazy's head, only snapping the man's head back, but at least momentarily stopping his chomping. Crazy reacted instantly, turning his anger on Brian, who appeared perplexed at becoming the focus. Crazy Man sprang off Jessica onto Brian in a single bound.

The springboard off her stomach took all of Jessica's breath away, and for a long moment, she remained on the floor, physically and emotionally paralyzed, while she gazed out the side of her field of vision in amazement. What happened next shocked her back into action. Crazy Man's mouth clamped down on Brian's neck, brutally. She launched like a rocket and leapt onto the two men in an attempt to pull Crazy off her now gravely injured comrade, but she tumbled off them. Crazy doggedly held onto Brian.

Jessica found the ship model on the floor. Rising to her knees, with all the strength she had left, she picked the model up and brought it straight down onto the Crazy Man's head, cracking it open like a melon.

But she feared she was too late.

Brian gurgled a hollow scream while pushing off the now unconscious, or even deceased Crazy Man.

Oh God, I think I killed him!

With the dead man off, Brian clutched his torn-up neck and blurted another weak scream.

She'd never seen so much blood, not thinking it was possible for a human to expel that much blood and still be alive.

Oh God, Brian was going to die!

Jessica was at once swept with feelings of overwhelming sadness and terror, and the strongest of desires to crawl into a corner and cry. But there was no time.

At the hatch, two more crazy people bounded through. One instantly locked onto her and pushed off the other to try and redirect his movement in her direction. But their legs tangled and they both tumbled to the ground in front of her.

Run.

There was no way she could make it to the hatch and exit the bridge: the crazies were between her and it. But she might be able to make it to the starboard swing deck.

If I leave now.

She bounded up, glancing once at the flailing tangle of crazies, desperately trying to right themselves and get at her. One of them was almost up already.

She focused on the swing deck hatch, putting all her effort on this. It was her only chance. Then she remembered Ágúst: he was in the bathroom still. She flashed a glance at the door, seeing the sliver of light shoot out the bottom. Then she remembered the navigation instructions, and she turned to look at her console; its warning light—the one she set to make sure she entered in the course correction—was flashing at her, giving her a countdown to their collision course into the Azores.

She turned back to the swing deck hatch, knowing she had one chance to make it out alive—the only chance she'd have to see her child and her husband, if they were even still alive.

She pumped her legs, but like a nightmare, she was too far away and going way too slow. She could hear the crazy behind her, snarling and huffing.

She chanced a glance back, knowing that it was the wrong thing to do, but unable to keep herself from doing so. She had to know.

He was right behind her, and he was reaching his hand out—

She smacked hard into the starboard window-wall, just to the right of the hatch, surprised that she was off her mark. *I should have been facing the door.*

She reached over to the hatch mechanism and pulled herself to the door, just as crazy man hit, head to metal.

Jessica put all of her fifty kilos down on the handle, the hatch clicking its response.

She chanced another glance, amazed that the crazy man, who should have been knocked out or at least dazed by his head connecting with the metal, was still doggedly after her. The crazy refocused on her much too quickly and even though his head was now gushing blood from the impact with the bridge's steel window-wall frame, he was clawing his way toward her. She still had to open the door, slip through, and close it tight. *She wouldn't make it in time.*

Jessica squealed, moments before the crazy was upon her, when a black-laced shoe hit the crazy mid-chest, sending him past her to the ground. She glanced below her and saw Ágúst there, now wearing his sunglasses, panting and trying to right himself.

"Let's go," he hollered, and she obliged, pulling the door open that Ágúst could slip out, followed immediately by her.

We might make it after all. Maybe I will see my family.

They yanked on the handle, four hands intertwined as one, sending the hatch shut with a *thunk*.

They released and scuttled back on their butts as the hatch's window was filled with the pale face of the red-eyed crazy man, silently snarling at them.

With their backs to the rails of the swing deck, they panted mutual "whews" at their just making it out of the bridge alive.

They glanced at each other, unable to form words from panting uncontrollably, large smiles covering their faces.

And then they heard the screeches again.

These were outside.

Both their heads snapped aft, to the solid wall end of the swing deck. There, only a few feet from them, were at least a dozen black birds, fighting over the torn-apart carcass of a seagull.

They had interrupted the black birds feeding. Now the black birds focused their red-eyed attention on the two officers. It was as if their fiery eyes were telling them, "Why fight it?"

Jessica glanced back at the bridge and now saw two crazy men silently growling out of frustration that their meal that got away, clawing their raw fingers at the closed hatch that they couldn't figure out how to open.

Unheard by either of them, an alarm rang out on her console. Its display read...

1:30:00

1:29:59

1:29:58

14

Crazy People Too

"Run to the Spa," Jean Pierre yelled.

Ted and TJ both knew the place and immediately moved in that direction, leading the way, and Jean Pierre following close behind. Ted briefly paused to snatch up a little table that had scooted out into their walkway, brandishing it by two of its legs. He liked the weight of it and that he could use it to keep the crazy people's mouths away from him. He also scooped up a pointed butter knife and slipped that into his back pocket, wishing he had one of Flavio's knives, or even one of the ship's steak knives they'd hurled at the monkey earlier. But as there was no meat being served in the Solarium—*except the raw human kind,* he thought—this would have to do.

"Come on," TJ insisted, also holding up. Her sunglasses flashed as she whipped her head from side to side to check out her perimeter for any potential threats to them. Her abrupt movements from side to side caused her Orion necklace to flop around onto the small of her back.

To Ted, she now looked like a living rendition of the warrior Orion, at least the necklace's version. And yet she acted anxious. *Of course, who wouldn't here, now.*

Ted couldn't help but take in the surreal landscape of the Solarium. It truly was stranger than fiction.

One of the performers in the cruise ship's drag show was there, dressed in full costume. He was attempting to escape one of the crazed people by jumping into the spa pool. The performer's dazzling feather-headdress hit the sloshing water first; his sparkling platform boots entering the water last. The crazed person didn't seem to care for the water much, immediately redirecting his fury at someone else less wet. That poor SOB was a passenger who was completely caught off-guard while gawking at the flamboyant performer's leap into the pool. The crazed person tackled the unsuspecting passenger, driving both of them into the slick and yet very solid pool decking. Both their heads hit hard, and the crazed person harder. Yet the crazy man rose and continued his assault on the now-dazed passenger.

The soaked drag show performer saw his opportunity and popped out of the water, sans headdress, white makeup sliding off his face. Mixed with the red of someone's blood, his was a macabre mug. He clutched his knees, panting and grinning. He must have known his luck wouldn't be so kind if he held there any longer, and he dashed off.

Passing in front of Ted and TJ was an obese man with frazzled white hair attacking a very small oriental woman. The woman appeared to be holding the crazed man back to protect her husband, an equally small person on the floor, wearing bright orange pants and white slip-on loafers. The man was screeching in a sopranic voice, sounding almost like a waterfowl. The frazzled-hair man was overpowering the much smaller woman, biting her and scratching at her, until she fell to the ground.

The crazed man then turned his attention to her orange-trousered husband, who tried to duck walk away without much luck. The crazed man caught up with the smaller man right in the middle of their path to the Spa.

Ted had a thought. He wasn't sure where it came from, but like many of his thoughts, his subconscious mind figured shit out before his conscious mind could give reason to it. But as usually was the case, he knew he was right. Just before his wife was about to thwack the white-haired man with her tray, Ted yanked out the butter knife and holding the blade-end, he whacked one of the table legs multiple times, generating echoing ping-noises, as if it were a musical instrument.

Apparently the *ping-ping-ping* sound was so loud, even TJ stopped in mid-swing, almost acting like the sound was piercing and hurting her ears. But it also had the desired effect.

The crazed man's head swiveled in Ted's direction, and he course-corrected, pushing off the oriental man.

Ted wasn't sure what he was expecting. He knew subconsciously that the loud noise would affect the crazy-person, he just hadn't thought through what would happen after he'd done it: it was not like they had time. Certainly, Ted hadn't expected the man to move so quickly, because he had barely enough time to push the table forward, using the top of it to deflect the man away. Luckily for Ted, inertia—both his and the man's—caused the frazzled-hair man to shoot past Ted and onto the floor.

When the crazy man bounded up, both Ted and TJ were ready. Before the crazy man could take more than one step, both pummeled his head multiple times, until he crumpled to the floor and lay unmoving.

They briefly flashed each other smiles, before TJ moved forward, Ted following. Jean Pierre still brought up the rear, swiping wildly with his own drink tray at a bird that seemed absolutely fixated on his chrome dome.

A flash of movement to Ted's left pulled at his attention. He didn't know how, but amazingly the oriental woman who was brutally attacked and bitten sprang up. She looked a bloody mess, but without hesitation, she sprinted toward a couple cowering in a corner of the Solarium under one of the larger tables.

Was it a bite that did that to her? he wondered. But that made no sense from what he understood about this parasite.

Ted must have not been paying attention, because he crashed into his wife, who was trying to hold the spa door open.

She said nothing, but scowled at him. Ted shrugged his shoulders as Jean Pierre breezed by them inside. Ted and TJ rolled in, clicking the spa door closed behind them.

The three of them stared out of the spa's double glass doors, chests heaving for air.

"Did you see that the people are crazy too?"

Ted and TJ swung their gazes at Jean Pierre. They didn't have to say anything; their looks screamed, "No shit, Sherlock."

TJ turned to her husband. "Is it the bite that turns them... crazy?"

"I wouldn't have thought it, but it seems so. Did you see that oriental woman bound up after being attacked?"

TJ grimaced behind her Oakleys. "Yes, but how? Why?" She reached around her back and pulled her Orion charm around her necklace chain, rubbed it a couple of times and let it drop just above the neckline of her soaked sports shirt.

In quiet, they studied the Solarium's chaos, while catching their breaths. Jean Pierre decided to check out the spa.

Ted hadn't answered TJ. And TJ didn't press him, as she knew he was chewing on the new sets of facts. "Did you see how they responded to sound?"

"Yeah, and you almost made me deaf."

"It wasn't that loud," he lamented. "Besides, I have a theory. The infected animals and now infected people are attracted to sound. I saw it with the birds: they attacked the loudspeakers while the alarm was going off, and then they stopped when it was no longer blaring. The screaming of the uninfected seems to draw the attention of any crazy humans or animals."

"Once infected, they don't seem too human. And did you notice they don't seem to care about their inj—"

A screech from the back of the spa stopped them both cold.

"Psst."

Jean Pierre was in front of one of the individual spa rooms, his hands waving them forward.

They quickly scooted in his direction.

Jean Pierre pushed open the door, and out poured Zen music: some sort of Indian musical montage, obviously meant to help their spa clients meditate or feel relaxed or something of which Ted had no idea, not being a spa-guy.

Jean Pierre slipped in through the door, followed by TJ and then finally Ted, who pulled the door behind him.

The three of them froze.

Inside were two couples. One of the two men, a bare-chested older man with wrinkled olive skin, brandished a heavy hardcover book, covered in splotches of blood and feathers. He was poised like a baseball player at the plate, about to swing for the fences. Then the older man's jaw dropped at seeing Ted.

He brought the book-weapon he had been holding up down to face level, pulled out a white handkerchief from a back pocket of his khakis and whipped off the gore from back cover—not even flinching at the blood and guts. He let the hankie drop to the floor, while glancing at the back cover, and then turned up his face again at Ted, his scowl building into a grin.

Ted recognized the older picture on the back cover: it was his big stupid-looking smile, complemented by a handle-bar mustache, his deerstalker hat tilted down to block out the sun, and the ocean surf spraying behind him from the balcony of their aft cabin of his first transatlantic cruise, some years ago. He never liked the picture, but his agent said it made him look like a "real person."

"Greetings, Mr. Bonaventure," said the man. "I'm David Cohen." He thrust out his hand as if he were at a book signing, and nothing else was going on in their world. All thoughts about adding more gore to his book-weapon were forgotten.

The Zen music was almost loud enough to drum out the screaming outside their room. Almost.

15

Collapse

All they could do at this point was run. It wasn't what Jörgen and his crew were trained to do, but who was trained for a riotous horde of crazed people, driven by an absolute desire to kill?

Somehow, they were able to pull Urban away from the crazed man who had taken a huge chunk of flesh out of his neck. But there were others now. What seemed like scuffles within the crowd were passengers and some crew attacking others. Both Jörgen and Wasano attempted to break up the attacks, but it was no use. In rapid fashion, they were being overwhelmed.

There may not have been any policy for dealing with riots like this one, but there was the rule about protecting your fellow crew members when invaders had boarded your ship. And this crazy disease had boarded their ship and was attacking it and his crew. And with Urban's injuries looking more serious by the second, Jörgen and Wasano thought it better to retreat to safety for now, while they still had a chance.

They followed the panicked passengers down the half-flight of stairs and then turned into the first crew access they could find, figuring that the numbers of frenzied people would be smaller, if only because of the smaller ratio of crew to passengers. They were correct.

Although there was some screaming in the crew stairwell below them, it certainly wasn't the all-out melee of the more public areas. They could stop here and collect themselves and figure out what to do next.

They found a cart of linens in the stairwell, abandoned by a room steward, and fashioned a make-shift compression bandage around the left side of the nape of Urban's neck. This they tied around his chest and under both arms. A lot of tissue was missing in his wound area, and more important, he had lost a lot of blood. His blanched features and sunken eyes were alarming. But all of this was alarming.

In the back of Jörgen's mind, he couldn't help but wonder if the Urban's bite-wound would turn him into one of those lunatics. It didn't matter. If he did, they'd deal with him. Right now, he was one of their crew and as his captain, Jörgen knew that he would do everything he could to protect his officer to the bitter end, no matter how or when that might be.

"So where now, Captain?" asked Wasano. "Officer Patel needs medical attention."

Jörgen wanted to get onto the bridge. That's where he belonged. From there he could captain them through this crisis. But Wasano was right, Urban needed immediate medical attention.

"Give me your radio."

Wasano handed him his walkie.

"This is Captain Christiansen. Repeat, this is Captain Jörgen Christiansen. Doc Chettle, report. Bridge, report. Engineering, report." He let go of the transmit button and turned up the volume.

Static and screaming sounds were followed by "Captain, this is Assistant Engineering Director Niki Tesler. Sir, we cannot get to engineering. This whole floor is overrun by these insane people…" she started to breakdown. "They ate Ivan, sir. It was horrible. I didn't know what to do…"

They thought she had stopped transmission, because they couldn't hear anything else. Then… sniffles. She still had her transmit button depressed.

"I'm sorry, sir."

Background static now, as she was done.

"It's all right, Niki." He almost never referred to someone by their first name in public, and certainly not on the radio. "Are you safe? Where are you?"

"I'm just off the control room, in Ivan's—I mean the Chief Engineer's—private office. I have two other crew here. We've been hiding and trying to keep quiet. They seem to be attracted to noise. But the place is overrun. So we're not going anywhere."

"Have you heard from the bridge lately?"

"No, sir."

"What about the engine room?"

Static silence. Niki was keeping off the air to let someone from the engine room chime in.

"Captain…" the speaker crackled, "this is Max Borne, from ER. I'm stuck in an access duct, port side aft of the main engine room. This place is a madhouse, sir."

"Sit tight, Mr. Borne, until this blows over." He said this, even though he doubted this would blow over any time soon. "To anyone else, do we have any control over this ship?"

Silent static.

Niki chimed in again. "Sir, I believe all those not affected by this have holed up somewhere, for safety."

There was a screech directly above them. It was close.

Jörgen turned the volume down and clicked transmit. "We're going off comm for a little bit. Sit tight, officer, and anyone else listening. Captain out."

Safety first, he thought. Then medical assistance for Urban, then figure out how to wrestle back control of the ship later. Everything should be on automatic, so they should be good for a while.

"Ye Olde Tavern," Jörgen whispered. It was only two floors down from where they were, and if they could make the turn quickly enough, and there weren't many frenzied people in the area, they might be able to escape inside. They needed to get to someplace safe to attend to Urban, who now appeared to be going into shock. "Ye Olde Tavern would be closed, and no one should be inside," he whispered once more, not wanting the frenzied person below them to hear.

Jörgen and Wasano hoisted Urban up, on each side of him, and they lumbered down the two decks, practically carrying the nearly unconscious man.

Holding up at the exit, they gave each other a quick glance. The low lights of the crew access stairwell masked their concern. At first, Jörgen didn't want Wasano to see his alarm. And Wasano had the same look, probably thinking something similar. At this point neither cared.

Urban did his best to just stay lucid. But he continued to lose blood, in spite of their best efforts to suppress the flow from his wound with their linen compression-bandage. It was obvious he was teetering between consciousness and unconsciousness. They couldn't get to Ye Olde Tavern fast enough. And even then, he still needed medical attention and they were moving much closer to Chettle's infirmary.

Ye Olde Tavern's door was immediately contiguous to the crew access door they were lingering behind. If the coast was clear, they could quickly unlock the door and close themselves in. No one else should be there.

Wasano carefully pushed open the door, just a crack and peeked out. An ocean of screaming and yelling poured through.

"How does it look, Wasano?" whispered Jörgen, inches away. He couldn't see a damned thing, and it was killing him not to be the eyes, but he wanted to honor his new head of security by ceding this part of their mission to him.

Wasano remained motionless, other than his head, which turned slowly, like a lighthouse beacon, taking in everything. "I think it looks clea—hold on." Without saying another word, Wasano bounded through the door, his feet squeaking on the floor.

Jörgen took over his position in the door and glanced out. He whispered to Urban, "Don't move," and then dashed out the door as well.

Urban wasn't sure if any time had passed, or if he had lost consciousness or not, because the world was swimming in front of him. His captain said something he didn't catch, before disappearing. Using his uninjured arm, he grabbed the doorknob above him and swung himself to the other side of the door, twisted the knob and peeked through. He now understood where his captain and security director went.

An older woman was fighting against a much younger woman wearing a spa bathrobe. The older woman kept beating the younger woman with her cane, but the younger woman was unrelenting, screeching anger and scratching at the older woman, who had her back up against the Ye Olde Tavern entrance.

The security director yanked the younger woman away, tossing her easily to the floor, while the captain helped the elderly woman up. She was trying to tell them something when several people burst out of the Ye Olde Tavern's door. The elderly woman must have been trying to hold the door closed when she was attacked.

The Spa Woman was already up and fixated on the security director, while captain and the elderly woman were racing back toward the opening Urban sat in. Urban used the last of his strength to move out the way and hold open the door farther to make passage easier. He hoped no one else would come through, because he wouldn't able to do anything. The captain, security director and elderly woman bounded through the opening and slammed shut the door, and the only thing holding Urban. He flopped to the floor, hearing his head clunk against the floor and the door being pounded on from the other side.

Another wave of dizziness hit, but he forced himself to stay conscious.

"My-oh-my. You gentlemen were just in time. Thank you!" said the old woman in between shallow breaths.

"It's our pleasure ma'am," answered Wasano.

Jörgen helped Urban up.

"I'm fine, sir," Urban responded.

"I guess Ye Olde Tavern was open already..." the security director stated what was obvious to all of them.

"How about the life boats, sir?" Urban croaked.

Both the security director and the captain shot each other glances, and then back to Urban.

"That's a terrific idea. There's a first aid kit for you, as well as provisions, and because they're locked up there won't be any passengers or crew there. We should be safe," the captain stated triumphantly. "And we're on the shady side, which should have fewer passengers, because of lack of sun. Wasano, would you lead us?"

"Yes, sir," the security director said and then took them down the stairwell and out a hallway that led to a separate crew access door out on the starboard Promenade deck, right in front of lifeboat #35.

A quick check both ways, and it appeared to be clear. So the four of them rushed out the door and across the rubberized decking to the locked gate. The security director already had the proper key ready, driving it in with purpose, and they were in.

The captain had his arm wrapped around Urban, who could no longer move on his own. The elderly woman seemed more agile than she had appeared at first. The security director closed and tried to lock the gate, but the tumbler seemed broken.

He threw open the door and hesitated momentary. When they heard a scream on the promenade deck, very close by, the four of them poured into the life boat and clicked the door closed.

Before Urban lost consciousness for good, he caught a glimpse of a large, hulking man standing in back. Then he was out.

16

Swing Deck

"Birds!" screamed Ágúst.

If just their presence didn't seem to do it, Ágúst's screaming did the trick. The dozen or so birds thrashed at the air, desperate to get to them as quickly as they could.

Jessica looked around for something to hide behind or to use to defend themselves with, but there was nothing on the swing deck. She had already slunk under a console, but there was nothing she could use to block the oncoming birds.

She'd read about horrific events, like a car crash, when everything appears in slow motion. She understood the science behind it: all of your senses becoming aware of everything at once; the firing of so many neurons to catch the input of a billion pieces of stimuli around you; your brain just trying to catch up. Still, it was something she had only read about. Experiencing this firsthand was amazingly intense as the birds came at Ágúst and her. And at that moment, which had slowed to a crawl, something very strange happened.

Images of her husband and her seven-year-old flashed in front of her. She had read about this too; it made sense. It was the human mind's escape mechanism, a way to cope with the unbearable. She suspected it would have been natural for her to accept these images, just as it was to not fight the inevitable about to hit her. But she was a fighter.

In fact, the images made her mad: she wasn't going to let these birds take her away from her family. She would at least try.

She looked up, remembering just then that there was a slide-out table above her, with keyboard. She clicked off the locks and slid the table out and off, the keyboard falling off its cradle and onto the deck. The birds hit at the moment she held out the table like it was a shield. They pummeled the table, as if individual fists were punching at her, pushing back her shield toward her. She pushed harder, locking her elbows, as they drilled down on her.

She felt one peck at her leg, out of sight and she kicked at it and the others flapping nearby. She couldn't see any of them. One attempted to come around and attack her side, but she was able to deflect its advance before it could get her face—they seemed to be going for her face.

She held back the assault of what felt like hundreds of birds, but she knew it was probably still only some of that dozen she'd just seen a millennia of moments ago.

Then she felt pecks at her fingers, followed by pain. Lots of pain. Several connected directly with her legs, despite her thrashing at them.

She was starting to feel pain everywhere and more so, a sinking dread that she couldn't keep this up much longer, when she heard *ping... ping... ping.*

And still the assault continued, but now with fewer birds than before.

Again she heard *ping* and something else. It was a grunt and then another *ping*.

When she no longer felt the birds attacking, she ventured a look over her keyboard table-shield.

It was Ágúst. He was standing in front of her, huffing and puffing, holding a small fire extinguisher. Before him were the dead bodies of at least a dozen birds.

He'd killed them all.

"You all right?" he begged, dropping the fire extinguisher and holding out his hand.

She thrust out hers.

"Oh no, your hands," he said, his face twisted with concern.

She pulled them back and examined them. Her hands were beat to hell. But they were still functional. She slid out from under the console and glared at the sky, sure another attack was imminent.

Other than the occasional bird in the distance, there didn't seem to be any interest in them. At least for now.

She glanced at Ágúst and was surprised to see he didn't have any injuries. She knew she must have looked like hell. She glared at her bloodied legs and then back at Ágúst. He didn't have a scratch on him.

"Don't worry about me," he said, watching her.

Then she remembered their larger problem. She spun on a heel and now focused her attention on the swing deck's console. It was supposed to have had ninety percent of the bridge's controls. She'd only used the swing deck controls for some basic system checks, since all the controls she needed had been on the bridge. But now she needed them.

She flicked the power switch on, but none of the monitors flickered on.

She toggled the on/off switch back and forth, but the screens remained black. "Dammit!" She pounded the middle of console with a balled fist.

"What's wrong?" Ágúst asked behind her.

"I left the bridge before I was able to reset our navigation. I was hoping to do that here."

"So we don't get our efficiency bonus this year by blowing through more fuel than scheduled. I can live with that," Ágúst snickered.

"You don't understand. Because I wasn't able to reset the controls, we're still scheduled to run into the Azores in an hour or so."

He gulped back a breath, spun and dashed past the bridge hatch, sticking his face against the glass, cupping his hands around his head. He pulled back and glared at her, his face slackening.

"What?" she asked.

"Look," he answered.

She did.

Inside the bridge were the two crazies, gazing slack-jawed at her console. It blared an alarm tone that warned there was 1:18.53 left until they'd run into one of the islands.

"Okay, so how do you fix this?" Ágúst begged.

Jessica ignored him and instead dashed to the most forward point of the swing deck. Reaching under that console, she found a set of binoculars.

She pulled them to her face, glanced through them, and then handed them to Ágúst so he could understand what she did.

Sao Miguel was just ahead and there was nothing they could do to stop them from running into it in a little more than an hour.

17

How Could It Get Worse?

"Please just call me Ted." Ted accepted the bare-chested man's hand and returned his enthusiastic handshake, attempting with difficulty to match the man's firm grip. He immediately noticed the Auschwitz tattoo on his forearm and thought, *This man lived through the Nazis and is probably a tough customer.* Ted suspected he would find this out firsthand, if they made it through the day.

David continued pumping Ted's hand, while his words tumbled out. "I'm a big fan, although I'm a little behind on my reading. Never finished your last one so I was starting it again, but was interrupted by the damned birds. Nice talk, by the way."

"I'm Evie," said an equally skinny woman, sitting on a massage table, towel around her shoulders, with two other passengers who looked nervous. Evie waved her palm tentatively. "My husband won't let you get in a word in edgewise; he's a bit of an author groupie."

David tossed a scowl behind him at his wife obviously practiced over the years.

Ted waved back at Evie and couldn't help but smile at how odd life was: they'd just barely escaped with their lives, and now were in a spa room filled with Zen music, while making small talk with a concentration camp survivor, who was also a Bonaventure groupie. He couldn't make this shit up.

"Enough of the meet-and-greet," demanded a rotund, bald British man seated in the back of the room, with an equally large pale-faced woman clutching his hand. He ignored Ted and David and focused his attention on Jean Pierre. "Staff Captain, what's going on out there? Is the captain still in charge?"

David's expression changed almost immediately, as did Evie's, a scowl finding what Ted suspected was a normal place on David's face.

Jean Pierre pushed past Ted and addressed the room. "Hello..."

"Boris and my wife Penny," said the large Brit.

"Hello Boris and Penny, and David and Evie. I probably don't know more than any of you. You saw the people attacking other people, didn't you?"

Ted suspected Jean Pierre had said this for the same reason Ted wanted to ask: it just didn't seem real.

"Yes, we did," stated David, his face very serious now. "That's why we're here, hiding from them, like you."

"You saw this coming, didn't you?" puffed Penny, glaring at Ted.

This comment took Ted by complete surprise. He didn't know this woman. And yet he'd been asking himself this very question over the last twenty-four hours. "Ah, no." His voice was weak. His eyes darted around the room furtively. It felt very small inside at this moment and he could feel his pulse take off again. "My book was fiction, and in it only the animals were crazy. Plus, it was a terrorist that caused it all in the book, which I don't believe is what we're experiencing."

Ted realized then it wasn't the woman's question that got his heart racing; it was his wife. She had been completely silent this whole time, and usually she would have said something snarky about David's adulation and certainly in response to the woman's accusatory comment. He turned to look at her.

"You're being somewhat coy about this, Ted, aren't you? I live with a man who's guarded about most things," Evie lobbed a knowing look back at her husband, "except when it comes to meeting his favorite authors." She returned her gaze back to Ted. "Please share what you think is going on."

Ted ignored her question, as his eyes had not left his wife since he had turned to look at her.

TJ was standing in the corner of the room, away from everyone. Her hands were planted on her hips, as she often did after a run. Likewise, her chest was heaving, mouth wide open to get air. Besides the oddity of her wearing a splash of blood across one of her arms, bare belly and cheek, she was still wearing her dark sunglasses inside. Further telegraphing her mood, her shoulders were hunched and head pointed at her shoes. She was upset about something, whereas she seemed fine after dealing with all the crazies in the Solarium.

"Hey Yank, do tell us what you think. Why have so many gone all barmy? Will we go barmy too?"

TJ looks distressed, he thought. "Hon, are you all right?"

All attention turned to TJ, and she seemed to know it. She caught her breath and tilted her head up to meet Ted's gaze, and shot him a weak grin. "I'm fine... Just a little freaked about the birds and the crazy people."

She huffed once and then stood up tall. She wasn't going to say anything more, and neither should he push her to answer, until he had her alone.

Jean Pierre seem to sense the awkward moment, and so he repeated the question, "Ted, please tell us what you think is going on."

Ted took a breath, turned to face the others, and started.

"It's a parasite; that's what's causing the fits of rage we've seen first in the animals, and then the people." Dr. Molly Simmons stood again, adjusted her skirt, and sat back down, readying herself for more questions.

"A parasite, you mean like a tapeworm? You think a tapeworm caused these people to go bonkers?" Hans shot a scornful frown at the elderly woman, as her fingers played with the contours of her odd-shaped cane.

She mostly ignored him. "Tapeworms are but one of tens of thousands of species of parasites. In fact, there are five times as many parasites as all other organisms on earth.

"This particular parasite is called toxoplasma Gondii or T-Gondii—"

"Sounds like a fauking sexual disease, raweyet?" Hans blurted and held his hand up for a high-five from his brother Franz, who also ignored him, and then readjusted the blanket around his shoulders. Franz kept his attention on the smart old woman, as if his life depended on it.

Molly disregarded this comment too, pushed her coke-bottle-sized specs further up her nose and continued, "And we are only just starting to learn how the T-Gondii rewires human and animal behaviors to do its bidding."

"Wait, Dr. Simmons," the captain barked. "Are you saying this T-Gondii planned this? Why would it want animals and humans to go insane and kill each other?"

"Yes, Captain, you're correct on the 'planned this' part"—she made quotation symbols with her two hands in the air— "of your comment, but not in the way you and I would look at it." She removed her glasses and rubbed away an invisible smudge on one lens and then polished the other, using one of the top ruffles of her long skirt. After a quick examination to make sure they were clear, she popped them back on her face.

It was her way of collecting herself when she was nervous—this time she was scared beyond reason. But unlike an academic lecture in front of a boisterous classroom or a presentation before her peers, this talk was about the scariest parasite she thought she'd ever encountered. Parasites had killed maybe a billion people over the years. This one might end up killing all the rest, making what they were all experiencing an extinction event.

Focus Molly, the captain, and others are counting on your knowledge.

"The T-Gondii is... a single-cell organism. So it doesn't have a brain, like you or me. But like us, the T-Gondii has DNA that tells it what to do, and we've seen many cases in the parasitic world where the organism transfers some of its DNA hard-wiring to its hosts, so that their hosts will do what it wants."

"But to what end?" the captain asked. "Why direct animals and people to attack and kill each other? Wouldn't that lead to every host's death?"

"Sounds like a stupid fauking bacteria," Hans chortled, raising his hand up toward his brother again in another attempt to get a high-five from him. After the moment lingered, when Franz avoided acknowledging him entirely, Hans lowered his hand and looked down.

Typical bully, Molly thought. But at least this bully is listening to you.

"No, sir. Far from stupid, in fact." She wanted to say, "unlike you," but such a comment would be juvenile, like him. "The protozoa has DNA, much like our own: a complex network, interconnected. It's very much like what goes to make up our own brains, at least for some of us." She couldn't help the small dig, but thought better of carrying it any further and inciting the large man ."Whereas a bacteria is just a bag of loose DNA and proteins, this particular protozoa is very smart, indeed. And like all other organisms—to get to your question, Captain—T-Gondii wants to survive and thrive, and to do that, it must take out all threats. Only those who are not infected are a threat. Somehow each host infected with T-Gondii knows who's not infected and desires to kill only those people or animals."

"What are you, some kind of damned expert on parasites?" the big German stated. It wasn't a question.

She turned away from the captain to address the man she had instantly disliked when they had arrived at this lifeboat: a skinhead, who must have instinctively known her Jewish roots. She assumed his brother was of similar ilk, although he wasn't as bellicose as his Aryan brother. "In fact, sir, I am an expert on this subject. I'm a parasitologist." She left off the "retired" part.

She returned her gaze to the captain, then across from him to the unblinking eyes of the ship's security chief and, head resting against this man's shoulder, the severely injured man, who was listening with his eyes closed. This one looked very pale.

"So I suspect that everyone who is not infected with T-Gondii will be attacked. Everyone who is infected will be mostly left alone."

"That makes sense, Captain," chimed in the security chief, addressing his superior. "Remember some of the passengers were not getting attacked by the birds and others were?"

Captain Jörgen considered this, and then looked back to Molly. "Please, no disrespect, Dr. Simmons, but how could you possibly know this with the limited anecdotal evidence we've seen?"

"You are correct, this is a supposition of mine, based on limited observations, but also a lifetime of studying parasites, like this one. This is what parasites do."

"So..." Captain Jörgen, looked upward to remember something, and then, as if he plucked the thought from an imaginary mental file cabinet above his head, he continued, "...explain how thermophilic bacteria plays a role in all of this."

"Yes, of course, you would have spoken to our author-friend." She grinned, just a little. "You cannot have the one operating without the other. Not on the scale we're seeing. You see, most of the time the T-Gondii doesn't appear to be active in most hosts. When it is active... Well, this is why, before this recent wave, we've been seeing more and more incidents of aggressive behavior by both humans and animals. But it still affects everyone it infects, having already done most of its work of reprogramming their brains, and then it lays in wait, for what we never knew. But I always believed it was waiting for some inciting stimulus to activate the T-Gondii and turn on the new programming in its hosts."

"That's where the thermophilic bacteria comes in," exclaimed the captain, nodding his understanding.

"Exactly. I don't know why, perhaps no one will, even if by some miracle our race survives this. But the thermophilic bacteria was just the inciter that the T-Gondii was looking for.

"And this bacteria was already unique, without the normal soft cell-walls of most bacteria. This thing is tough as nails—almost indestructible. And when it infects a host that is also infected with T-Gondii, it appears to set the

T-Gondii's new programming off, so that the hosts then do what the T-Gondii told it to do: kill or destroy every non-infected species of mammal."

"Sorry, Ms. Simmons," interrupted the security head—she couldn't remember his name, nor see far enough to read his name-tag. "You said, 'if our race survives this.' There must be some way to stop this?"

"It's Dr. Simmons, actually." Molly wasn't one for titles, but she didn't want her words to be taken lightly. "And it is I who am sorry. I'm not sure there is any way to stop this. We've known for decades about the Plasmodium parasite that causes malaria and kills two to three million people a year. And yet the best we can do is practically kill the patient with arsenic. So instead, the medical community had been focused on prevention, because we simply don't have a cure. I don't suspect we'll ever find a cure for this either."

The six occupants of lifeboat 35 fell completely silent, weighed down by this shocking piece of information.

A loud tone startled all but the security chief and the captain. The security chief reached around his belt and unclipped his radio, and to Molly, he said, "Someone has put out an 'all hands' call on the radio. Mine was turned down so as not to attract the attention of any of the crazy people."

He turned up the volume.

"... Repeat. This is First Officer Jessica Eva Mínervudóttir. We are stuck on the swing deck. I'm asking for any officers to respond, or anyone from engineering."

The radio responded right away. "Hello, First Officer. This is Staff Captain Haddock."

The security chief held the radio to his mouth. "This is Acting Security Director Wasano Agarwal. I'm here with Captain Jörgen, Deck Officer Urban Patel, and three guests."

"Jörgen, you're safe, sir?" bleated Jean Pierre.

Wasano handed Jörgen the radio.

"Yes, we're safe. But Deck Officer Patel was seriously injured. Where are you?"

"We're holed up in a room in the spa. What about you?"

The captain quickly gazed at Molly, and then Hans and Franz before speaking. "Staff Captain, we're in life boat 35, with *three* passengers." The captain's tone had changed like he was reminding his officers to keep up their radio decorum. Molly was a widow to a ship's captain and understood protocol very well. "First Officer, who's OOD?"

Oh-oh!

There was a long silence, before Jessica—*the one trapped on the swing deck*—answered, in a much more obtuse manner. It was as if she knew, after the captain's subtle reminder, that there were passengers within earshot.

"No one is, sir. And I didn't get the new navigational instructions into the ECDIS. We are still on a 296 degree heading, at fifteen knots, and we'll hit our destination in just over an hour."

Jean Pierre let his head droop down, his chin practically coming to rest on his chest, the walkie held suspended in the air, where he'd been listening. After a deep breath, he stood up straight, radio finding his ear. "Have you been able to raise anyone from engineering?" He suspected he knew the answer, but he had to ask to confirm this.

Jessica answered, "No, sir. Since Safety Officer Helguson and I were chased off the bridge, we've been trapped on the swing deck by a couple of those crazy people. I've been trying to raise someone for the last fifteen minutes."

"Merde," was the only thing Jean Pierre could think of saying, before he let his body fall into a soft chair, pushed up against the wall of their spa room.

Ted stepped over to him. "Did I understand your first officer's veiled point correctly?"

Jean Pierre looked up to Ted and then over to the four passengers who heard much more than he wanted to have to explain, but he knew he had to now.

"We're all in this together now. Best tell them what we just heard," Ted exclaimed, while rubbing a temple.

"Yes, JP," TJ huffed, the first words any of them had heard from her in awhile. "Spill the damned beans."

"If we don't find some way to get to either engineering or the bridge and change our course, in just over an hour, we will slam into Punta Delgado at fifteen knots."

18

Eye in The Sky (A few minutes earlier)

Deep had been watching and listening to everything, but that's all he could do.

When he first saw the ship's captain and the others about to make a break for Ye Olde Tavern, Deep tried to warn them on the radio that this would be a problem with all the crazies running around that very public deck, and those in the bar. But his base unit wouldn't transmit, even though it was receiving most everything, albeit weakly.

Best he could figure was that the connection to the radio's antenna, which ran up through one of the conduits and out to the antenna outside—so he and the bridge, just forward of him, and engineering, below and aft of him, had the best radio reception—was broken, no doubt from the tsunami. The fact that he was receiving anything seemed a miracle. Worse, like an idiot, he'd forgotten his portable in his cabin. So while he'd glanced at each of his monitors, he was busy fashioning an improvised dipole antenna for his base unit, using strands of wire from a coil pulled from a dead generator.

After a few minutes of watching the captain's group, the staff captain's group, the bridge, starboard swing deck, engineering, and a few other key areas, it was obvious to him that they had lost control of the ship to the crazies. This was, of course, bad. But he wasn't immediately worried, because he knew everything on this ship, including navigation, was on autopilot.

They still had some time. At least that's what he was thinking.

Now, all Deep wanted to do was tell everyone with a radio that he was right there with them watching.

He thought about some American news programs, which received periodic reports about traffic accidents and safe routes for morning commuters, all coming from a news helicopter, which called itself their eye in the sky.

He would be the ship's 'eye in the sky' and maybe point out possible routes to safety for crew members and passengers. He also wanted to promote the conversation further among the officers and crew about what was going on and how they could fight against it, together.

Deep keyed the microphone, "Hello, this is Deep, speaking from the MR. I'm putting a call out to all officers. This is Deep in the *Intrepid's* Monitor Room. Do you read me?"

"What was that?" asked the staff captain, his signal weak and scratchy. "Something just cut you out, like someone was transmitting over you."

"Dammit!" bellowed Deep. The steel surrounding the MR was too great. His antenna wouldn't be enough to transmit his signal outside the MR and then to each location, many of whom were also deep within the ship's bowels. This is why his base unit was connected to an outside antenna. He needed to get his new antenna outside. But he had no idea how to get it outside while he was stuck inside the MR.

Deep stepped to the MR entrance and glared out the small window to the outside world, currently owned by the crazies.

He heard a muffled animal-like screech and saw a shadow shoot by, the beast's screech-sounds trailing behind it.

"How will I get an antenna out there?" he wondered out loud, shoulders drooping. It seemed impossible. He wished he could talk to Buzz, their know-everything-electronic fix-it guy, more than anything right now. Buzz always knew what to do.

Deep was lost in thought, staring through the window, when something large consumed all light in the window.

He stepped back and saw it was a man in a head waiter's uniform. The name tag flashed by before he could see it, but he saw the colors of the flag.

Ukrainian or Romanian, he thought.

There were others huddled around the waiter.

Deep caught a brief view of the side of a ferret cradled carefully in someone's palms, followed by the faces of his friends Jaga and Yacobus and one more familiar face behind them. They were mouthing something.

Deep disengaged the lock, and the four men and one ferret poured inside, with the waiter slamming the door shut behind them.

"Tha-thanks for letting us in, Deep," Buzz stammered.

"You are exactly the person I needed. So glad you're here, and you're safe."

Deep turned to his other two friends, wearing chasm-sized grins. "Hello Jag—" Deep nearly bit his tongue when he caught the full-view of Jaga's ferret, cradled against Jaga's chest. The ferret was eyeing him. Exactly like the other crazy animals, Jaga's ferret had blood-red eyes.

"Don't worry about Taufan; he's fine, even though he has those crazy eyes."

"Enough pleasantries. You contact bridge? What is status of crew?" demanded the big Slavic waiter. This man was serious looking: more like a general in the military than a waiter. The uniform looked too small for him, like it had shrunk or he had grown out of it.

Deep wondered, even though the accent sounded right for his nametag, if this man killed the waiter whose uniform he was wearing: it was coated in splotches of blood. There were other oddities: long sleeve shirt, leather work gloves duct-taped around his sleeves, and large bandanna bunched around his neck. Finishing his ensemble were two sheathed knives—one on each side—and a large wrench clutched in his hand, also covered in blood. He was ready to do battle; rather, he had already done battle.

"This is Flavio," said Yacobus. "He helped us get here safe. He wanted to get to the MR too."

"Hello Flavio," Deep offered, making direct eye contact with the man who towered over all of them.

Flavio didn't change his expression, blurting, "Status please?"

Deep knew who was in charge, in spite of the uniform. He obliged the man. "The ship has crazies everywhere, including on the bridge and in engineering. And I haven't been able to reach anyone on the radio yet, because my connection to the antenna is broken."

"How do we connect?" Flavio asked. He scooted closer to the video screens, his arms now folded and cradling his blood-soaked wrench. His eyes flitted from screen to screen.

"Well, I don't exactly know. But I'm hoping Buzz here could help us figure that out." He turned to Buzz, whose eyes had been searching around the MR, "So Buzz, I've constructed a dipole, but it won't work in here because of the heavy steel around us. Maybe we could—"

Buzz cut him off, "Actually, that's simple. You have plenty of coaxial cable. Connect that from the radio to the dipole antenna you created. Then someone needs to get outside the crew areas, where you're not dealing with the thicker steel skeleton around the MR, for instance, inside the atrium."

Deep's mouth dropped. He was going to suggest some way to connect with the broken antenna, or push wire through the conduit. This was so much better. And yet it was impossible.

Who would be nuts enough to volunteer to leave the safety of this room, and then snake a coax line from there through the crew access hallway into the atrium, where there were bunches of crazies waiting to murder him?

Flavio turned to Buzz, with the same serious expression he had when he came in. "Thought you said this was simple."

"Simple, yes. Easy, no."

"So, if antenna is placed outside in public area," Flavio tilted his head upward to do the calculations, "roughly eighteen meters away, assuming you have enough of this cable, we can speak to the crew?"

Deep's mouth snapped shut before he spoke, "Yes, I have more than thirty meters of cable."

"Okay, I go, now."

"But..." Jaga looked out the window of the MR door and watched another two crazies pass by. "There are so many of them out there. We just barely made it. How will you get through them?"

"I can handle it." Flavio hoisted his bloody wrench in the air and tapped the handle of one of his knives with his free hand to demonstrate his intent, which was already obvious to the others. He didn't blink an eye as he studied the screens, especially those on deck 8—their deck.

Flavio tracked Deep who had returned from the other side of the room with a roll of black cable and another roll of thin metal cable and said, "Would be better if you can make diversion noise, but I can still do it without."

Deep nodded and quickly twisted the two wires connecting the coaxial cable with the antenna. He grabbed a roll of electrical tape and spun it around and around the splice, cut the tape and smoothed out the edges.

While Deep was focused on the antenna, Buzz paced around the room, stopped suddenly, and then addressed Jaga.

"Say, does your ferret still do that run-away-and-return game?"

At that moment, Jaga started fidgeting as he did when he was nervous. He knew exactly what Buzz had in mind.

"This is stupid idea," Flavio told them. "My life is depending on big rat?"

Jaga flashed the big man a scornful glance, but Flavio had already turned away to receive instructions from Buzz on how to set up the dipole antenna so that it would work throughout the ship. Jaga returned to reassuring his ferret Taufan, while Deep adjusted the animal's straps. Attached to the straps was one of the two portable radios Deep had retrieved from the lost and found. They were almost his, as the guests who left them ten months ago hadn't requested their return. After twelve months, lost items would go to the crew in an auction, held once a month. The funds from the auction were used to add supplies to their crew recreational areas. Deep had already told the potential bidders that the radios were his. The auction was to have occurred in a couple of days, if the world hadn't ended.

Oh well, maybe the radios will help to save us, he resolved.

"Taufan will do as he's told," Jaga announced, while looking up at the hulking Slavic. "Are you sure the angries won't eat him?"

"Angries"—Flavio smirked at this—"only attack people or animals not like them. Can't promise it works for big rats, but I guess better than nothing... unless one of you want to be diversion?" Finally, Flavio's small grin evaporated, as if it never existed before.

"It'll work, Jaga," Yacobus insisted. "Remember how he was with those dogs? They weren't after Taufan; they were after that man hiding behind the water bottles."

Jaga seemed to accept all of this, deciding absolutely that Taufan would do this. It was certainly less risky than one of them going out there, as Flavio had joked.

Jaga leaned over to his ferret. "Okay Taufan. When I tell you to run, you run, all right?"

Taufan seemed more interested in preening himself than anything else. And at that moment, all but Jaga felt dubious the ferret would follow his commands.

Flavio humphed a sigh, and then grabbed the rolled-up cable and attached antenna. "Make sure your rat goes in right direction. Don't want crazy people chasing both of us."

"He's not a rat. He's a ferret." Jaga rose and stood tall, in defiance. But his face was not even close to that of the larger man.

Flavio grinned again, just a little more this time. "I know." Then he turned serious again. "Let's do this, now."

Deep stood ready at the MR exit and when he received a tepid nod from Jaga, he slowly unlocked and cracked open the door. He turned his ear to the opening, while the others waited directly behind him. Deep must have felt safe, because he pushed his head outside just enough that he could see in both directions of the hallway. Then he withdrew himself back inside and took a knee.

"Okay, now!" he whispered and threw open the door wide enough for them to do their part. Jaga darted into the hall, facing forward, laid Taufan down and held him pointed away, so that he'd run in that direction. Then he commanded, "Run, Taufan. Run."

Taufan took off, and Jaga withdrew back through the door. Their door clicked closed.

Jaga lifted the second portable to his lips and yelled, "Run!" And then clicked on the emergency button that comes with these radio units.

Even muffled, all of them heard the loud tone echo down the hall, followed by the louder tone's reverberation from their walkie. The sound changed slightly, telling them that Taufan had just turned down the U-shaped hallway, that followed around them. It would be out of view of their cameras, until he returned or ended back up front.

All but Jaga glared out the window. He didn't want to see this.

Several shadows dashed by their window, running forward, in Taufan's direction.

"They're taking the bait," exclaimed Deep.

"Open door, quietly," Flavio commanded.

Deep obliged and Flavio slipped out, clutching the loops of coaxial and antenna cable in his left hand and clutching his heavy wrench with his right. He held up at the edge of the doorway.

Two more crazies ran by, screeching their dislike at the loud noise, but running toward it just the same.

Flavio shot an eye aft, holding for just two seconds. Then he darted in that direction, letting loops of cable fly out of his left hand. His wrench was held up, ready to strike. He didn't look back, even though he should have.

Yacobus held tight on the other end of the coaxial line, while Deep clicked the door shut, although with some difficulty because the thick coaxial jammed open the bottom corner of the door.

"Not yet," Deep insisted to Jaga, who held the radio at his lips, ready to issue the next command.

"Okay, Jaga, turn off the tone."

Jaga let go of the button.

"Now."

That was Jaga's invitation to call his little buddy back.

"Return, Taufan. Return." Jaga let his hand, squeezing the radio, drop to the floor, and he sprang up to look out the window with Deep. They waited.

No sign of Taufan.

They were startled to see several crazies running past their window, headed aft. They were headed toward Flavio and their antenna.

Jaga, Yacobus, and Buzz crowded around the small window to the insane world outside the door, with Jaga bouncing from heel to heel.

Deep stepped back. He knew there was nothing he could do, other than hope the ferret and Flavio made it.

He dashed over to his table and gazed at the lone camera located at the crew entrance to the hallways around the MR, but didn't see Flavio or the ferret. Really, he had only one measurement for success. He turned up the volume to his base unit, and waited to hear voices.

It was nothing but static.

19

A Flawed Plan

Their plan had been full of flaws. After ten minutes, both Flavio and Taufan were still missing. No signs of either. And with the infected running past the MR window, in both directions, their hope had ebbed further away with each tick of the clock on the monitor wall. The staticky blare from the base unit's speakers, turned up high so that they wouldn't miss anything, had been only occasionally interrupted by distant incomprehensible voices, before they too had bled back into the radio's static murk.

Yacobus and Jaga had stood vigil at the door, glad it was more of a reinforced hatch than a regular door, even though there was a little opening at the bottom where the coaxial snuck through. They took little comfort in their wall of protection. It had kept the infected out, but it also kept them locked in. They knew they couldn't stay there forever.

Jaga's angst had been the heaviest. "I don't know what to do. I'm afraid to call him again; I don't want to risk any more noise and attract more angries to him."

Yacobus had put his arm around his friend and offered reassurance. "He'll be fine." But his words didn't sound believable when they had come out.

They had continued to stare out the window and anxiously tapped at the floor with their heels.

Buzz had made himself useful by working on a burned out circuit board, the one which had caused two of Deep's monitors to not function perfectly and had seemed to set up a chain reaction in other systems. It wasn't a high-priority task. But it was all he had thought he could do while they waited.

Deep had simply focused his gaze at the base station's speakers, as if that would improve the reception.

Still nothing.

Then it had come.

As if someone had thrown a switch to give them instant reception, the speaker's constant crackle had been replaced by a mélange of voices seemingly speaking over each other. Then the sonorous sounds of the most beautiful officer on the ship, Jessica Eva Mínervudóttir, the bridge's navigational officer, sounded over all others.

Deep would have known that voice anywhere. He was in love with Jessica, even though she was already married, with a child. Even when he would occasionally bump into her in the crew mess, she talked to him about her husband and son constantly. It was Deep's little secret that he never shared with anyone. And upon hearing her voice, his whole persona changed. All he could think was, *Thank God, she is safe.*

Then his heart had sunk upon hearing her plight.

He could only imagine what she was going through on the swing deck, and that she'd be terrified not knowing what happened to her husband and child. Or with the outside world in chaos.

Deep was then knocked out of his lapse when he realized he had an audience. Jaga and Yacobus had sprung up behind him, knocking their knees into the back of his chair. Buzz laid a palm on his Deep's shoulder; a sort of attaboy for Deep's accomplishment. All of them had silently gawked at the speaker when they heard the familiar voice of their staff captain, followed by the booming voice of the captain. They were all just connecting for the first time.

When the captain had asked Jessica who was on watch, their hearts sunk further. They knew the answer, but they were hoping they had somehow hoped they heard it incorrectly. Jessica then destroyed that hope.

What she said next was at first confusing, and then shocking: "we'll hit our destination in just over an hour."

They were supposed to be in the middle of the ocean, and their next port of Nassau was at least four more days away. It was the use of "*hit* our destination" that was so jarring. It was code.

When the radio paused, as the officers chewed on Jessica's response, Yacobus and Jaga whispered, "What did she mean by that?"

"It's code," Buzz answered. "They know passengers might be listening and don't want to alarm them."

Deep went slack-jawed when he got it, and in case the others didn't, he said it out loud. "Jessica just told us that we're going to crash into land in an hour, unless they can take back the bridge or engineering and readjust our course."

While his friends gasped, Deep didn't waste another moment, clicking the transmit button. He also didn't waste time mincing his words.

"This is Whaudeep Reddy from the Monitor Room, I read you, First Officer, and you, Captain, and you, Staff Captain. I can provide you eyes above in your efforts to get to either the bridge or engineering. But I'm afraid there are many crazies between you and both locations."

"This is Captain Jörgen. Thank you Mr. Reddy."

Jörgen clicked transmit once more. "Staff Captain, can you try for the bridge and help the first officer, and we'll head to engineering?"

"We'll do it, sir," Jean Pierre's voice crackled back.

"First Officer, do you have an exact time of arrival?" asked Jörgen, his voice as steady as normal.

"I would have to guess forty-seven minutes, sir. The bridge consoles and the swing deck console are all dead. Punta Delgado is close enough to see without binoculars."

Jörgen immediately set the timer on his watch for forty-six minutes and released it. The second hand exploded forward and raced toward a finish line that seemed impossibly short. He clicked transmit once more. "Not to worry, the staff captain is coming to get you. And I'm heading to engineering, just for insurance." His words were offered with the same steady cadence his officers had come to expect.

"Mr. Reddy," barked Jörgen. "What is our clearest route to engineering, then report the clearest route for the staff captain's group to the bridge?"

The static barked back.

Jörgen's heart skipped a beat as he wondered if they had lost communication with the MR. But when Deep finally responded, Jörgen knew the man was simply checking his monitors for their safest route.

"Captain, I'm afraid I don't have a clear path for you. Outside of your emergency craft are at least five or six crazies... they're ah... murdering a crew member. If you can get past them—maybe you can if you don't make any noise—then take the crew access stairwell above you on Deck 6. Walk forward to the crew stairwell, which appears clear right now, up to deck 7. Then go aft, down the hallway for the senior crew quarters. You'll have to exit the main hallway, where you'll probably encounter more crazies. At least they're intermittent. Again, if you're quiet, it should be a few steps to the mid-ship crew stairwell. You can then take that all the way down to engineering. Getting inside engineering is another problem. The whole area is swarming with them. Sorry, sir."

"Thanks, Mr. Reddy. We'll tell you the moment we're set to go. Then, if you can, keep watch for more of the... what do you call them, crazies?" He hadn't heard the term before, but it was appropriate.

"Aye, sir. As for the staff captain, the news is worse... I don't see—"

"—Don't worry, Mr. Reddy," interrupted Jean Pierre. "We have an idea. We're going to take the zip line across. If you can get us the best route to the aft access, we'll take it from there."

"Sir, I don't think that's a good idea," Deep pleaded.

"Thanks, Mr. Reddy. Are we clear from the crew access to the stairwell and finally the crew exit to the zip line?"

"Hold on, sir... I thought I saw a crazy running around the spa... I don't see him anymore. Stay on guard for him. Otherwise, you're clear."

"Thanks again, Mr. Reddy. We'll also tell you when we're headed up. And we also need you to eagle-eye our passage too."

"Aye, sir."

Jörgen glanced over to Urban. His face was slack and ashen, motionless. Then he looked at Wasano, who shook his head in answer to the question he knew he didn't need to ask. Urban Patel, First Officer and member of his bridge for three years, was dead.

"Wait," Hans exclaimed, popping out of his seat. Jörgen figured the man's addled brain just connected the dots to Jessica's obtuse message. "You mean there's no one driving this thing? Don't you have a baby-captain or something?"

Jörgen ignored him and looked back to Wasano. "You ready?"

Jean Pierre clipped the radio to his belt and gave an unsure glance at his group. "All of you wait here, and either I or someone else—"

"I have your back," TJ barked and stepped forward, sunglasses glinting from the overheads.

"So do I," Ted stated, although with much less surety than his wife. "It sounds like you'll need at least a couple of sets of hands."

"We're not staying here," declared David. "Besides, if two sets of hands are good, four more are better still."

"Don't we get a vote on this?" begged Penny, anticipating her husband's response.

"We're both going too," Boris croaked.

Jean Pierre opened his mouth to say "no," and then hesitated. Under normal circumstances, he'd never have allowed guests to participate in something that was bound to result in one of them getting injured, or worse. But if they didn't reach the bridge, and the captain didn't reach engineering, in forty-five minutes, they'd all be dead. No, he did need all the help he could get. "Fine. But you all must do exactly what I say. No exceptions. Anyone who disobeys me will be left behind with the... the crazies. Am I clear?"

All heads nodded, except TJ's. She was already at the door, clicking it open.

20

Abyss

The zip line spanned almost three hundred feet, easily one third of the length of the ship. Falling the thirty or so feet from the line to deck 10 would normally cause serious injury, perhaps worse if you landed on your head or if you plummeted the additional twelve feet to the sun deck and pool. Today, falling from the line would certainly result in death, as both decks 9 and 10 appeared full of crazy people, infected by a disease of madness, all of whom appeared to need to kill anyone not infected. And lest they forget, there were dozens of crazy birds still buzzing around outside, searching for the opportunity to nibble on any human stupid enough to slowly work their way across the zip line.

Ted, like the rest of his group, considered this insurmountable span and their mission. He mentally climbed the entire span of the line from the porthole they looked through to the broken antenna tower and out of sight to their final destination, the bridge. Even if they made it there, they still had to somehow lower themselves from the outside into the nearly impregnable shell of the bridge that mostly withstood a giant tsunami. And if they managed to make it inside the bridge, they'd have to battle more crazies to save two officers and wrestle back control of their helm. And because that wasn't enough pressure, added to an already near-impossible situation was the fact that they had to do this in around forty minutes, or they'd crash into an island and die.

"So are we all ready?" TJ bellowed.

This elicited a scowl from everyone.

Ted's wife often demonstrated acts of fearlessness that surprised him, in spite of her rabid fear of animals. But bravado now seemed reckless in this situation. Then again, a lack of fear would be welcomed: Ted felt practically paralyzed by it at this moment.

He stared at his wife, wondering what was going on in her head. Curiously, she was standing away from everyone, staring at her feet while rubbing the Orion necklace he'd just given her. Maybe she was trying to call up her inner warrior.

"Please, Lassie. You go right ahead," quipped Boris. He waved his palms in the direction of the zip line, a taunt to her, obviously viewing her as some sort of rah-rah, I-can-do-anything, body-Nazi. Ted guessed the rotund man was just as scared about this as he was. So what came out of Ted's mouth next, surprised even him.

"I'll go fir... first... to help everyone off," Ted barked, though he heard his own voice warble a little at the end. He instantly hated his volunteering to go first. He had no interest in doing this at all, but he felt every second evaporate and knew if they didn't do something quickly, everyone on the ship might die anyway.

Jean Pierre, thankfully asserting his authority, stated, "I'll go first. Penny, you follow, and then Bor—"

"There's no blooming way I'm going across that," Penny cut in with a nervous chortle. Then her face crumpled into a panicked scowl. She appeared close to tears.

"I second what she said," protested Boris.

"Fine. Anyone who wants to sit this one out, stay here," Jean Pierre peeked out the porthole, no doubt eying a couple of birds fluttering over one of the corpses on the pool deck. "Just stay inside here. When we've secured the bridge, we'll send someone back for you."

"I'm going too," David stated resolutely and then turned to Evie, "but I want you to stay here with Boris and Penny."

"Wherever you're going, so am I," she responded, equally resolute. Evie's arms were wound around her chest like a tight garment that constricted everything. It was her way of saying she was intractable on her not going.

He softly squeeze one of her arms and gazed into her eyes, "I'm worried you won't make it across the one hundred meter span, upside down, especially with your arthritis." He spoke almost at a whisper. "You were having difficulty holding onto a pencil this morning. This is far more difficult. And if you fall, I'll never forgive myself. Please allow me to go and help these people, and I'd ask you to stay and look after our new friends."

While listening to David's plea, she slowly released all of the tension in her arms, until she finally let go. "Okay," she huffed, "Just promise you'll return to me."

He wrapped his arms around her, "I'll do my best."

David let go, turned to Jean Pierre and said, "All right, let's do this." Even though he sounded resolute, gravity pulled at his wrinkled face abnormally. He looked very tired and very old, completely different from when they first met in the spa.

"All right then. I'll go first, then you Ted, then David, and TJ will bring up the rear. How's that?"

Everyone nodded.

"Wait until the person in front of you is halfway across. I don't know if the line could take more than two of us at a time."

"Guess I shouldn't have eaten that full breakfast then," Ted joked. His voice had raised at least an octave over normal. He glanced at his wife, who usually laughed at his jokes, no matter how stupid they were. She was stoic. No, focused, and now eying the other side, almost like she didn't want to be here, with them. Everyone else ignored him too. He couldn't blame them; there was a lot riding on their success, or failure.

They filed out of the hatch, one by one. TJ stopped upon exit and double-slapped the portal window, a signal to lock them out. A heavy thump sounded behind the door.

Jean Pierre, already at the edge of the platform, grabbed the line with both mitts underneath. Then he curled one leg around it, followed by the other so that he was hanging.

Like a piece of meat on a spit, Ted thought.

Ted turned to his fellow adventurers, just to confirm that he didn't actually say it out loud. He didn't.

He turned back to watch Jean Pierre dangle just above the edge of the tower skirting they were all standing on. The wind whipped at Ted's clothing and batted at his eyes. As Jean Pierre slowly crawled upside down, one hand and foot over the other, sliding along the line, Ted let his mind wander. He, the storyteller, had difficulty imagining what lay ahead of their little group on this life-or-death mission. Harder still was imagining what promised to be their new world, even if they miraculously got command of the helm of the ship and steered it to safety.

They talked around the periphery of this larger question inside, but Ted hadn't until this moment considered what it might be like to live in a world where fifty percent or more of the human population might be so crazy that they wanted to kill everyone else who wasn't infected. Then add a trillion infected mammals, picking off the survivors. This truly was an apocalypse, more vast and horrible than he could have ever imagined. Worse than all of those he had conceived, combined.

In his book called Madness, he'd only considered fifty percent of the animal population going crazy. That logically would result in a near extinction-level event for humanity. But in this real-life scenario, it was not only most of the animals, but half of the humans too. How could they possibly survive this one? Would they?

He was jolted from his daydreaming when he heard his name. He looked up and his wife was beckoning him forward.

"Ted, you're next. David will follow you and I'll be behind to make sure everyone gets across safely." She expressed this without a hint of emotion.

A bird squawked above, raising their heads. It flapped about a hundred feet away, folded its wings into its body and barreled downward, aiming right for Jean Pierre, who was more than halfway across the line.

It zipped past the line and buried itself into the lifeless corpse of a passenger floating on the swaying surface of the reddish pool water.

At that moment, Ted panicked. He wasn't ready yet. "But..."

TJ shot him a glare, through her sunglasses. It was her, and not the stoic person who'd been possessing TJ's body the last thirty minutes or so. Her look said, "Not a good time to wimp out on me, buddy."

Ted didn't say anything more. He swallowed hard and did what Jean Pierre did. And within a couple of minutes, he was a third of the way across the line. That was when he made the big mistake of looking down.

A momentary wave of faintness washed over him. While dangling, he felt himself being blown around by the stiff breeze and swayed by the rocking of the ship. He shot a glance ahead of him, in a vain attempt to gain a solid visual footing. He saw an upside-down Jean Pierre move all around his field of vision, making his nausea worse.

But that feeling went away the instant Ted's phone sang out the William Tell Overture—it was his text tone.

He couldn't see it, and was glad for it, but he imagined the Azores were close enough now that his phone was picking up one of their cell towers. And even though his phone was nested deep in his jeans, the sound was loud. Too loud.

In response, he heard and then eyed several crazies below, screeching up at him.

They want to eat me.

Like some macabre choir taking their lead from the music coming from his pocket, the hordes below howled their rapturous reply. They growled and screeched, all while congregating underneath him, willing him to let go, to fall into their clutches.

Ted drilled his eyesight back down the metal line, aft to his wife, where he had started. She was still glaring at him.

Was that concern for him, or disgust at him?

He couldn't tell.

He carefully moved one hand after another, one foot over the other, not slowing down even when he felt the pinprick-bites as his hands scraped over some sharp surfaces in the line.

Then he felt a steady hand on his shoulder. It was Jean Pierre helping him off the line.

He'd made it.

Ted gave the thumbs-up to the rest of his party and was surprised to see David already crossing.

It all looked like it might work.

The growing hordes below growled in contempt.

David was halfway across, pausing for a moment to glance forward at Jean Pierre and him, when a loud cracking noise sounded.

It reminded Ted of the sound of ice breaking off a glacier.

The two men looked around the glass flooring underneath them, thinking maybe it was breaking underfoot.

"We couldn't break this if we tried," Jean Pierre stated emphatically. Yet he didn't know what it was either.

When part of the zip line snapped back at them, they understood at once.

Somewhere in between TJ—she was already swiftly moving across—and David, two of the line's three metal strands broke free. With the tension released, the broken ends snapped back to their starting points.

When half of the line shot by David, under her legs and through his arms and hands, it tore through his skin, knocking his hands away. His top half fell, but his legs and feet remained curled around the remaining strand, holding him.

This final strand groaned at the undue strain of two humans pulling at it, even two skinny humans.

TJ ignored her own pain from her own cuts, the slickness from her blood coating the surface of their life rope. She raced across the remaining distance between her and David. "I'm coming, David. Hold on."

The roar of the breaking lines and their commotion brought more crazies into a foaming frenzy just below them. The crazies' dinner bell had just been rung. A few of the birds, previously occupied with the dead, took flight, and made way for the human beacons calling to them.

Ted motioned like he was going to hop back on the line, but Jean Pierre held him back. "I don't think the line can stand any more weight, Ted. If anyone can get him across, it's your wife, TJ," insisted Jean Pierre.

David seemed stuck, dangling by his legs, thirty feet above a horde of crazy people, feverishly hoping he'd let go and drop.

When TJ slid over the area that broke, she saw that the single line that held the both of them up was frayed too. It wouldn't be long before it also would snap. She slithered the remaining distance. Now ignoring how loud her voice projected, she yelled out, "David, I think this line is going to break soon. Can you reach up and grab or do you need a boost."

This did it. He swung his arms back and then forward, grunted and stretched upward with one hand just hooking the line. He pulled himself up the rest of the way until he had both hands on the line. He didn't hesitate then, he bolted.

TJ held back a little, giving David some room and then mirrored his speed. David shimmied the remaining amount of the line and reached out one bloody hand to Ted and then the other to Jean Pierre, both clasping David's wrists.

It was then that final strand snapped and TJ went flying.

For a moment, TJ looked weightless, as if still suspended in the air. Then she was falling, even though she was still clutching the line. She was falling too fast to shimmy up in time. She curled one arm around the strand and gripped hard. As she swung down, her forward and downward motion drove her into a trellis beam. She hit like a rock, bounced once, and then she let go.

She fell into the gathered horde of crazies that brayed at the expectation of killing another human.

"Noooo!" Ted screamed as he watched his wife disappear in the crowd of crazies that swarmed over her.

She didn't scream even once.

21

Jörgen

Captain Jörgen felt the weight of his command now more than at any time of his career. Before this, he would have thought he'd dealt with every conceivable problem, including a terrorist boarding. Was he ever wrong.

Besides the absurdity of mad dogs and birds attacking his guests and crew, he now had zombie-like crazy people roaming his ship, each with an insatiable desire to kill. And because the outside world was in total chaos, they were entirely on their own. And finally, they only had forty-three minutes to race to engineering and change the navigation or they'd all die. And yet, he liked his odds.

In spite of everything being stacked against them, he had the best crew in the world. He had every confidence in them to find a way around whatever problems were thrown at them, no matter how impossible they seemed. And as long as he was still breathing, with his crew's help, he would captain his ship to safety. He'd already lost an uncountable number of crew and guests. Whatever power he still possessed to change their fortunes, he'd make sure no more lives would be lost.

He asked Wasano again, "Ready?"

His current head of security nodded resolutely.

Jörgen then glanced at the two German boys, and they half-nodded. He didn't want to take them, but the older one said he wouldn't stay, and he just didn't have time to argue. He nodded to Dr. Simmons, who looked dejected and just scowled at him. She didn't like being left behind, but they had little choice. She would have slowed them down and there was no way she could do what they needed her to do next.

He held his glare one final time at Urban's body, covered with one of the emergency boat's blankets, resting peacefully on the most forward bench seat. Jörgen would make sure he was accorded a proper burial at sea, when they got through this.

If they got through this.

Wasano cracked open the door and slipped out, followed by the Jörgen and the two German brothers. Dr. Simmons held the door to the lifeboat open just a crack, enough so she could watch them. She promised she'd lock it the moment they were out of sight, or any of the crazies came close.

Their plan was to quietly exit the secured area, walk a few feet to a ladder attached to the inside wall and climb up ten feet to a large steel strut supporting the ceiling. From this, they'd climb over to a deck 6 crew access balcony, hanging cantilever on the other side and just above the promenade deck they were on. Their plan depended on two of Dr. Simmons' assumptions. First, that it was sound that caused crazies to react. So they'd have to sneak by the crazies without them hearing. Second was the assumption that the crazies wouldn't climb up after them to the balcony, because they seemed to lose some motor functions after turning into whatever they were now. Those were two giant assumptions which must be true for their escape plan to work, and he hated to assume anything.

They slipped out of the gate of a jail-like structure that protected the lifeboats, each of them holding it for the other to pass through. Hans, the last out, turned to deal with the gate.

Jörgen eyed the cluster of crazies tearing apart one of his crew. It was even gorier than what he saw with the rats and the dock workers in Malaga. He couldn't help but wonder what possessed them to do this. It was one thing to hear about this from their resident expert on parasites; it was another to see it front and center.

Wasano had swiftly climbed up and over and was already beckoning them from the other side. Jörgen would go next, followed by Franz and then his brother Hans, who boasted he could climb anything.

Jörgen may have not been as nimble as he was years ago, when he was on the Norwegian gymnastics club team, but he was healthier than most sixty-five-year-olds. Up was simple, but over became difficult with his dress shoes. Rubberized soles like those worn by his crew in the galley would have been much better for this kind of task.

When Jörgen's foot slipped a second time, he took a moment to examine his footing and just happened to glance behind him. That's when he saw the gate was still open.

The gate to the enclosure was supposed to have been clicked closed by Hans—*that was the boy's only damned job, except to not slow them down.* But the gate was not only wide open, it was starting a slow swing inward.

Maybe with a little luck, it would clasp shut on its own.

Then it stopped, as the ship swayed to starboard, and the gate picked up the sway and began to swing the other direction.

It gathered speed, until it reached its limit and clanged loudly against its metal frame.

The sound was so jarring it startled Dr. Simmons, who was hanging out of the lifeboat hatch to get a good look at them. She lost her grip, fell out and landed face-first on the hard deck. The crazies heard all of this too, screeching their displeasure—or was it pleasure? He wasn't sure.

Jörgen peeked sideways at the crazies racing toward the lifeboat and Dr. Simmons, who lacked the physical capabilities to retreat back in the lifeboat in time. At the same time, he watched Hans flash the oncoming crazies a wide-eyed look, then Dr. Simmons—who was squinting back at him and the crazies. Just as they were a few feet from him, Hans decided it was every man for himself. He jumped up on the ladder, going around his brother, who had just grabbed a rung. Hans scurried up two rungs at a time.

Dr. Molly Simmons was one more passenger who was going to die if Jörgen did nothing. He wasn't going to let that happen.

Jörgen jumped, landing squarely on the lead crazy's back, just as it was passing underneath him. He heard something crack, like a bone, and hoped it wasn't one of his. His muscle memory from his gymnastics days kicked in immediately. Somehow he rolled and landed on both feet.

A definite 10.0, especially on the dismount.

He must have spent too much time relishing his success, when another crazy blindsided him, knocking him backwards.

Before getting flipped around, Jörgen caught a glimpse of Wasano leaping off the balcony and racing toward him. Close behind was Franz, who raced after two crazies who were headed toward Dr. Simmons. He guessed Hans was hiding.

Jörgen felt a sharp pain on his wrist. He was shocked as he rolled once more that the crazy's mouth was clamped down on his left wrist. While continuing to roll, Jörgen balled up his right hand and punched the crazy on the side of his head. Each punch caused more excruciating pain, as the crazy bit down harder, holding on like a pit bull.

Still Jörgen kept pummeling him, until the crazy lurched to get a better hold with his teeth and instead received a solid blow. The crazy's head wrenched back at the same time Jörgen's shoulder hit something solid.

With the crazy dazed, Jörgen pulled his right elbow back and delivered one final blow, sending the crazy man's head sideways, into the metal panel he'd found himself against. The crazy's head bounced hard and he was out.

Jörgen recognized the man who had just attacked him. He was from Florida, some sort of banker who, with his wife, had taken a picture with Jörgen just before the dinner in the MDR. He couldn't remember now if that was one or two nights ago; it seemed a lifetime. Now this man, who had gone crazy, lay in a heap, bleeding. Maybe he'd even killed the man.

A snarling bray, followed by a scream, pulled Jörgen's attention back toward the lifeboat. Molly was whacking at the head of one of the crazies with her cane, while Franz tugged the feet of another trying to get free and attack the old woman. Wasano was dashing toward them to help, after he had just dispatched another.

Jörgen pulled a handkerchief from his back pocket and wrapped his mangled wrist and stepped toward the lifeboat to assist. He knew this thing was going to hurt like hell when his adrenalin wore off.

In a flash, Wasano was up the stairs and beating the crazy man attacking Dr. Simmons.

Jörgen held up in front of Franz, rolling around with another crazy, thinking maybe he could use his dress-blacks for something useful, rather than ceremony. While Jörgen waited for an opening, he noticed something interesting. This crazy wasn't trying to bite Franz. In fact, to the crazy, Franz was nothing more than a clutch of seaweed it had accidentally gotten entangled in. It simply kicked and wriggled, attempting to free itself, only gnashing its teeth wildly when it caught sight of either Wasano or Molly, who was now being helped up.

When Jörgen saw an opportunity, he looked at the crazy like he would a football, and not the American kind. He lined up, took one step and drove his foot through his target. Score!

Jörgen was also a pretty good footballer in his day, stepping past the delirious man to get to Molly. "Come on, Dr. Simmons. You're coming with us now."

"Thank you, Captain, but please call me Molly."

They all turned and scowled at Hans, who had wandered back to the enclosure, examining his feet.

With one arm around Molly, Jörgen announced, "Let's go. I hear more coming."

22

Outside The Bridge

"A little farther," huffed Jean Pierre. There was no response.

"Did you hear him?" David brayed at Ted.

Ted nodded, though he was staring in the other direction. He released some of the tension on Jean Pierre's leg, causing the man to slide down farther. David did the same.

Each held one of Jean Pierre's legs, who was stretched out, face-down on the long slope of the bridge's windshield. His target was the area where the window had broken from the tsunami a day ago. The area was temporarily covered in plywood until they could make home port, where it would be replaced. It was there that they thought they'd make their entry into the bridge. Deep had told them the crazies were on the starboard side of the bridge and they might be able to enter unnoticed. Getting in without a sound would be difficult at best.

As he slid closer, Jean Pierre noticed one of the windows beside the broken one was left partially open. If Jean Pierre could reach the window, he could slip his hands inside and manually crank it open far enough for them to slip in.

"Almost there. Maybe a foot more." He said this with his head tucked back, so that he was facing them, and a palm directing his voice away from the opening, so that the crazies inside didn't hear him.

"Hey Ted," David cracked. "Please get your head back into the game. Your wife would want you to survive this."

Ted mindlessly nodded and lowered Jean Pierre as far as they could. Now he and David held onto each of the officer's ankles.

"Make sure you've got his weight supported by his ankles and not his shoes," David directed.

Ted wasn't listening. His mind kept flashing the images of his wife's expression as she fell into the horde below. And then their undulating mass on top of her in an instant. He couldn't believe she was gone.

"You're losing him," David barked.

It was too late.

Jean Pierre's foot slipped out of the black dress shoe Ted had been clutching. Jean Pierre's body started to slide down sideways, David's grasp providing the only resistance. But as Jean Pierre's body started to twist, David who didn't have full function of his hands because of cuts from the zip-line, lost his grip as well.

Jean Pierre pressed his palms hard against the glass in an attempt to slow his progression. Their squeaky protests were no help. He slid faster.

Now he was both sliding downward and fishtailing around; his feet were moving faster than his upper body. He eyed the direction he was headed. That's when he saw his one chance to stop himself and avoid slipping off and crashing five decks down onto the forecastle. All he had to do was snag the bottom of the open window.

His slide sped up, as his heart pounded painfully. With his eyes drilled onto his target, he waited for the right moment. Then he sprang outward, extending his left arm and fingertips to their limits.

His pinkie brushed by the low edge of the window, and his heart sank as he thought he'd just missed it. But somehow, he hooked the bottom of the open window with two fingers. It was just enough.

With his downward progression abated, he swung under and was now able to grab with his other hand, giving him a firm grip.

"Made it," he breathed.

When his motion stopped, he pulled himself up just enough so that he could venture a better peek inside the bridge. With all the squeaking, he'd thought for sure it would have brought all the crazies to his port side. But he didn't see any there.

Hauling himself up farther, he looked to his left, toward the consoles on the starboard side of the bridge, where most of their work was done. That's where two crazies were taking out their anger, pounding away on one of the consoles. It was Jessica's; the one emitting an alarm. He knew it was the alarm she had set to warn her to change the ship's navigation. It had been blaring the whole time. Both crazies were beating with their fists so hard against the console that glass, skin, and bones were breaking. Each fist lifted revealed a red pulpy mess, and yet they were completely focused on their mission: stopping the alarm. This was their opportunity.

While the crazies were occupied, it was their best chance to surprise them.

Jean Pierre heard a noise from above. It was Ted and David trying to make sure he was okay. "Yes," he mouthed. *In spite of your letting go of me,* he thought. It was Ted, but he couldn't blame him. He was surprised the man was functional at all after watching his wife die. But they all had to focus right now on the task at hand. With a little luck, there'd be time for mourning.

Jean Pierre reached inside and worked the hand crank slowly to open the window wider, one centimeter at a time. Just a few more turns and he could slip in all the way. Each crank, though, creaked a loud chirp, and so with each squeaking crank, his nervousness grew. While he turned the crank, he glared at the crazies, willing them to not turn his way.

When the crank stopped cranking, Jean Pierre examined the opening. It was plenty of room. Glancing once more at the crazies—they were still pounding away at the offending alarm—he slid in head-first.

Jessica watched wide-eyed from the starboard swing deck. Ágúst was at the opposite end, because he'd vowed to take out any more crazy birds that showed up. She gave him the thumbs-up and he returned it, without the smile she expected. He adjusted his sunglasses and then re-glued his face against the swing deck windows to watch Jean Pierre and the others take back the bridge.

She was surprised by her staff captain's brash plan. And it might just work. The crazies—they were all calling the infected people this now—appeared to be dead-set on beating her console to death. And that is what concerned Jessica more than just their presence on the bridge: she still needed that console functional to change the computer's navigational instructions, and she had maybe thirty minutes left. She sure hoped her staff captain would stop these crazies from their equipment pummeling. They'd tried to do this themselves and it almost got her killed.

First Ágúst and Jessica pounded on the starboard bridge windows, and for less than a minute, it seemed to work: the crazies stopped pounding, and momentarily glared at them with their creepy red eyes. But their pause was brief as the two crazies returned to assaulting her console and its non-stop alarm. Each subsequent attempt to divert their attention by pounding was ignored by the crazies. Then she tried something stupid.

Ágúst was against it, but she insisted. They cracked open the hatch and she screamed at them through the opening. The crazies ignored her. It's like they knew they couldn't get to her. She slipped through the door and screamed some more, and still they did nothing. But when she took two steps toward them and screamed, that drew their interest. They darted toward her, much quicker than she expected. She turned and jumped through the door. In mid-dive she could feel one of them swipe at her shoe, but it couldn't get a hold on it. When she hit the swing deck floor, Ágúst slammed the hatch. They agreed that neither of them would try that again.

Probably ten minutes passed since then and now they just watched and discussed what they saw.

The root of the crazies' fury appeared to be the console's alarm. And Jessica and Ágúst pounding on the windows just wasn't a loud enough substitute. It was only when she was yelling close enough to them that they turned away from the alarm. They confirmed this with Deep on the radio, who told them of other witnessed occasions when crazies attacked the loudspeakers inside and outside during the general alarm. Just like the birds did.

Jessica would have loved to have gotten more feedback on the radio from Deep, but he said he wanted to keep the radio open for emergencies and to steer the captain's group and staff captain's group to their appointed targets. So they waited, and watched the crazies pummel her console. Until the staff captain slid into the bridge.

They held their breath as they watched their superior slide inside the bridge window, their eyes floating from him to the crazies and back. He must have been quiet enough because the crazies continued their unceasing pounding.

When he was all the way in, after also confirming the crazies were occupied, he slipped the top half of his frame up and through the half-opened window and signaled his team above. That's when something happened.

From the outside, they couldn't really hear the alarm or the crazies' pounding, so they couldn't tell what happened. But all at once, they stopped their pounding. They glared at the console, like it was telling them something. Both crazies held their fists halfway up in the air, in between putting them down, or raising them to continue their pounding. It was as if they didn't know what to do next.

"Is the alarm still going?" Jessica asked.

"I'll check," Ágúst said, already running forward to the leading edge of the swing deck and the beginning of the bridge windows.

"No! I think the alarm is off. The screen looks dead. I think they killed it," he reported, hands cupped around his face, sunglasses pressed to the glass.

"Oh no!" Jessica breathed.

Then she screamed, "No!" and started pounding on the bridge windows.

"What?" Ágúst begged. But then he saw.

23

Infected

Jean Pierre signaled David and Ted. It was their turn. David gave a slight wave and whispered, "You're up" to Ted, who gave a weak nod.

Ted glanced down the course from below his feet to where the top half of Jean Pierre was beckoning out the broken bridge window, some twenty feet away. And beyond that, an abyss. If Jean Pierre didn't grab him, or if Ted slid down wrong, he'd careen off the bridge's bank of windows onto the forecastle, at least thirty feet down, to certain death. Yet he wasn't at all nervous about this. And for just the briefest moment, he considered taking a dive down the twenty-foot window span, purposely missing Jean Pierre's grasp, followed by the thirty foot drop. Then he might be where TJ was right now.

Why not?

Something squeezed his arm, vise-like. He turned and saw David, gazing at him with compassion. "Look Ted, none of us would fault you for sitting the rest of this out. But you need to decide right away."

David was right, of course. He couldn't just sit this out. They would probably need another body on the bridge to help take it back. Mourning for his dead wife would have to come later. And if there wasn't a later, so be it. At least he'd try to make TJ's death matter.

Ted glanced back at David, took a breath, and said without any bluster, "I'm good. I need to do this." David gave a weak, unbelieving smile back.

With his back to the bow, Ted knelt down and thrust out his hands, and David gripped them firmly.

Ted extended his legs and arms, and David lowered him over the bridge windows face-down. Ted's tennis-shoe'd toes squeaked against the glass. Once David's arms were outstretched and he was on his own belly, he shot glances at Ted and then Jean Pierre. Ted waited for the moment of release, trying to guess when that might be from David's face and body language. And although everything in him told him he should try to flip over on his back so he could see, he stuck to the plan, held his breath and braced for it when David nodded.

And then he let go.

Ted's slide was very slow at first, as he pressed his hands and sneakers against the thick glass for traction. But just like Jean Pierre had sped up, so did he. He realized too quickly that traction was impossible because the windows were coated with a layer of salt that made them slippery.

Ted accelerated with no control.

He told himself that it was out of his hands: he'd either be stopped by Jean Pierre, or he'd sail over the edge. When it felt like he had traveled at least the estimated twenty, Ted was about to panic. Then he felt Jean Pierre clasp onto his legs and tug.

Weightless, as if he were floating, but only for a moment, when he hit hard Ted did all that he could to take up most of the impact with his knees, but he felt one of his ankles give way and he tumbled to the bridge's solid floor.

Muting a painful grunt—ice picks in his ankle—he glanced up and watched their plan go completely to hell.

Two crazies screeched and dashed toward them—he assumed his loud landing must have drawn their attention.

He'd written about and even read about situations like these in books and stories, and it was true. Everything around him slowed down to a snail's pace. And it was during this elongated moment that he had three thoughts all at once: he'd never see his wife again, this plan was a bad one, and he knew what he had to do next.

A quick head-snap back confirmed to Ted that Jean Pierre was more concerned with Ted's hard landing than the crazies running toward them. Only when one of the two crazies brayed did Jean Pierre's features change. But his reaction would be too slow.

Ted returned his gaze to the first oncoming crazy, and at the same time he leapt upward. His left ankle screamed for him to stop, but he sucked in the pain and hobbled two more stutter-steps forward. That's when his ankle gave up completely, sending Ted sailing forward, toward the first oncoming crazy. Keeping his arms up like goal posts, he tucked down his head, and braced for impact.

The first crazy didn't anticipate this, and because somehow Ted was able to snag the crazy's legs, it flipped over him and hit the decking with a deep *thunk*, just before it could reach Jean Pierre. Ted held on. The crazy convulsed violently, all in an attempt to flip itself around again—*some part of the infecteds' brains must have been turned off, or confused. They weren't able to control or figure out some of their normal motor functions.*

Ted let go and spun out from under the crazy who, now free, fairly quickly turned itself around. And faster than he would have thought, it now scuttled its way toward Ted.

Ted wasn't sure what he was expecting: maybe the crazy would stay down when it hit the ground. And it was why Ted remained on his belly when the crazy barreled toward him.

Again he didn't think; he just reacted.

He spun himself around and onto his back, taking a cat-like defensive posture. If he had thought about it, he probably would have tried—albeit unsuccessfully—to run. When the crazy fell on top of him, Ted was able to deflect it using his legs and arms. His left ankle roared in pain. But he ignored its pleading. He had bought another few seconds.

Jean Pierre was now in motion, but in the other direction, while Ted watched, still on his back.

For a long moment, Ted thought he was running away. Even more surreal, he grabbed a large model of the *Intrepid*—the plaque read 1:50 scale—from the floor. Clutching the model—its smokestack looked damaged just like the original—with both hands, Jean Pierre took two long strides to the crazy, who was once again trying to right itself. But before it could, Jean Pierre swung and connected solidly, sending the crazy into the wall just below the window they'd just entered. The timing was perfect, because David slid in hard, landing right on top of the crazy, taking him out, perhaps permanently.

That left one.

Ted spun around again, not sure why the other crazy hadn't struck yet, but then he saw why.

Jessica was wrestling with the other.

The crazy was moments from biting her when Jean Pierre and David arrived. They pummeled the crazy—David with a foot and Jean Pierre with the ship model—until the crazy no longer moved.

Jessica squirmed out from under the unconscious crazy and dashed to one of the consoles. It appeared to be the same one Ted and TJ had seen her working on earlier today.

Jean Pierre bounded over to Jessica, while David stepped over to Ted. No one thought to look after Ágúst, who had disappeared from sight.

David hoisted Ted up off the floor. Ted swung his arm around him and the two men slowly moved to the back of the bridge without making a peep. The last thing they wanted to do was interrupt the officers' attempts to do what they needed to do. From what they saw, it didn't appear to be going well.

"David," Ted whispered, a quiet call to his human crutch that he was about to let go.

Ted released himself and sat heavily in one of the bridge's only two chairs, behind a long console of computer and radio equipment. The other chair was the captain's, at the very front of the bridge.

David must have realized that the bridge's hatch was still open, because he dashed the ten or so feet and locked up the bridge. He then grabbed a tape dispenser from inside a glass bookcase and darted over to each crazy and wrapped their legs up tight. Perhaps he thought they would wake up, even though Ted suspected they were both dead.

Inside, they were safe, but outside...

Ted pointed to the bow, past the captain's empty chair.

David, now standing behind him, followed Ted's finger forward. He shuddered, instantly understanding it wasn't the bow Ted was pointing to. He was looking beyond the bow.

When they were up top, although their view was even better, they were more focused on their mission: to get into the bridge and regain control. Now that they had to wait impatiently for the two officers to do their work to regain the helm on one of the broken consoles, they couldn't help but plainly see the perfectly framed Sao

Miguel Island. It was so close now that it occupied a good portion of the bridge's windows.

They needed to fix the navigation problem quickly.

Jessica tossed a glance and some hurried words in their direction. "Can one of you go check on Ágúst? He has a nervous stomach and ran into the bathroom."

Ted only half-heard her, because at the same time the pretty Icelandic officer was speaking, he was wracked with overwhelming grief. All he could think of at this moment was that he would never see his wife again. Even if they somehow got themselves out of this mess, she was still gone. Forever.

He dropped his face into his hands and wept.

David glanced down at Ted and immediately felt sorrow for this man. Ted was cocooned, head cradled in his hands on the table-top. He watched the man quietly sob; small convulsive quivers buffeted Ted's body every few seconds. The shock phase had passed, and this was the first moment the man had been allowed to mourn. David understood quite well what it was like to lose a loved one to a horrific fate. He'd lost more loved ones than he could count to the evils of this world.

"I'll get him," David said. He glanced back at Jessica and Jean Pierre. They were frantically working away at the console. Neither was going to respond.

David had never been on the bridge of a cruise ship, and he suspected the makeup of the bathrooms—didn't they call them heads on these things?—was probably different than what land-dwellers like him were used to. At first, he wasn't sure he'd be able to find it, but since there was only one other doorway besides the entrance and the ruined doorway to some room on the other side of the bridge, he assumed this was the bathroom. A small sliver of light stabbing out from the bottom of the door was the exclamation point to his assumption.

David approached the door and tapped on it lightly at first. He waited a few seconds and then put a little more authority into his tapping.

There was no answer.

"Hello, sir. Are you all right?"

Still no answer.

David grabbed the handle and was about to open the door, but then wondered if this was the smartest idea. What if this Ágúst was one of those things now?

While clutching the door, David turned back and glanced first at the staff captain and then first officer, now working on a different console without lights. Then he glared at Ted. "Hey Ted! Ted, please!" David's words came out in short puffs of air. He wanted only Ted's attention, and not the others.

Ted slowly released his head out from under his own clutches. He lifted his face up, his teary eyes meeting David's.

David put aside his compassion for the man. "Sorry to interrupt, but I may need you to back me up..." These words came out even quieter. "In case... You know."

Ted nodded and pushed himself up, using the table while holding up his injured ankle. He put some weight on it and immediately pulled it away, his face screwing up. But then he tried it again, as if he were testing it.

Ted nodded again, this time more resolutely.

David nodded back and pivoted back to the bathroom door. He gave one more light tap and then twisted the handle.

He pushed the door open.

A bright splash of light shot out, causing David to squint and hold a hand up to hold back some of its brightness.

Quickly his eyes adjusted, and he saw the officer.

Safety Officer Ágúst Helguson was lying on the floor in the fetal position.

For just the briefest of moments, David wondered if the man was dead. Then he saw the man's rapid breaths. And slight convulsions.

Was he crying?

This wasn't the action of a crazy, and immediately David's demeanor changed from alert to feeling sorrow. He was feeling lots of that lately. He offered his hand and said, "Hey, Mr. Ágúst. The crazies are all incapacitated." He thought of saying "dead" but wasn't sure if this man would be able to take the added stress: he obviously wasn't dealing with the attacking crazies very well. Who would be except Holocaust survivors like him and his wife?

"Are you hurt?" He thrust his hand out farther, palm up.

The officer seemed not to hear him. But he was definitely crying. Again, always being alert—that's what kept him alive all this time—David became more convinced this man wasn't a crazy, but someone ill-adjusted to a world where people kill other people.

David took another step toward the officer. Then another. Now standing over him, David knelt down a little.

"Sir?" David tapped Ágúst on his shoulder, causing the man to shudder.

Ágúst lifted his head slowly and eyed David.

David's first reaction was to run.

He shuffled back the few steps to the door, not lifting his eyes from Ágúst's.

Ted had advanced closer to the door, now holding a pen in one hand as a stabbing device and a clipboard in another. Ted's face twisted from anticipation to confusion, now begging the question, "What is it?"

"Ah, folks," David bellowed as he continued back-stepping out of the bathroom until he bumped into Ted. "We have a problem."

Jean Pierre and Jessica both turned from their broken consoles. Jean Pierre had been talking on a handheld and he continued to hold it out in front of him, while they both gave David their attention and then the bathroom doorway.

Framed by the doorway, Ágúst was slightly hunched over, silhouetted against the bathroom's bright lights. His hair was disheveled and sticking straight up, his shoulders hung low. And there was something else they couldn't quite see. That was until Ágúst took a step into the bridge.

To the two officers who knew the man well, it was almost like a birthmark they'd never noticed before. Then it was obvious. And now it was the only thing they could see.

It was Ágúst's eyes.

They were blood red.

24

TJ

The experience had been surreal.

TJ would have sworn it was someone else, not her. Someone without fear. Someone without anxiety. Someone who didn't feel fatigue or pain. Someone fully alive. Someone—anyone—but her.

But it was her.

No, it was a *new* her.

She felt like some meta-human, chronicled in a graphic novel; this person who couldn't be her had not only lived through the hard fall from the zip line, but the horde of crazies below. She didn't feel injured. And somehow, she was surviving, even now.

No, big correction—she was thriving.

It seemed impossible, but the horde of crazy people had not hurt her.

She was covered in blood. But she knew, just as she did about so much more, it wasn't her blood.

And yet, she couldn't explain why, but the coat of blood she now wore felt to her like a new protective skin, a skin made from the blood of all of these crazy people.

She felt impenetrable as she beat and kicked and punched and elbowed every crazy around her. One by one, the crazies around her fell to the ground. And she did it all without a weapon.

And then there was the swearing.

Like a drunken sailor on shore leave, she was hurling profanities as rapidly as she landed each swing. And behind the profanities was her anger.

She didn't know where any of this came from. She only knew that she was filled with the most putrefying outrage: she was angry at the line that broke and deposited her unceremoniously on top of these crazy people and then this deck; she was furious at these insane people, who at first seemed dead-set on killing her and now didn't seem to care about her at all; she was resentful of her husband, for leaving her to deal with these crazies; she was irate at her weaknesses, or previous weaknesses; she was infuriated at her being angry. She was filled with an uncontrollable bitterness for everyone and everything. And with each crazy she slugged, her heated desire to cause more destruction to everything that affronted her grew, like a wellspring of hate that had pooled up from the darkest part of her soul.

Her fears were completely gone now; they were replaced with her bountiful anger.

Her fear of animals... gone—she hated them now; her fear of hurting herself... non-existent—her previous aches and pains pissed her off even more; her fear of being weak... history—she felt completely intolerant of all fear.

Instead, she had an uncontrollable need to hurt these crazy people, who were mindlessly flailing around her, keeping her from something she needed right now, but just didn't understand.

The new TJ felt like for some unknown reason, these crazies were the cause of all her woes, previous and current. And so she took it out on them.

With even more fury, she pounded away at each crazy, leaving a trail of unconscious and broken people and sometimes the occasional bird still fluttering about. Everyone and everything in her path suffered her wrath.

Before long, she found herself inside the ship running.

It was as if she had blinked in the middle of her battle royal and transported herself seconds or minutes later to where she was galloping to her destination.

But what destination?

She had no idea where she was going, but without the hindrance of the crazies standing in her way, she only knew she had to get there.

With several possible routes to her goal, she turned and darted toward an open crew access stairwell she'd never been in before. Oddly, she seemed to know it was the shortest route to where she was going.

Another thought struck her, and it was odder still.

The new TJ felt as if she were being controlled—a marionette, and her master tugged at her strings, making her lurch in one direction, and then another, all setting her upon this unknown course. Yet she almost didn't mind that she had little control over this. In a way, her life had felt out of control for a long time now. This somehow felt better, like she had a purpose. Whatever that purpose was.

Just as she blew in through the doorway, she held up momentarily to take in the most exquisite smell. She'd never smelled something as glorious as this before. And when she turned her head to examine the source of the smell, she was both shocked by what it was, and even more, her reaction to it.

It was a small cowering Filipino crewmember, curled up and literally shaking in a fetal ball. His wide eyes glared at TJ, and then he reflexively shrank even farther from her. He was utterly horrified... of her.

But it was TJ who felt all at once horrified. Not of the Filipino's reaction to her, but her reaction to him: she was possessed at that moment with a desire... no, a complete need, to kill him. To pummel him to death. To rip him to shreds. To bite and tear and to... drain him of his life-giving blood.

At that moment, the shock of these feelings was too much to handle. The repulsion of these desires was enough to push her away from this fearful little man.

She stutter-stepped back from the Filipino. And although her maddening desires were still there, just as pronounced as they were moments before, she could now gather herself and instead refocus on the other desire that still pulled at her, the one that tugged at her from the opposite side of the ship.

This other force she also didn't seem to have control over. But this force seemed like a good one. With the almost uncontrollable urge to kill now gone, she followed the other urge, which gathered strength as she found herself dashing down a stairwell in leaps, three stairs at a time.

An old image filled her head. It was the Iron Rattler roller-coaster in Texas. She and... it was someone whose name she couldn't remember, even though he was important to her. They were on this roller coaster. Their roller coaster soared down a multi-story drop, and she was momentarily flying—like now. A small part of her allowed herself to feel the fear she would have once felt, along with the desire to get off. But mostly the feelings were exhilarating: the feelings of not knowing where this coaster was going next. And the whole time, she screamed with joy. Like she did now.

She felt that same abandoned exhilaration of the unknown, as she popped out of the stairwell and dashed down the hallway. She sprinted by a group of crazies beating on a partially-open cabin door. Its occupants losing the battle of holding these crazies back. The crazies screeched their desire to get in. And it was like she understood why, and she could have joined them.

But she had another desire.

None of the crazies turned their heads or even acknowledged her, even when she bumped shoulders with one of them, almost knocking it down—it was as if the new TJ didn't even exist to them.

I'm not a threat to them, she thought.

Another crazy was feasting on the body of another guest. Her old self would have stopped, though she wasn't sure why. The new TJ didn't slow one bit. She leapt over what her old self would have thought was a gruesome sight. But now... she just didn't care. Her puppet master seemed to be giving her two options. And this unknown path was the one she wanted to continue to follow, even though she still didn't understand it.

And yet the hallway she was running through was very familiar. She didn't think about the why. She was only aware and knew that finding out the why wasn't important. Not right now. Only getting to her destination was important. And the not caring part felt so freeing. Once again, she screamed her joy to no one but herself.

She arrived at a door and reflexively pulled something out of her back pocket and slashed at the door with this object. The door opened and then it closed itself.

She turned, reached down and pulled on another door and leapt inside, where she hit the cool floor and a wall of what she instinctively knew was a bathroom.

She had come to rest, having found her destination and unfolded herself from the heap she had landed in. Breathing labored breaths now, she remarked at how rapidly her chest heaved, so much so she thought her lungs might explode.

Finally, after many minutes, she pushed herself up from the floor and pulled herself up farther by the counter. She glanced at the woman staring back at her. She wasn't sure if this woman was the new TJ or the old one. This person looked like the victim of a horrendous homicide: every square inch of her was covered in blood, some dried and some bright red and dripping from places like her nose, chin and ears.

Her undone hair was no longer blond. Parts of it were sticking to one side; the rest looked ragged: a homeless wreck of a person.

She held herself up, elbows slightly bent, and scowled at her image for the longest time. And still her breathing was rapid and irregular.

A thought hit her and she reached up with a forefinger and hooked her sunglasses and gave a small tug; they didn't want to let go. They were caked into her face and matted hair. She gave them a larger jerk, and they fell from the bridge of her nose, but still clung to a dangling lock of hair.

She ignored them and stared at her face.

To get a closer look, she pushed her nose up against the glass, smudging the mirror. Her gaze held onto the woman staring back at her. Her focus fell to one of her eyes: gone was the familiar blue ring of her iris resting delicately on a round white eyeball. Instead, the blue color was now replaced with a vibrant red; its color almost mirroring the blood seeping off her.

She pulled back a little and gathered in both eyes. One of her irises was the same color as the crazies she'd just battled with. It was the tell-tale symptom of what made the crazies crazy. She had the same crazy red eyes—well, one of them; the other was more pinkish. If she had the same eyes, she was now a crazy too.

At that moment, all the strength she had felt left her.

She collapsed onto the cool surface of the bathroom floor.

Everything went black.

25

Engineering

"It's nonfunctional, sir," Jean Pierre reported on his walkie, eyes glued on Jessica's console, in case something changed.

"Have you tried..." Jörgen closed his eyes and went through a mental checklist of all the possibilities Jean Pierre had told them they'd tried, just in case there was something they might have missed. But Jean Pierre was always so thorough, as was Jessica. There was nothing else they could do. The only previously fully functioning console on the bridge was officially beaten to death by the crazies. And there was nothing they could immediately do to resurrect any of them before they ran into Sao Miguel Island. There was only one hope for his ship now.

"I guess it's up to us then," Jörgen stated, his mind whirling.

"What's your status, sir?" Jean Pierre crackled over the handheld.

Jörgen gazed at Wasano, Molly, and his two German troublemakers. Then he thought about what he'd say and clicked transmit. "We're just outside the deck 2 crew entry. We're still waiting on Deep to give us the all clear"—that was a reminder to him for an update—"and then we're going in."

"Sorry, sir," Deep chimed in immediately, his voice solemn. "There are still three or four of them hanging around that entry."

Jörgen rose from his crouch. "We don't have any more time to wait, Deep. I'm going—"

"Hold on, sir," barked Wasano. His heavy flashlight lifted, ready to strike at whomever or whatever they all heard, fast approaching them.

A large shadow arrived from a connecting hallway. Their skin crawled, until they saw the man attached to the shadow float in and then kneel in front of them.

It was Flavio.

"Let me go first, sir," he huffed, breathing in long, measured puffs. Flavio looked like he was dressed for some macabre Halloween party. He wore goggles, rubber gloves taped to long-sleeved arms, and his ankles were taped around some sort of extra padding. Everything was coated in blood, as if he had just butchered a live animal. His eyes were serious and mostly dispassionate, except there was a hint of annoyance: as if the world was conspiring to keep him from what he should be doing, which was most certainly not this.

Adding further to his surreal costume, in one hand Flavio clutched what looked like a long work glove—the kind used with heavy equipment. Each of the glove's black fingertips hung heavy, as if weights were inside. Upon closer inspection, recent splashes of blood cleft off the glove's finger-tips sprinkling the floor below where he held it suspended. In his other hand, he clutched a two-foot long wrench, its heavy end also coated red. Two sheathed knives, one on each side, were tilted at the ready.

"I go in and distract them in one direction; you go the other, to engineering."

Jörgen shot Wasano a look of disbelief, and then quickly studied Flavio; his immediate thought was, *Isn't this guy a waiter? Looks like he's better suited to security. No, the military.* "Yes," Jörgen said and nodded. "You take them port-side, and we'll go starboard, to engineering."

"Roger-dodger, sir." Flavio said. He leapt up, opened the door, burst through it, and mostly closed it, leaving a small crack so they could see through and know when to move.

"Hey, you crazy bastards. Come get some of this tasty Romanian meat," the macabre ex-waiter taunted.

Even louder, "Hey crazies. Come herrrre."

This deck 2 area had a reception-like desk just inside the door that separated two hallways: one going to the left to a couple of engineering offices and other equipment rooms; the hallway to the right led to engineering.

Several screeches and groans responded from both hallways: one crazy from the port side and two from the engineering side hollered their anger at his taunts. Flavio turned to the crack in the door. "When they've followed me down port hallway, you run to engineering. I can give you one minute. Don't waste time."

Flavio didn't wait for a reply. His eyes were on a single crazy coming from his left, just turning the corner. He leapt toward that crazy.

Flavio's movements were precise and fluid: he swung the weighted glove backhand with his left hand, connecting with the crazy's head and knocking it sideways and off balance. Then almost simultaneously, with his right, Flavio brought the wrench down hard on the crazy's Achilles' tendon, collapsing it to the floor, where it screeched its absolute hatred at Flavio.

Flavio took a knee behind the writhing crazy, ignoring its screeches, seemingly unconcerned with its movements toward him, while he glared at the other hallway. He rose up, standing tall, and waited stoically for the other two screeching crazies to arrive. He didn't flinch as these two beasts burst out of the hallway, turned at the reception desk, and barreled toward him.

Flavio held his position, a statue of the ultimate bad-ass man: *a rarity this day,* for sure, Jörgen thought. Flavio's gaze was fixed on the crazies, up to the moment before they were on him. The anticipation of their eminent conquest was almost too much for them to take. Each crazy groaned in anticipation.

Just before they reached him, Flavio stepped sideways. The crazies reached for him, missed, and tumbled over each other, entangled legs and arms clawing, colliding and one of them breaking with a loud crack.

Flavio immediately sprang down the left hallway, holding up after twenty steps. "Come on, you stupid crazies. You missed me. Now you got to kiss me," he bellowed. He almost seemed to be enjoying this.

Jörgen's group edged farther through the crack of the door, waiting for the right moment for their dash to engineering.

"I love this faucking guy," huffed Hans, behind them.

"Shhh," demanded Wasano. He didn't even look at the German, not wanting to miss their opportunity.

"Captain," stated Dr. Simmons, "did you see how they don't think about their movements? They're clumsier than children. Wonder if they'll have to re-learn their basic motor skills?"

The doctor was almost mumbling, more or less talking to herself, like a scientist in a laboratory dispassionately studying a dissected animal, while dictating observations into a recorder for future study.

Franz was quiet, as he had been almost the entire time. He looked like a smaller, more demure version of his brother. "Hey! Shouldn't we get going?" he whimpered.

"Go now!" Deep crackled through their radios. He was obviously following their every move, and was on top of their plan once Flavio had sprung into action.

Jörgen yanked open the door and Wasano led, followed by Dr. Simmons, Jörgen, and the Germans.

They raced down the right hallway, only slowing when they'd reached their destination, engineering.

So far, so good.

The small and simple placard on the door seemed to belie the importance of this area, especially now.

Knowing their time was short, Wasano immediately swiped his card and pushed the door open upon its clicked acceptance. He slipped into the doorway first, heavy flashlight raised above his head, ready to strike anything or anyone who rushed him from the shadows. He snapped it on because the overheads were off and the room was murky. While dousing the room with a cone of light, he worked at the switch to the overheads, confirming the lights weren't working—little on their ship seemed to be working now. At least the computers seemed functional: all the monitors were blinking their minimal light, coating the room in misty Regal European Blue.

Most important, there were no crazies.

The room was fairly compact, with one long row of three monitoring stations, crowded with half a dozen flat-screens per station, and a single desk in the left corner of the room, with its own flat-screens. On both sides of the room, connected to the ceilings, but tilted so they were visible to the whole room, were giant flat-screens with multiple views of the ship's engine room areas, various mechanical areas and the bridge. All the walls were papered over with multiple layers of deck-plans, charts, schedules, and other items Wasano didn't really understand, nor did he care to. This place was all about utility. There was nothing else to it. Certainly no place for crazies to lurk.

All three stations were abandoned, their chairs spun around. The butts which had occupied them must have left in a hurry.

"It's empty, sir," whispered Wasano to Jörgen and their group. They all quickly moved inside and clicked the door shut behind them.

Jörgen immediately went to work on the middle console, thinking if one didn't work, he'd move over to one of the others.

"Tell JP we're here," Jörgen said while tapping on the keyboard.

Several monitors sprang to life, blinking from murky blue to blazing white, removing more of the room's ghostly shadows. Jörgen brought up the Electronic Chart Display and Info System or ECDIS and saw their position: only 8.64 kilometers from the island. A red light flashed its concern about their proximity. Their ETA was still twenty minutes, probably because with the stabilizers out and down, providing maximized resistance, their overall speed had crept down to 14 knots. Their ride was much choppier, but it had bought them time. Just not enough.

First step was to engage the ship's rudder and steer them away from Sao Miguel Island. Jörgen brought up the Navigation and Command System or NACOS, which would allow him to steer the ship using its rudder.

There was a knock on the door, and Wasano prepared to answer it, holding his flashlight up high. He felt a little stupid, because he didn't see any evidence that crazies would knock first. But he wasn't taking any chances. Dr. Simmons stood fast, while the Germans shrank back deeper into the room.

Expecting Flavio, Wasano was startled instead to see a blonde-haired woman, wearing large designer sunglasses, an orange swimmer's nose-clip, and a crooked smirk.

"Are you going to leave a lady hanging outside, or do I have to beg to come in?" she said, her arms folded over her chest, acting impatient to be let in.

Jörgen turned from the keyboard—he had been waiting for the computer's program to respond to his commands—to take in the woman at the door, whose voice sounded somewhat familiar. "Hold on." He erupted from his seat. "Theresa-Jean?" he called out. "Is that you? Let her in, Wasano."

All eyes watched the athletic woman, clean and sporting a fresh coat of makeup, stride in and wait for Wasano to close the door. Her sleek jogging outfit appeared pressed and perfectly fitted to her form; her ponytail glistened. She looked like she had come from the spa, refreshed after a treatment, and certainly not someone who they had heard had fallen two stories from the zip line and then tangled with a horde of blood-thirsty crazies.

The oversized sunglasses and the swimmer's nose clip seemed out of place on her. And other than her sporting a clean bandage covering part of one wrist, she looked good. Really good. She certainly didn't appear deceased, as they had all assumed, including her husband Ted.

"Thanks, Captain. Did my husband and JP make it onto the bridge?" Her smirk was gone, crossed arms still in place over her chest, which appeared to be rising and falling rapidly. Her voice had a more nasal quality than usual.

"Yes, they did."

"I must talk to Ted and let him know I'm alive. I lost my radio in the fall." Her words were rushed and she offered a smile, but it seemed forced. She was not at all like the jovial woman he'd witnessed at dinner. She wasn't right, even though she more than looked it.

Jörgen said nothing, and simply beckoned her to the seat beside him, where a microphone telegraphed at an angle, waiting.

When she sat and rested her elbows on the long counter, Jörgen overtly pressed the transmit switch to the left of the microphone, now a few inches from her lips.

A cacophony of voices burst from a small speaker in front of her.

She shuddered slightly and pulled away. But when Jörgen nodded for her to go ahead, she leaned forward into the microphone and spoke.

"Ted?" Her head remained frozen, her lips closed, as she waited. Then she spoke again. "Ted, are you there? This is TJ."

Jörgen, sensing she was done, visibly clicked off the button so she could take over, while he continued with the ship's controls.

Radio static bled through the speakers for many long moments. Even the crew who had been just speaking were quiet.

"TJ?" a shaky voice answered. "Is... Is that really you?" Ted's voice raised an octave with each word. "My God," he said, his voice cracking, "how?"

"What can I say, I'm—"

Jörgen abruptly put his hand over the microphone and bent the flexible boom in his direction.

"Sorry, Ted. This is Captain Jörgen. I need the radio back. She looks fine. In fact, she seems almost completely uninjured. Let's hope you two have plenty of time to catch up. Jean Pierre, can you hear me? We still don't have any helm controls here. Unless we can discover some other way to gain control or reverse the engines in the next twenty minutes, we will collide with Sao Miguel."

26

Sao Miguel

São Miguel Island, although the largest of the Azores Archipelago, was still nothing more than a tiny spot on a map of the vast Atlantic Ocean. Its closest landmass, Lisbon Portugal, was over nine hundred miles away. To the *Intrepid*, it was supposed to be a transitional point on their navigational compass. Almost as if a harbinger of what was to come, São Miguel burst out of the ocean depths from a violent undersea volcanic eruption many millennia ago. Now, the island's three-thousand-foot high peak filled up the bridge windows from port to starboard, a looming target which grew larger with each eye blink.

This sub-tropical island had been a growing favorite stopover for Europeans and transatlantic cruise ships. If the *Intrepid* had intended to port here, its crew would have long switched its controls to manual, slowed its engines to less than ten knots and guided the ship around the island's southern exposure, and then north into Punta Delgada, the island's cruise port terminal and the archipelago's chief port. But that was not their destination.

Jessica had programmed the Intrepid's nav computers to take them directly into Nordeste, the easternmost town on São Miguel. Unfortunately for them, Ted heard that Jessica always hit her mark.

Of course, Nordeste was only meant as a reference point. Several miles back, they were supposed to have changed their course, resetting their heading for Nassau Bahamas. It was all part of the captain's simple plan to track along the path of the least dense cloud configurations, those coming from the ongoing volcanic eruptions. Because some in the media had suspected the volcanic clouds as the root cause for the Rage disease, striking first the animals and now people, the captain had thought it would be good to stay out of the clouds and have the added effect of keeping their passengers happier by giving them warmer temperatures and sunshine. That was before they lost control of the ship.

Now, with dark clouds thickening above and around them, and with the island growing closer by the second, the *Intrepid* crew sounded as if they were in a full-on panic.

The NACOS had automatically adjusted their stabilizers, and that had slowed the ship somewhat. But without helm controls, they were fast running out of options.

The team on the bridge and the one in engineering were shooting ideas back and forth over the radio. With staff captain Jean Pierre and first officer Jessica still working on their consoles, Ted manned the radio and repeated their words from the bridge to the captain in engineering. "The staff captain asked if you were able to reach anyone in the engine rooms?" His words were careful and without any emotional inflection.

Ted repeated Jean Pierre's words and waited. But he wasn't really listening.

Ted was jumping out of his skin. More than anything, he needed to be with his wife, TJ. Besides just the simple desire to see her, a part of him relented that they were probably going to crash. And if that was their fate, he didn't want to waste any more time being apart from her. He wanted to leave this world holding her.

But he also needed to confirm she was really all right: his logical mind told him it was impossible, replaying as evidence the scenes of her falling from the zip line and then disappearing into the writhing pack of crazies. *There was no way she could have survived this,* his mind argued. And yet, he had heard her. And so she did survive, his emotional side debated back. Even with the captain's confirmation, he still needed to verify this with his own eyes. He just needed her, and he needed her now.

He beat his fist on the table, demanding his logical mind's silence. *Focus, dammit!*

There was still a chance, no matter how small, that they could come out of this alive. But to do so required that he pay attention and not miss all that was going on. He could play a role in helping their success. But if he screwed up or delayed the crew's efforts, it could lead to all of them dying.

Did Jörgen just say, "No!"?

The captain continued on the other end of the radio conversation, "I'm going to go down myself and hit the automatic shut-off. But we have another problem." Jörgen paused. When Ted heard nothing but squeaks coming from the speakers, he twisted the volume control to its limit.

No one on the bridge could see the captain furiously scribbling computations on one of the flat-screen monitors with a wax crayon.

"Please, sir. Don't try both shut-offs on your own..." Jean Pierre hollered from the other side of the bridge, in between rapid puffs of air, "...with all the crazies out there..." Ted watched him, as he dashed across the span of the bridge; with Jessica in tow, each clutching paper navigational charts.

"What problem, sir?" Jean Pierre huffed.

Jean Pierre and Jessica were now on the port side of bridge, spreading their navigational charts out on the long table. Jessica pointed enthusiastically at some point on the chart. Ted's heart was racing uncontrollably. For just a moment, he stopped thinking about his separation from TJ.

Ted had the microphone open, but he feared the captain didn't hear what was just said. "In case you did not hear that, the staff captain was worried about your going at it alone and attempting both shut-offs, especially with all of the crazies out there. Though I don't know where those are, I'd agree about the futility of such a lone endeavor because of the crazies. They're now both examining some paper charts... Oh, and the staff captain asked what was the other problem you mentioned?"

Ted let go of the button and turned up the volume to its highest level. He didn't know how much time they had left, but he looked forward out the bridge windows and was shocked at how much closer the island was to them, just in the span of the last minute.

Two ridiculous thoughts leapt out of Ted's mind simultaneously: *it was so close, they could swim from here. And why don't they try that?*

He looked back down at the radio, unsure he'd let go of the transmit button, even though he could hear the background sound from the captain's own microphone being open.

An echoing voice from he guessed the security director said, "I'll go with you, Captain." It sounded like it was meant for the captain and not their consumption. But then Ted heard TJ's voice. His heart skipped a beat, and he gulped back his breath, as he heard her say in a colder than normal voice, "One officer should stay here; I'll go."

The microphone remained open for several seconds and some hushed words were barked, and then the booming voice of the captain erupted. "Thanks. But even if we're able to stop the engines, we still need helm control. Otherwise, we're too close to the island and we'll have too much speed: at this point, we'll still hit."

Oh shit! Ted thought. Or maybe he said it out loud.

"We could use the anchor," hollered Jessica from the opposite end of the bridge. "What do you think?" She said this facing Jean Pierre.

Ted punched the button. "Jessica, I mean the first officer said we could use the anchor?" Ted repeated, but it came out as a question, even though he knew it wasn't meant as one.

"That's not a horrible idea," Captain Jörgen answered in a flurry of words. "If it weren't for the depth... We'll need all twelve shots just to scratch the surface, and by then, it would be too late, because we'd be too close."

Static.

"But what about the Nordeste Bank?" Jean Pierre barked. A quick glance to Ted told him to repeat quickly. He held up his finger like he wanted to add something.

Ted kept his eyes on the staff captain, while clicking transmit. "The staff captain wants to know what about the Nordeste Bank? There's something more..." He waited for his next instruction, still maintaining eye contact and still holding the mic open.

"Tell him..." Jean Pierre trotted over to the base unit, stopping on the other side of the workstation and leaning over, "Sir," he yelled, "it's as little as 245 feet deep nearly two miles offshore. That should be enough, if you can use the stabilizers to nudge us over it. Jessica figures we only need to change our heading by two degrees to starboard, but it must be done right away."

Static.

Jörgen clicked open the mic and mumbled to himself, just barely loud enough that Ted and Jean Pierre could hear. "...if we dropped the aft anchor at the tail end of the Nordeste Bank, assuming the automatic release wasn't engaged, as it was designed to be, severely damaging the ship... It might be enough to stop us, if we can also cut off the engines..." Finally, Jörgen puffed out a loud breath, his mouth up against the mic. "That's a great idea. But get someone there right away, and I'll work on the stabilizers."

Ted knew from the All Access Tour that the release was on deck 1, and on the other side of their long ship. It seemed too far a distance for someone from the bridge. Engineering was right there. Someone from their team should be going.

The radio's pulsing static droned on while everyone listening waited for some heroic volunteer to go on this newest suicide mission.

Ted would have volunteered, if only to break the silence, but he couldn't get there quickly with his bum ankle and he didn't know which buttons to push; they didn't tell him that part on the tour. And thinking it through further, that was the key: knowing what buttons to push or levers to pull and when. And other than the captain, no one from their group in engineering would know what to do. It seemed impossible.

And while Ted waited helplessly, as time raced by, he once again considered belting out, Why don't we abandon ship?

"Sir?" pleaded a meek voice from behind Ted.

It was Ágúst, who'd been sitting on the floor, arms resting on top of his knees. David had been watching him like a hawk the whole time to make sure he didn't become a threat: none of them still understood why someone infected and symptomatic wasn't violent.

The officer shot up abruptly. David countered with a two-step back, taking a defensive posture. Ágúst glared at his staff captain with his odd-colored eyes. "I'd like to volunteer for that."

Jean Pierre had since walked around the table and was also now standing beside Ted. Jean Pierre didn't hesitate. He spun around, punched the mic and stated, "Captain, First Officer Helguson volunteered to go now." He glanced back around, while touching the transmit button, to scrutinize the Ágúst.

"Should he go alone?" asked the captain. He asked this, but they knew he wasn't really looking for an answer. There was no time to question the decision. He would have to depend on Jean Pierre making sure this was the most viable option. And of course they'd all have to stake their lives on Ágúst.

Again, Jean Pierre didn't hesitate. "Trust me when I say he'll be fine."

Ted immediately knew this to be the best solution. So did everyone else on the bridge. Ted had explained to them earlier that the crazies seemed to ignore those who were also infected, even those like Ágúst, who were infected but hadn't become violent like the others. He'd be perfect for this, assuming he remained sane, and they had enough time. He didn't want to even look out at their looming target.

They could all *feel* its proximity.

27

Becoming

Jörgen busied himself on his console, focusing on the only thing he had control over at this moment. He had had an idea. And it seemed to be working. Like other helm controls, he didn't have manual controls over the stabilizers. They were automatically being controlled by their systems. But he was able to feed false compass data into their NACOS, causing it to automatically adjust the port stabilizers and move them slightly to port. If he'd thought of this sooner, he might have been able to steer them completely away from the island. But they were too close for that now. With a little luck, it should be enough to place them over the Nordeste Bank, a low-lying underwater mountain of sand and rock, barely two hundred feet from the surface. His ECDIS display, as well as movement of the island across their bridge windows, told him this was working. *Thank God, at least these controls are still functioning,* he thought.

With the port stabilizer no longer providing resistance to the port side of the ship, and the starboard stabilizer continuing to provide the only resistance, he could feel the ship's stutter through the water beneath them. His eyes were glued to the ECDIS display, eyeing their speed and heading, his mind going through the computations to make sure it was enough. It was. He could leave now.

Jörgen spun in his chair to face his acting security chief standing guard at the door. "Wasano, if you're ready, let's get an update from Deep on the status of our hallway."

"Captain," TJ demanded from the back of the room, stepping closer. She had found a back wall in engineering after the captain had cut her off from the radio. "You need me to go—"

A double-pound sounded from the other side of the door.

All heads but one turned to the door.

TJ cast down her gaze, huffed out a frustrated humph, and ratcheted her arms around her chest.

Wasano cracked the door open, his flashlight raised, just in case.

This time, it was Flavio, who slipped inside, pushing the door closed behind him.

The former waiter, and now the ship's chief bad-ass, was a little more scratched up than before, and wore a few new splotches of blood, but he otherwise looked fine. He had halted just inside the door and quickly flashed glances at the captain, the German brothers, Dr. Simmons, Wasano, and then finally TJ. "Are we... Mrs. Villiams? Good to see you," he said to her.

TJ half-nodded a confirmation, without any smile or show of emotion. This was different than the Theresa Jean that Jörgen had met with several times. But on the other hand, she'd just escaped certain death.

Flavio continued, returning his gaze to Jörgen, "Sir, what's our status?"

TJ jumped in, "We're basically fucked. We've got ten minutes to get someone to the engine room now to stop the engines. Wasano volunteered and so did the captain. I told them both I should go, if someone would tell me where to go."

Flavio ignored her and responded with an immediate flurry of words to the captain. "No, captain must stay here and run ship. I get to engine room. Someone tell me where is stop controls. I am only one who can do this." Flavio's hand was already on the door handle, his body pointed in that direction.

"What makes you think you can get through all of those crazy people and make it to the engine room in time?" Wasano asserted.

"I deal with crazy passengers all the time, and now everyone crazy. No time to discuss. You and I go. Captain and others, vith Ms Villiams stay." He twisted the knob.

"Wait!" bellowed TJ. "I am going with you." Her arms were down, her shoulders squarely pointed toward Flavio.

"Absolutely not," the captain, now standing, demanded.

"We don't have time for this," Wasano yelled, taking a place behind Flavio, almost pushing him forward.

TJ stepped in front of Flavio and pulled off her sunglasses.

Wasano jolted backwards, hoisting up his flashlight to strike.

Everyone in the room either gasped or loudly caught their breaths.

Jörgen squinted and now understood why TJ seemed so different.

Flavio didn't flinch. "Okay, you come then. We go now. Follow me, I know shortcut to engine room." He dashed out the door.

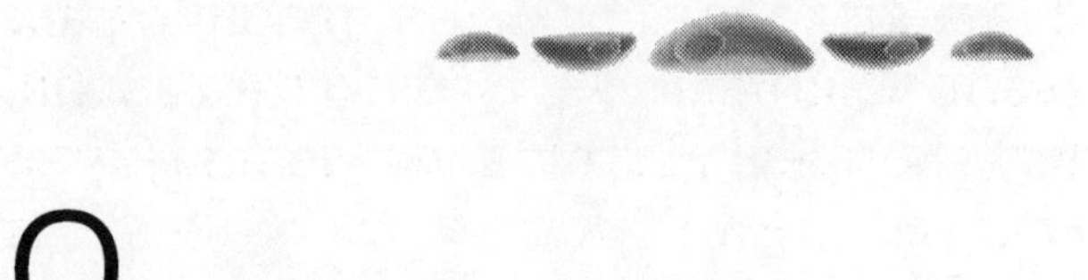

O

nly moments ago, Eloise had felt satiated. Fulfilled.

But she had also known that she still needed... something.

She had had her fill of food and felt better in what she'd become. It was a warm feeling, like a... *soft blanket* came to mind; this made no sense to her, though the thought felt right. And although she had a strong urge to sleep, she fought it. She just didn't know why.

She could have slept right where she stood. This part made sense. She was exhausted. But at the same time she felt exhilarated. It was better than after sex. That was one thing she remembered very well, and another urge she needed to fulfill. But she would satisfy that urge another time. Sleep was needed now.

She glanced at her misshapen wrist and the missing digit on her hand. She understood instinctively that her body needed sleep, if only to repair what was damaged. Her wrist was swollen. She remembered that it was called a sprain—she'd had had one of those before... she couldn't remember where. Her finger wasn't bleeding anymore. Another instinctive thought instructed her that her body was already healing. This instinct also told her that it wasn't yet the right time for sleep: something else needed to be done.

But what? a voice in her head yelled.

She started searching, first with her eyes. Then her search moved her and she lumbered around the open Promenade deck.

The public deck was littered with discarded cups, towels, purses, splotches of blood, and an occasional body. She had no idea what she was searching for amongst the debris. Only that like everything else that now came to her, she knew what she was searching for would come to her soon. She stumbled around, one foot shuffling after another, until she tripped over a corpse.

No, it was another person like her. This person was resting, just as she wanted to be doing.

Eloise took a few more slow steps and stopped over the body of a pretty officer, lying on her back, eyes opened, pupils dilated. Eloise knew instantly several things about this woman: she wasn't someone who had become like Eloise, and that was the reason she was dead.

Eloise examined the dead officer more closely, sensing she'd find a clue to her search.

She started her inspection with the dead woman's hair. At one time, before her rebirth, the old Eloise would have been interested in how this woman prepared her hair—what was this called? She would have thought it cheap-looking, but still pretty. The new Eloise had no interest in such things. But she felt there was something else important about this officer. So she continued her examination.

Eloise scrutinized every part of the dead officer, knowing now what she was searching for was here. It must have been something she had glanced at that made her stop. The dead woman's mouth was wide open—a scream interrupted: her jaw slack and silent; her neck a ragged mess, but no longer releasing her life's blood; her chest unmoving; the tag above her breast told others that she was Cruise Director; her ripped shirt was made from a cheap polyester material, just like her faux leather belt; the radio…

That was it!

Eloise snatched the radio from the officer's belt and fumbled with the controls. She'd never worked one before, but she knew she could figure it out. She twisted a miniature knob marked "V" and the radio came to life.

People were speaking on it. They were people who had not become like her. They were the Other People who she needed to kill.

They were talking about stopping the ship. They were saying that they needed to stop the ship before it hit an island.

Eloise realized right then that she needed to be on that island. She needed to get off this ship and get on the island. Her mind searched for the reason why, but there wasn't any. Nor was there a struggle with this decision. Once again it came to her intuitively, just like how to hunt, or eat, or kill. She knew that this ship was now useless to her. Most of the people had already become like her, or they would eventually; everyone else on this ship would be dead by tonight. But on the island, she felt... No, she knew, there would probably be many more Other People on the island, rather than on this ship. So she had to get there.

Right at that moment she knew what she must do: get off this ship and get to the island. And to do this, she needed to stop these Other People talking on the radio. She didn't know how, but she knew this, just as she knew everything else, and that this too would come to her. She listened intently to everything the radio told her.

A scream from an Other Person—she definitely knew this was not one of her people—forced a small tick in Eloise's face, but she didn't turn her head from the radio or adjust her position. She remained mostly still, crouched down beside the dead officer. After another terror-filled scream, she reluctantly lifted her eyes from the radio, and glanced sideways.

It was a woman in a one-piece bathing suit, perfectly sculpted to her body—a Ballet Maillot by Amaio, with the French mesh. This wasn't one of those things that just came to her intuitively. It was an old memory, from the old Eloise... She had had one just like it. Before becoming. The old Eloise would have stopped this woman and told her how good that suit looked on her. The new Eloise only wanted to kill the woman. But she'd leave that to one of her own people.

The woman raced by Eloise, a feline yowl escaping from her rapid puffs for air, her strides choppy but quick. The woman's head snapped to her right, just as two people who had also become tackled her to the floor. The woman screamed once more, and then was silent.

Eloise returned her glare back to the radio when she heard one of the ship's officers say they were going to deck 1 aft... Eloise knew for some reason that she was already aft and near a crew stairwell that went to deck 1. She remembered now that one of the officers told her about the aft stairwell—she glanced at its door a few feet away from where she was at that moment.

Someone on the radio said that First Officer Helguson was going to disconnect the anchor automatic release. He was already headed that way. Again, she didn't know why, but she knew that she had to stop this person. Somehow by preventing this Officer Helguson from doing what he was about to do, she could get onto the island.

Eloise quickly learned not to question these thoughts, where they came from or why. She just accepted them. It was all part of her becoming.

She sprang from the dead officer, surprised at how quickly she was already at the crew access door and inside. She felt so alive and so full of anticipation once again.

28

TJ

"This way," Flavio stated in his usual matter-of-fact tone. He grunted as he struggled with a large hatch in the floor. It moved an inch, but then his wrench slipped out of one of his hands and he lost his grip. The door and wrench *thunked* back to the decking, with a deep thunder-like tremor.

TJ pushed past Wasano, who was doing nothing but stand in her way, grabbed the handle and heaved. The thick metal door flew open, its metal clanging hard against the steel frame. Flavio shot her a stunned glance, one that said both "What the hell?" and "Damn, you're stronger than you look."

TJ turned away, wincing at the pounding reverberation in her head: a throbbing echo of the hatch's banging sound. Her features bunched up, as if she were in horrible pain, while she focused on quelling something worse than pain that wanted to come out: a darkness, more loathsome than the most abhorrent pain she'd ever felt. And like her body's previous responses to pain, she felt jolted and unable to stop its coming. Also like pain, which she used to just accept, this dark urge didn't give her the luxury of choosing. It rose up and demanded her acceptance. But she couldn't. If she did, she would lose control over that urge. So she dug her fingernails into her palms, nearly piercing skin, and pushed it back harder.

Then she stopped to listen. They all did.

The sound echoes from the hatch-banging must have vibrated throughout the metal structure of this hallway, as there was a growling response forward from them, just out of sight.

TJ looked up at Flavio, who was studying her with suspicion, just as he had been since they left engineering. "Are you going down first or am I?" she flared. They had so little time left and she wasn't sure she could hold it together much longer.

"Follow me," Flavio said, grasping the ladder with both feet and one hand—the other now clutched both the bloody wrench and glove-weapon. He slid down the ladder with dogged determination, until he hit the deck 1 flooring with a teeth-rattling *thud*.

TJ followed, sliding down in one fluid motion, her landing cat-like. She waited until Wasano was with them, after shutting the hatch. "You see, the... crazies, as you call them, are both attracted to and hate loud noises." She whispered this not only for their benefit but for her own. She was desperately trying to understand all that was going on in her and around her. Recalling the clang-echo which had thankfully started to fade, she continued, "It's like ringing the dinner bell, but at the same time, you're rattling their mental bells. In other words, when you make a loud noise, you might as well be calling them to you."

"You know this because you're one of... th-the infected?" Wasano stammered, his voice a little too loud and shaky. He didn't want to hear her answer. His eyes darted around the area in which they were standing, in an attempt to gather in any movement: it was a narrow utility hallway, marked with emergency lights that faded into the darkness in both directions. Flavio continued to study

TJ, his demeanor also jumpy, but in a different way. She sensed no fear in him; he was simply ready to strike her down the moment her actions became aggressive.

Yeah, she *knew* the whole sound-thing quite well. And while she culled some of this from recent observations and suspicions, she mostly perceived it instinctively, like so many things she seemed to just fully know, ever since her… *what, rebirth?* When she had the time, she wanted to mentally explore and understand why a simple loud noise made her head scream. And not the dull banging pain that she'd always felt… *no, scratch that, pain she used to feel in her head and side since the dog attack.* This wasn't pain. The urge that she pushed back was rage, pure and simple. She wanted to wallop on that hatch for making that noise, but also on everyone around her, including Wasano and Flavio. So yes, she understood this, because she knew exactly what the crazies felt.

She glanced back at Flavio, still scowling at her, and she motioned to the aft-side of the darkness. He nodded and then held out his two makeshift weapons, in preparation for combat against more—*dementeds* came to her mind and seemed like a better word than crazies. Crazies felt demeaning, and far too close to home.

Flavio waddled into the darkness, with her close behind.

"Okay, fine. Don't answer me," Wasano whined. He kept a couple of paces behind TJ, watching her more than anything else.

Flavio abruptly stopped and turned to face TJ. He leaned in so close TJ could feel his breath. She reflexively twisted back a little at the move, almost as if she were repulsed by his breath. She couldn't smell him. Mostly. With her nose plugged, she couldn't smell anything. But it was reflexive, because she knew what he smelled like and that terrified her.

He breathed, "You're not going to try and eat me, are you, Ms. Villiams?"

Once again, she had to suppress a natural emotion. This time, it was something she hadn't felt since all these changes took place: laughter. She gulped it back, but enjoyed the moment and said deadpan, "I do have a weird hankering for rare Romanian meat right now."

At least I haven't lost my sense of humor.

"Humph," was Flavio's only response.

He turned back and continued walking a few more steps before stopping once more, this time less sudden. He pivoted to face a sealed hatch in the wall pulling up the latch with his glove-whacker hand until it clicked. Then he pulled at it.

A shaft of light shot through, illuminating them.

Flavio gestured at the thin opening. "What is it you Americans say... Ladies first."

She nodded and slipped through, the hatch swiftly closing behind her.

Almost immediately, she thumped twice from the other side.

It was their agreed upon all-clear signal. There were no dementeds on the other side.

Flavio cracked the door open again and whispered through it, "Nothing?"

"Nope," she said.

"Do you smell them?" Wasano breathed.

"More like, I don't smell them. But I do smell both of you, ah... very strongly." She positioned the orange nose-clip back over her nostrils and squeezed.

"It's my manly scent," Flavio quipped, as he slid past her and continued his track aft.

"What do we... non-infecteds smell like?" Wasano glared at TJ.

She suspected he would be less likely to ask this question if she'd taken her sunglasses off and he had to stare directly into her eyes. "If I told you, you'd freak out." She moved past him and caught up to Flavio, leaving Wasano with that thought. For the second time since her change, she felt her cheeks crease into a smile. It felt good, even though she had to work hard not to think about what both of them smelled like. Again, thoughts of a dinner bell came to mind. In truth she was more afraid of freaking herself out.

Flavio held up at another door. He leaned forward, beckoning them both to come closer, so they could hear him.

"This starboard engine room," he told them. Then he faced Wasano. "You must enter security key."

Wasano tapped in the numbers on the pad below the handle. It clicked and so did a solid lock in the door.

A blast of heat and noise pushed through the door and spilled into their hall.

TJ didn't wait for the offer. She pulled off her nose-clip, letting it dangle around her neck, and slipped her head and part of her body in, stopping midway. She tilted her head back and whispered, "Wait here for a moment." She silently stepped through, clicking the door closed behind her.

Flavio put an ear to the door, while Wasano eyed him and waited to glean something from his facial reactions, or for some sort of report from him.

Wasano shrugged his shoulders. *What?*

"I hear struggle. I hear thump. I hear another thump. I hear nothing."

Two knocks on the door.

Flavio pointed to the door lock again, and Wasano quickly entered in the code and the door once again clicked open, sending in a blast of heat.

TJ stuck her head through, nose-clip on. "Okay, there are no more dementeds... at least conscious. Find the shut-off quickly. We have little time."

Flavio stepped past her and glanced at the two human shapes lying silently on the metal flooring a few feet in front of them.

"Did you kill them?" Wasano asked as he slipped by her.

"No, of course not. They're still people, you know... Please, the shut-off?"

"Yes, of course." Wasano nodded and then took a few quick steps to an opposite wall with his back to Flavio and TJ, who watched him attentively. Wasano's head fixed on an unseen point on the wall, then darted around, before he pushed his radio to his ear and yelled something they couldn't hear.

"What's the problem?" TJ asked Flavio.

"Don't know. I know ship's deck plan well. Never been in engine room."

They both rushed over to Wasano to ask what was wrong and why the engines weren't powering down.

Then they saw.

A large electrical-like box hung by wires from where it obviously once fastened much higher to the wall. On its face, now bent and distorted, was a hole and below it a placard announcing that this was the "Emergency Shut-Off." Pieces of bright red plastic littered the floor below the now nonfunctional device. It was destroyed. And that meant that someone, or more likely something, had sabotaged the emergency engine shut-off.

29

Ágúst

First Officer Ágúst Helguson scampered down the stairs, out of control, as if something were chasing him. In reality, he was running from himself.

He turned a corner and dashed through a crew doorway, barely slowing. When the door swung back and slammed shut, he twisted his head to shoot an angry glare at it for making so much noise. Still barreling forward, not watching his path, he pile-drove into a rotund passenger.

It was like hitting a wall. A soft wall.

Ágúst bounced off the much larger man, and tumbled to the floor. He glanced up at the moving shadow above him, and was surprised to see it was one of those lunatics, and it was snarling at him. *Oh God, I ran into that?*

The beast wore a Hawaiian shirt, with one panel ripped and hanging open, revealing a huge belly with deep scratched troughs that were raw and oozing. The beast roared bear-like at Ágúst, spewing flecks of dark coagulated blood from its mouth, while the thick gold chains that ringed its neck flopped in a frenzy. Then it stopped and just bored holes in him with its fiery eyes.

Ágúst reflexively pushed away from the loony, but he realized almost immediately that he wasn't scared of the man at all. In fact, he felt angry at this thing for snarling at him and being in his way. The feeling passed.

Ágúst stood up, ignoring the beast, who now seemed to have grown disinterested in him as well. So he continued his race once again. He didn't care about the loonies anymore; they certainly weren't going to bother him, unless he ran into them. He had to get to the aft anchor. His staff captain asked him to do this.

As he zipped through the large expanse of the deck 5 public areas, he marveled at everything he observed: all seemed out of place, and at the same time, just right. With each stride, he gathered in the scenes around him: objects that seemed different or that he'd never noticed before—it was his job was to notice things—or people running in terror, or the loonies running after them. With each object or person or loony he studied, he came to know more of what was happening to himself.

When he leapt over an overturned table full of useless pamphlets about the ship's various spa treatments, he knew he was stronger than he could remember. He felt like he could take on anyone and anything; he could beat up anyone, even that big loony he'd just ran into. He felt indestructible, like a superhero.

When two loonies were stumbling in his direction, he knew he was no longer afraid of them, and the loonies didn't pay any mind to him either. It was just as the author had told him would happen. And it wasn't just the fear of loonies that had left him; he no longer had any fears, about anything. He scoffed at himself, at how he used to shiver at night, thinking about what others would say about him. Even when he made first officer, he was sure he overheard others talking about him. None of that seemed to matter now.

And the smells. He wasn't much of a foodie, as Jessica called it, so the smells coming from their mess never turned him one direction or another. Eating was just something he had to do. But now there was a bouquet of both the most foul and most delightful smells, and none of them he recognized. He felt like he could smell something many meters away too, even though he didn't know how that was possible.

His eyesight seemed better as well. He noticed this in the darkened hallway and again when he dashed by blackened windows of the Computer Center. He often gazed in to see who was there, but he could never really see inside, even when he stuck his face up against the glass and cupped his hands around to block out the light. Now, as he breezed by, he could clearly see inside. Further, at some point he realized his glasses had fallen off and he didn't seem to need them anymore. But along with the better eyesight, everything seemed so very bright. The overheads felt like they burned holes into his skull. He found himself squinting and looking down while he ran.

But the biggest change of all was his anger. He was so angry now. And the smallest things made him angry. It was worse than simple anger. He felt almost insane with rage right now. He knew it was all part of the disease. But he also really didn't care. It felt strange that this didn't bother him. He would have been paralyzed by all of this... Before.

Really, nothing bothered him now... except for the urges. Those bothered him a lot.

Before this, he lived a life of regimentation and planning. He didn't have urges or yearnings. He took pleasure in his work and that was all he needed. His one desire in life was to improve to the point that others recognized him. In everything else he was careful and hesitant, never wanting to make noise. Now, he had overwhelming urges that he felt compelled to pursue, and with wild abandon: sex, violence, murder, and the hunger... For what he didn't know.

During all of this, he never connected the dots, assuming his urges, no matter how bothersome, were something that would pass. Then he came across a slight woman—he remembered her from the spa. She was hiding underneath a table, eyes owl-like, obviously hoping no one would see her. At first, he didn't see her; he smelled her.

He tried to ignore it, even running past her, but the glorious smell was too much to ignore. He halted, desiring to know what that smell was. No, he desperately needed to know. He pivoted on his heels and followed the unknown scent until he was upon the table. The woman's head swung up to catch a glimpse of him. She shrank back in terror. He shrank from her too when he realized what the scent was: he was smelling her, and he knew right then what he wanted desperately to do. And this so disgusted him, he almost puked right there. He pedaled back farther, away from the woman and her hiding place, just as another loony reached in and grabbed her.

Ágúst turned and continued his run, daring himself not to look back at that sight. He didn't want to admit it. He wouldn't acknowledge it. But he knew it, like everything else: he was a loony too.

Now on auto-pilot, he zoomed from hallway to stairwell to hallway, until he crashed through a final entrance and dashed the final stretch of hallway before he would be at the entrance to the aft anchor area. He could almost see it.

That was his whole purpose. He had only one mission, and that was the only thing that mattered. He was to drop the anchor and make sure that the auto-release mechanism didn't engage and the anchor chain held, slowing or stopping them before they hit the island. The whole ship was depending on him.

He rounded a pallet of recyclables and was five short strides from the door, and the realization of his mission. But he abruptly held up, stopping just short of his goal.

In front of him, blocking the entrance to the aft anchor area, was a completely naked woman.

30

Engines

"You're kidding, right?" TJ huffed, as she first heard and then watched the group of dementeds rush toward them. *They didn't have time for this.*

She exhaled and then ran at them, targeting the first demented, who was oak-tree-sized, and like the others, wore a black jumper. Her immediate thought was that if she'd make like a bowling ball and knock this one pin down, some of others would tumble behind it. *With a little luck, because this demented was so big, maybe he'd take out all of the others.*

This supposition was more of the combo of intuition and observation. For reasons unknown to her at this moment, she had more dexterity and control over all her motor functions than the dementeds did over their own. Most dementeds appeared to be either lumbering or spasmodic, with the spasmos acting like they were running downhill and were easily tripped up. Rather than take them on one on one, and risk any of them getting through to Flavio or Wasano, she knew it would be better to trip up the whole group of them.

Just before she was in striking distance, TJ threw herself up and somewhat sideways into the air. But at the point of leaping, she twisted her body hard, reacting to another crazy who had pulled up quickly beside the big one—*the two pin was off kilter now and wouldn't automatically fall when she took out the one pin. She'd settle for a one-two split.*

She wasn't sure where these thoughts were coming from, or what exactly they meant, only that they were correct.

Her body moved more slowly in the air than she would have thought, and so she had to gesticulate more to get the second one. But this caused her to lose sight of her second target as her head and torso rolled around to face Wasano and Flavio, who gaped at her actions. When her right foot connected, she couldn't really see the impact, but she felt the hard bone of her ankle connect with the soft jowls of the number two demented's face, almost at the same time as all her body weight smashed into the big one.

She expected her forward motion to continue, toppling the big one, but was instead jarred to a sudden stop. Her body was forcibly wrenched down and then sideways. She felt the beast's giant arms clamp down around her, and then deftly fling her away from it and the rest of the horde. She was airborne again, this time traveling in the opposite direction.

Once more, she wasn't anxious or fearful about any of this—more like surprised. Just before she crashed hard against a wall of pipes, she saw the big demented barely acknowledge her. The beast turned only slightly, and then continued its barreling toward Wasano and Flavio, with others close behind.

A splash of stars filled TJ's field of vision; her head had struck the steel exterior ship-wall.

What just happened? she wondered. *The dementeds weren't supposed to move that way. They weren't supposed to react so quickly.*

Her legs were above her in an awkward position, her body contorted at an odd angle. She swung her feet down and around until they slapped the floor.

Droplets of liquid slid down her face. Blood? A disconnected set of her fingers wiped above her brow, her wet fingertips held up for inspection and confirmation that it was only her sweat. It was hot down here... At the same time, rather than the expected feelings of fatigue or injury, she felt invigorated. More so, she was enraged and ready to do battle, more than any time in her life.

The engine room roared its unstoppable rumble all around her—a mind-numbing rattle that infuriated her even more. And with this was a chorus of other sounds too: screams, growls and grunts, all coming from the horde attacking and the two men now fighting this band of dementeds. She glared at the hubbub like she wasn't a part of this, but her mind still analyzed her best target.

Upon seeing the big one beat down on Wasano with its giant paws, this vision lit a fire under her. She resolved then that they would lose, and therefore she would lose, if she didn't immediately help.

She quickly pulled herself up, using her elbow, already hooked around a cross-beam. The wooziness was sudden and struck all her senses. And yet she fought through it. Oddly enough, there wasn't any pain. Shouldn't I be in pain?

Before all of this, if her head had connected as solidly, she would have just stayed down and taken her time, making sure she didn't have a concussion—she was most certain that she did now, and yet she should have had deep flashes of pain. She felt none and had no worries about this or any of the other injuries she must have sustained. Instead of pain or worry, she was filled with more overwhelming waves of irrational anger: killing and maiming were the only things that seemed to offer her comfort. She would oblige these feelings.

Right beside TJ was a fire extinguisher, as if the ship handed it to her. She grabbed it, hoisted it high, and focused her sights on the biggest demented. The beast towered over the much smaller security man, who would lose this battle in seconds. She sprang forward, almost fell over before straightening herself up, and rushed to the back of the horde, ready to strike.

When she reached the group, she pile-drove the extinguisher's hefty base into the first demented she came upon—one away from the big one—striking the back of its head. She knew she hit hard, because she felt the crack through the extinguisher, and watched the demented crumple to the floor.

She lifted the extinguisher up high once again, intending to now target the largest demented's head. Using the unconscious body of the one she'd knocked out as a vault, she catapulted herself up and came down on her target, striking its head with much more violence than the last one.

Her body rattled back, and she landed on her feet directly behind the giant. The huge demented stopped, but didn't fall. It swung around and glared at her, as if the horrendous knock on the head was but a light slap from a fly-swatter. It fixed its red eyes upon her and howled a spittle-laced blast of air into her face.

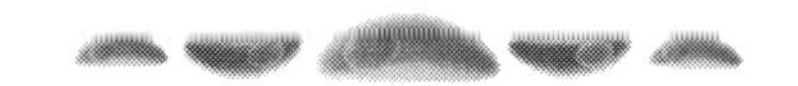

"We'll be approaching the Nordeste Bank at any moment," boomed the captain over the radio microphone. This was an announcement to Wasano and his team to let them know they needed to do whatever they could to get to the engine shut-offs immediately. It was also meant for Ágúst, in hopes that he would chime in and let them know how he was doing on the anchor. Finally, he wanted to update Jean Pierre and Jessica too, even though they were busily working on a different console, with Buzz over the radios adding some instruction—they were onto something, but Jörgen feared none of it would matter. They were all just about out of time.

Jörgen had finagled the stabilizers to steer them slightly north, toward the Nordeste Bank, but with half the resistance offered by one stabilizer, they were picking up speed again. If the engines didn't get shut down and the anchor dropped properly, they'd only have one option left: they'd have to brace for impact.

"What's their status, Dr. Simmons?" he asked.

"They're still stuck battling with the parasitics," Molly stated in her measured tone, eyes drilled into the big TV screen tilted from the far wall. It was far enough away that Jörgen couldn't see each of the little screens within a screen clearly. "I still don't see the officer by the anchor-thing."

Hans watched attentively from the entry of engineering, his back to the door. Earlier, he had been asked by the captain to check the door and make sure it was locked. The captain didn't—for good reason—trust that the man had properly secured the door after Wasano, Flavio and TJ had left. Hans had simply glanced at the door, assumed it was good, and then flipped around so he could watch what was happening next on the large monitors, and the console where the captain was working. His brother Franz was busying himself in another seat next to the captain, disinterested.

Jörgen furiously typed in commands. He still wasn't able to wrest control of the helm, and was fearful of turning off the automatic systems because they were the only ones running. He just didn't know what the hell was going on with the controls. There was a loud bang beside him. He stopped, fingers poised over the keyboard, and glared at Franz, who was spinning himself around in circles in the leather chair beside him, like some little kid bored to be visiting his father's office during *Take the Brat to Work Day.*

"Oops, sorry." Franz shot a demure glance at the captain. He rapped his feet onto the floor and stared at the screens in front of him. A red blinking light attracted his attention. Franz knew he probably should say something to the captain, but was fearful of garnering more ire. He'd already been a nuisance. A second red light started flashing in unison with the other.

TJ shot a glance at both men: Wasano was now swinging his large flashlight at other dementeds, connecting with one, and Flavio was knocking one wiry demented away with his wrench, while thwacking another with his work-glove weapon. Other dementeds attempted to push through openings in the melee to get at the only two non-infected people there. But there were too many for them to handle.

She glanced back at the big tree-of-a-demented, roaring at her, unfazed by her strike. She wished that she were battling an overweight blob of a passenger, rather than...

That's when it hit her. A latent memory flashed in her mind, back before she had become. It was a classic sci-fi movie called The Blob. Its star, Steve McQueen, used the cold of a fire extinguisher—like the one she held—to stop the blob. He froze the blob so that the other characters could get away. *Maybe this would work too.*

She flicked the safety pin out, clutched the handle, pointed the hose and squeezed. A white spray of liquid billowed out, splashing the giant demented directly in the face.

The demented became statue-like, his mouth gaping, now full of foam. Its head then listed, as if it was disconnecting from its neck. Then it righted itself. Its mouth closed, squishing out the white chemical spray. It slowly fixed its sights back on her, but she sprayed again, catching him once again right in the face.

It worked.

She held down on the lever and sprayed the giant demented again, just for good measure, followed by each demented in the horde, one after the other.

The results were the same: one by one the dementeds received a blast of cold white spray, first on their heads and then on their faces as they turned to see what this was. And one by one, after receiving the blast in their faces, they stopped, as if each of their internal go-switches had been flipped off.

Finally, she released the handle, stopping the spray.

The two men were no longer fighting. They watched, stunned like the dementeds. Their faces were almost clown-like: clenched and serious, but covered in splatters of white as well; their weapons fixed in the air, eyes riveted on their near-motionless targets.

"What are they doing?" Wasano huffed. He was mostly covered in white spray, over red splotches of blood; one of those splotches oozed red over the white.

Wasano remained still, back almost pressed to the wall. But Flavio marched forward to examine the dementeds himself, as if he had to convince his eyes what he was now seeing.

Except for their rapid breathing, each demented was stationary on its feet, though wobbling from side to side, looking as if they might fall over at any moment. Their faces were slackening with each second, mouths slinging open. Their reddish eyes glazed over. Their chests heaved unabated, faster even. "It's the cold," TJ replied.

One by one, the dementeds started to fall to the floor, their eyes closing after they hit. And then, as if it were normal, they all fell into a sleep. *They were hibernating.*

"I should announce on radio," Wasano breathed several long breaths, "the cold stops them."

"We must get to other engine," Flavio said as if this were the normal course of their mission. He stepped over each of the sleeping dementeds and shuffled down the metal walkway. TJ followed, still holding the fire extinguisher, with Wasano behind her on the radio.

Very quickly, they were through another hatch and into the next engine room.

Wasano identified the shut-off button and rushed to it while Flavio and TJ kept an eye out for more dementeds, even though TJ said she didn't smell anything.

Wasano held up his palm to slap the big red button, but before he could hit it, the rumble of the engines hitched and then shut down.

The engines did this on their own, without their help.

31

Down With The Ship

"I think they were successful, Captain," Dr. Molly Simmons announced jubilantly. "The two men are high-fiving each other. The symptomatic woman, Mr. Bonaventure's wife, looks... bored."

Jörgen didn't look up. He didn't need to. The shuddering, followed by the absence of rumbling below his feet, told him the engines were powering down. He glanced up at the same monitor Molly had been studying and caught the screen showing the aft anchor. It should have been released by now. "First Officer Helguson, please report." He bellowed into the radio. Staticky feedback was the only reply.

"What does that light mean?" Franz begged from beside him. He'd been as quiet as a church mouse since being scolded.

Jörgen glanced at a screen beside his and its two flashing lights. On his screen, he pulled up the data, but the reason for the lights didn't immediately make sense. *We've run out of fuel?*

"Captain? Ah, you need to see this," Molly alerted, her voice fluttering.

"Oy, what is that guy doing?" asked Hans, who had stepped away from the engineering entrance and padded closer to the screen, a couple of feet from Molly.

All eyes studied the monitor, and the images none of them expected to see.

Jörgen squinted, thinking he wasn't seeing clearly. He typed in a quick command and brought up the questionable video feed onto his own screen. The video images now filled up his entire monitor. His mouth sagged.

It was Ágúst Helguson, the first officer on whose actions their very survival depended. He was standing hunched over the anchor release assembly, staring into space, drooling. In his hand he held something.

"Another light is blinking, captain," announced Franz.

Jörgen craned his neck back at that monitor, to his right, and watched a number accelerate...

50—150—350.

It was the counter announcing the length of aft anchor chain spilling out. But it wasn't stopping, as it was supposed to.

He turned back to his video feed of Ágúst. He zoomed in farther to look at Ágúst's hands and confirmed what he was holding. "It's the release pin."

Jörgen was gut-shot with realization. His first officer not only released the anchor, which he was supposed to do, he also pulled the pin that would prevent the anchor chain from stopping when it hit its max length. The anchor would now automatically release all of its chain, as it was designed to do, so as to prevent any damage to the ship. That meant even if the anchor had snagged the Nordeste Bank, as they had hoped, it wouldn't then stop and hold. And that meant it would do nothing to slow them down.

There was now no way to avert their crashing into the island's shore.

"Oy, look at the naked woman. She's a looker for a red-eye."

Jörgen slowly turned to look up at the overhead and immediately found the video feed that Hans had called their attention to. It was the feed outside the entrance to the aft anchor assembly. In the middle of the screen stood, slightly hunched over, a naked woman he instantly recognized. It was Eloise Carmichael, the woman who had killed her fourth husband and was presumed to be washed overboard. She looked very much alive and she was staring with determination at the camera.

She is staring directly at us, he thought. It was as if she knew they were looking at her. She was now one of the infecteds, although she didn't look completely crazy. She tilted her head; it was the look of a predator considering its prey, from a distance.

And even though the color was far from perfect in this video feed, there was no question that Eloise's eyes were blazing the same blood-red color that coated much of her nude body.

All four of them were so focused on the monitor and the bizarre vision in it, they didn't even notice, until it was much too late, the two crazies that burst into engineering. The door that was supposed to have been locked by Hans when Wasano, TJ and Flavio left was left open.

The two crazies crashed through the partially open door, screeching animal-like brays and immediately targeted one person: Molly, who was now closest to the door.

The captain sprang from his chair and just before they could get to her, he struck first, tackling both crazies to the floor.

Hans dashed the other way, toward his brother Franz, who was already shrinking into a murky area on the other side of the room. Molly assumed because Hans had missile-locked on his brother, he didn't see she was in his way until he was upon her. Yet, using a shoulder, he blasted through her, knocking her to the floor. Her cane clattered against the other side of engineering.

Hans didn't even look back—she knew this because Hans' locomotion spun her around in his direction, away from the attack. He snagged Franz, who still had his blanket wrapped around him, and they both grabbed the darkest corner of the room, in an attempt to hide behind the overhanging end of the large three-station console the captain had just been using.

Stars filled Molly's field of vision, though if her head had hit something other than the rubber strip hiding some electrical cords, she might not been able to attempt to recover so quickly. It was knowing her life was in immediate peril that fueled her to move quicker than she could remember doing over the last several years.

She pushed herself up from the floor onto her knees and did a quick assessment, while her cane-hand blindly searched for its crutch in vain. Her mind reminded her hand that the cane had hit the other side of the room. It wasn't important now.

The two parasitics appeared to be focused on the captain. Both were pounding on him and one, she was shocked to see, looked to be biting his neck. The captain's pleas for help came out as low gurgles, while one of his hands weakly struck at the biter.

That should have been me, she thought.

But she could see the captain was gone, or would be soon, and so would her only opportunity to move while the parasitics were occupied.

She couldn't race for the exit, because she'd have to run around them, and even with her cane, she couldn't outrun them.

She reflexively turned in the other direction to confirm what she already knew: there was only one way out. She saw the anti-Semite who had just mowed her down when attempting to get away. His eyes were wide, like a little child, afraid for his own skin; his brother was partially covered in his blanket behind him.

There was no getting out of this.

Then the certainty of what she needed to do clicked in her brain, like the solution to a math problem.

She bounded up, wobbled, but regained the leg strength she needed to get to her target, a few feet from the captain. She ratcheted forward, but she couldn't help but throw a quick glance at the captain first. He lay bleeding on the floor as the parasitics tore into him further.

Molly lumbered the last couple of steps to the wall, below the big monitor they'd all been gazing at moments ago. It was on that monitor that she had seen her only salvation, offered to her by the symptomatic wife of Mr. Bonaventure.

Molly had eyed the fire extinguisher on their wall after she witnessed TJ spray the parasitics in the engine room, and then the security man announced on the radio about how cold from the fire extinguisher affected parasitics.

Molly did exactly what she witnessed TJ doing, although she had to clutch the heavy extinguisher against her chest: she pulled the pin, squeezed the handle, and pointed the nozzle and its billowing spray in the direction of the murdering parasitics.

Unfortunately, she just didn't have a good hold on it and either the pressure from the spray pushed at her or the thing was just too damned heavy and she was too damned weak. It fell out of her hands and clanged down onto the floor, and she tumbled over once again. This time, she hit her side on the floor, and she hit hard. It knocked all the wind out of her.

She rolled over onto her back, dazed, expecting that at any moment, one or both of the parasitics would be upon her.

A flash of a shadow shot past her, but from the other direction. The shadow grunted, as if dragging something heavy.

She tilted her head to the grunting and was surprised to see it was that obnoxious German, Hans, who had knocked her aside moments ago. He finally grew some balls, after she had done all of the heavy lifting. He was emptying the fire extinguisher she'd dropped onto the two already incapacitated—thanks to her—parasitics who had killed their captain.

"Save some for later," she croaked. Her voice sounded strange to her, like it was someone else's.

A loud noise on the other side of the room diverted her attention to the front of the room.

The other German brother, Franz, was standing before the door, which she had guessed had been closed. Finally.

Molly laid her head back down and took in a long sigh of relief.

A shadow enveloped her and she screwed her eyes into the dark face staring down at her, features not clear because of the room's low light. She could definitely make out the stupid I'm-proud-of-myself grin plastered over his demented mug. His hand was thrust out, a surprising gesture of help.

"Damn Jew. You're one tough old broad, ain't you?"

Yes, she guessed she was.

32

Rewired

She accepted his hand, and he easily hoisted her up as if her weight was that of a leaf. She wobbled—she was doing a lot of that lately—while standing and feared if the ship pitched or rolled in the slightest, she'd fall over. As much as she hated holding his hand, she had to wait until the wooziness passed before she could let go. Her spine tingled and her skin crawled at the feel of his sweaty mitt.

"Thank you," she said. Her eyes were closed, and her voice barely a whisper.

She felt the familiar form of her cane being placed into her other hand. At first she shuddered at the unexpected act of kindness. But she didn't question it and gladly shifted her weight onto it, feeling instantly stronger.

"How did you know about the fire extinguisher?"

She finally let go of Hans' hand and flicked open her eyes, but didn't make eye contact with him.

"If you hadn't only been staring at the naked woman, you wouldn't have asked me."

"Well, at least I..." Hans finished his sentence in a mumble, or she simply tuned him out.

Her focus was now on his brother Franz, who had paddle-stepped over to the two parasitics, who were in some sort of hibernative state now, just like the ones they had witnessed on the screen, after Mrs. Bonaventure had blasted them with her fire extinguisher. These two were lying beside the barely moving form of the captain.

"Wait," she huffed, and then waddled carefully over to the captain. Using her cane, she lowered herself down to her knees.

She could see there was nothing they could do for him. He was violently ripped apart and surely dead.

"Wow! Look at that, Hans!" Franz said beside her. "They clawed the ever-living shit out of his neck." She scowled at the young man, angry at the man's insensitive comments. The younger man wasn't interested. With a blanket shrouding his shoulders, he gawked at the captain, just like a typical little boy who'd just witnessed something gory, and liked it.

The radio chirped at them, "Captain, are you there? We need you to try something."

Molly glanced at the radio and then back to the captain

Again, her spine tingled as Hans sidled up beside her, rubbing his leg against her shoulder. "What now?" the dumb buffoon asked her, as if she would know.

With her eyes fixed on the captain she replied, "Maybe we can't do anything, at least about the controls, but we can at least tell them their captain is dea—"

Just then, Captain Jörgen gurgled something. His throat was barely held together by the thin strands of tissue that threatened to let loose. She certainly didn't think he could speak. She leaned over him. "I'm here, Captain," she said, her ear almost touching his lips.

"Tell the... About the fuel... Tell them use... thrust..." His voice trailed off to nothing. She waited, hoping he'd finish, while she held her own breath. After a few long moments of silence she realized he wasn't going to say anything more because he was dead.

"Yeah, that makes sense," Franz said, on the other side of the captain's body. His loud words were jarring. "The gas was off. I mean the red warning light said the gas was off or out."

She had thought the kid was just stupid, but he did have a brain.

"Captain, are you there?" the radio bellowed.

Molly gritted her teeth and clasped one hand onto Hans' arm and the other on her cane, using both as support. Then, pushing herself up and then forward, almost tumbling again, she raced over to the console, falling into one of the three swivel chairs. She spun to face the microphone and punched the transmit button, her face thrust into it. "This is Dr. Molly Simmons. I'm afraid your captain is dead. But he wanted me to tell you that we had run out of petrol, and I believe he said you should use the thrusters, whatever those are."

Jessica's head was loosely cradled in her hands while she sobbed, "Oh my God, not the captain."

Jean Pierre put a hand on her shoulder and squeezed. Then he let go. He let a few seconds go by before he said in a firm voice, "First Officer Mínervudóttir, I need you to focus on the problem at hand. Now that we have most helm controls, I need you to confirm our fuel supply."

Jessica stared at him, her eyes irritated and watery. She sniffled and asked the question they all thought, "How could we run out of fuel?"

"Have no idea. Doesn't matter right now. Check the controls."

"Aye, sir," she snapped, and began typing on the console she had just activated, while Jean Pierre stepped lively to the microphone.

They had both been working furiously for the last few minutes, and even surprised themselves at being able to somehow rewire the only other undamaged console, bringing it back into service. But they still couldn't get control of the rudder. They had limited control of the engines now, but without fuel they couldn't stop their forward motion into the island. "That's it!" she exclaimed. "I think I understand, Staff Captain."

"Go," Jean Pierre gave Jessica his full attention, while he hovered over Ted, who continued his vigil at the radio.

"It's the fuel! I still don't know how we could run out of the heavy fuel." Jean Pierre's head nodded in affirmation, knowing where she was going now. "However, we still have our MGO."

"Do we have thruster controls?" Jean Pierre huffed. *Could it be that simple?*

Jessica smiled, now completely sure of what to do, completing the taps of her new commands into the working console.

"Please explain," Ted begged. David, behind him, also nodded at Jean Pierre.

Jean Pierre held up one hand and punched the microphone button with the other.

"Thank you, Dr. Simmons. Please hang on. We think we understand the captain's command." *His very last command,* the thought burst his bubble of excitement just then.

At that moment, they could all feel the rumble of the ship's engines reverberating through the ship's hull beneath them. And almost as quickly as they felt the rumble, they could feel the gentle nudge of them being pushed forward. Ever so lightly at first, and then more prominently a few seconds later.

"The captain must have realized," Jean Pierre explained to Ted and David as well as the ship, as he also held the microphone down, "that we had run out of heavy fuel for some reason, but that we still had MGO—a different kind of fuel that we also carry—located in a different tank. And if we could get control of our port-side thrusters, we could steer away from the island."

"You mean we're saved?" Ted and David bellowed at the same time, almost sounding as one voice.

Jean Pierre waited to answer this and when they felt the movement hard to their starboard side, a giant grin enveloped his face. "Yes, I think so," he finally answered, and breathed out a long sigh of relief.

Jessica's head shot up and she joined them in watching their view of the island, which had filled the entirety of the bridge windows. The island slowly moved from right to left, until after a few seconds, there was nothing in front of their bow.

They joined in the cheering they heard on the radio. But theirs was far more muted. Still, they would enjoy this hard fought success, but just for a moment. They all knew it would be short-lived. Their next battle would be their hardest.

33

A Pause

They weren't going to take any time to lick their nearly mortal wounds. They didn't have time.

Somehow, they had averted a complete disaster by narrowly avoiding collision with São Miguel. Yet their losses were mind-numbing: their captain and many crew and passengers were dead or missing. Bodies littered the ship, like discarded debris from the morning after an epic New Year's Eve bash.

They had some control of their helm. Having one functional bridge console and the use of their thrusters gave them very limited maneuverability. And for now, they were gliding at just under a knot, with their engines off. Jean Pierre had cut off the supply of fuel to their stuck-on engines—they still couldn't figure out why they were like this—to temporarily stall their screws and with them, their immediate worry about running into any other islands. At least for now.

These solutions felt to all of them like small Band-Aids applied to a giant gaping hole in their collective guts. And if their ship were to ultimately survive this apocalypse, each knew they'd have to eventually deal with their most devastating of injuries: they had lost total control of the interior of their ship, with the only exception being the bridge, engineering and a few rooms or cabins they had radio contact with. None of them had any idea how or when they would regain control anytime soon.

To complicate their troubles, the bridge was mostly blind, and they were unable to regain the video feeds on their two working consoles. At least they could hear what they couldn't see via Deep's regular reporting. He radioed constant updates, laced with many verbal flourishes, describing all of the gruesome images flashing before him from the ship's working cameras.

From his reports, they gathered that it was still chaos outside their secured areas: enraged parasitics—Dr. Simmons coined the term for infecteds appearing violent—still dashed around the public and crew areas. The parasitics chased, maimed or killed their fellow passengers and crew, just as they had done for the last few hours. Some of the parasitics even appeared to be eating their victims.

The only good news was that the incidents of attacks appeared to be dwindling as most of the survivors were now hiding or were hunkered down somewhere, waiting for the crisis to pass. The ship was huge and there were quite a few hiding places for the survivors. It was the survivors on which they now focused their collective attention.

While Jessica was tirelessly working to regain control of another console under the direction of Buzz on one of the portables, Jean Pierre, Ted and David were on the base-unit attempting to identify crew and passengers and to help them find safe places around the ship. Deep continued calling out the potential perils to all involved from the MR.

They communicated with crew members who had radios—many had been listening to the drama unfold before them—and told them what they needed to know about those who were infected, and how to stay away from them. It appeared that if they could get to a cabin or other clear room, simply locking their doors was enough to keep the parasitics back. Ultimately the infected person would grow tired or would so damage themselves from incessantly pounding on the door, it would stop and run to some other location. Many of the crew were trapped, but at least safe. And because it was still insanity out there, they remained where they were until some help could be arranged or they had somehow muted the threat. They would deal with that part later, they all decided.

Ted and David did their best by manning the big port-side table in the bridge with the deck plans. When a group made themselves known on the radio, Jean Pierre would call out the location, and they'd mark down the number of survivors using a black wax pencil. They also marked down reports of those hiding or those still out in the open but headed to someplace identified as safe. These were indicated by an arrow. Reports of parasitics were marked in red with their number. An arrow was added if the parasitics were on the move, showing their direction.

With this system, they were able to track the location of survivors and parasitics, so they could visually keep track of each group. Each survivor was told to hold tight; they'd be retrieved later, when they figured out what to do about the parasitics.

After a while, they were all beginning to feel like they were gaining an upper hand in the chaos. And within an hour, there were few crew or passengers they could help, at least over the radio.

It wasn't long before Ted and David began to feel like third wheels to the process. Because of the few frustrating moments early on, when neither knew a location, Jean Pierre decided to relieve them. He grabbed a portable and took residence at the giant table with now more than a hundred scribbles in red and black pencil littering all thirteen deck plans.

Meanwhile, each time Ted put pressure on his damaged ankle, by moving or just standing, he'd unconsciously grunt or groan. David offered that now would be a good opportunity to thoroughly check out Ted's injury.

They proceeded over to the captain's chair, the only other unoccupied seat on the bridge, and David carefully examined Ted's ankle. Though not a doctor, as a child, David found himself helping his fellow Auschwitz survivors with all sorts of various physical maladies. Because of what he learned, he became pretty good at properly identifying and patching up injuries, using whatever was on hand.

"It's a bad sprain, but not broken," he told Ted.

Using strips torn from a blue bathroom towel, he tightly wrapped Ted's swollen ankle. It wasn't pretty, but Ted could now hobble around, with fewer grunts and groans.

With the added mobility and feeling unneeded, Ted was even more anxious to leave. He desperately wanted to see his wife, who was still somewhere in one of the engine areas. He didn't want to wait any longer to see her. And when he did finally see her, he would hold her tight and not let her go. After thinking he'd lost her, he was practically going mad himself to make this happen.

"It must be killing you to be locked in here, while she's out there?" David asked, mostly to give him a chance to talk about it. David's wife Evie often reminded him that talking out those things you had no control over helped you feel a sense of control. He had done a lot of talking with his wife over the years.

Ted lifted his head and shot him an embarrassed glare. "That obvious, huh?"

David nodded and smiled. He didn't need to say anything more. Besides genuinely wanting to help Ted, he figured talking about it might also help the man better focus on whatever it was they would be tasked to do next. He didn't hold it against Ted that his head wasn't altogether there: if he'd thought Evie had died, he'd be beside himself.

Of course, he didn't know Evie's status. At least not yet.

"I just keep remembering her fall, seeing her fear, and knowing I could do nothing but watch. This very thing had happened to me before... I lost my first wife and a child. And when I thought it happened again, I swore I'd do what I could to protect TJ. And with our spending so much time apart for so many years, it just seems ridiculous now that I know she's alive and she's so close, yet we're not together. I just don't want us to spend another moment apart."

"I get that. Evie and I have had our long periods of separation too, and of course, I really miss her now..." David stopped and glanced down, collecting himself.

"I'm sorry. You don't even know she's safe yet." Ted's shoulders drooped, and his pensive look turned into a glower. "I'm being selfish."

"Nonsense. Evie's alive. She's too much of a pain in my side to pre-decease me." David snickered at this, not sure Ted knew it was a joke. "Guess you spend so much time together as a couple over the years, you feel like a part of you is missing when you're apart."

"Except when they drive you crazy, huh?" Ted said with a wry smile, obviously doing his best to add a little humor to their otherwise serious conversation.

"That's what I love about Evie. She knows what buttons to push. I've long since ceased being a mystery to her and that just suits me fine."

Ted studied him with scrutinizing eyes. "Listen, David. I appreciate what you're doing. But I have to do something—hell, anything—right now or I'm going to go bat-shit crazy just sitting here. Either I find something useful to do to help here, or I'm leaving to go find my wife, regardless of how stupid that may sound." Ted pushed himself up out of the captain's chair, suppressing an under-his-breath-grunt.

"I'll go with you. But let's first ask the staff captain... I'll bet there's something we can do just outside this bridge."

David put an arm around Ted to help him along the short distance to the port-side bridge. Ted gladly accepted and they waddled to the front-facing area of the deck-plan table, where Jean Pierre was slunk with a black pencil touching the white area of the Regal Crown Lounge on deck 11. His ear was pressed against speaker. He nodded every now and then. He wrote the number sign and then "6" with an arrow pointed to the Concierge Club.

He'd just put out another of his many calls to any who hadn't checked in yet.

"Okay. Just remember that curiosity killed the dog." David couldn't help but smile at that one. "You hold tight until we send some crew out there."

After the pause was long enough, Ted asked, "Jean Pierre, do you want us to go up there? If not that, we'll do something else that the ship needs. David and I need something to do. Don't care if it's dangerous. We're going flipping stir-crazy here, just waiting."

David chimed in before the staff captain could answer. "We want to help, but we're kind of limited with our lack of knowledge about the ship."

Jean Pierre looked up, flashing a forced smirk at each man. "You're probably not going to like it, but I do have a suggestion."

"The answer is yes, whatever it is," Ted burst out.

"I need you both to go to the next door cabin, number 8000, on your right." He handed Ted his key card. "You'll need this to get in. It's a luxury cabin and it's one of the only places on the ship that has a satellite connection to the outside world's television broadcasts. It would be good to know what's going on out there, as we'll eventually need to make land at some point."

"Why wouldn't we enjoy luxuriating in the Queen's Suite and watching TV, just so we can soak in more bad news?"

"It should be a piece of pie, but it would be helpful to know what's going on." Jean Pierre didn't crack a smile, even after his bad idiom. He scoured the notes hand-written all over his table, as if he'd missed something, and then looked back up again. "Please be careful when you leave the bridge: the, ah... parasitics, are still running up and down the hallways."

They both nodded, each remembering the occasional screech running by the bridge's entrance.

"Perhaps, before we step outside, you could ask our eye-in-the-sky if our coast is clear?" David asked and then looked to Ted. "You ready?"

Ted had removed his hat and was scratching his temple, focused in the other direction at something on the bridge. "I was just thinking... Maybe we could secure the area around the bridge entrance and 8000 beforehand, so any of us can come and go and not worry about getting eaten."

"What did you have in mind?" Jean Pierre asked.

"How about those dead consoles? I figure two or three of those, standing side-by-side, should block the hallway access on each side. Maybe we even shore them up with tables or chairs from the luxury cabin?"

Jean Pierre smiled. It was the first time they saw him smile since their ship was overrun. "That's a great idea. I'll help you drag them to the hatch. Then we'll have Deep tell us how it looks and when it's clear for you guys to set up the obstructions."

They all worked quickly, dragging the five dead consoles, and a few heavy pieces from the busted conference table lying in the wrecked conference room. After getting the okay from Deep on the radio, who said he hadn't seen anyone in the deck 8 hall in the last twenty minutes or so, they cracked open the hatch.

Each man carried a hefty broken leg from the conference table, which made a substantial club.

David edged his head out the door first, listening for any sign that he needed to retreat.

He slipped out the door, followed closely by Ted. Both held their makeshift clubs above their heads, ready to pummel any crazy who threatened to attack them. Even though they were just told by Deep that their hallways were clear, David was still surprised at how quiet it was. He wasn't sure, really, what he was expecting... maybe some sounds in the distance or signs of what had been going on the last few hours. His eyes were immediately drawn to a splatter of blood on and around cabin number 8001, right next to their destination 8000.

He turned his head in the other direction, towards Eloise's Royal Suite and saw the slaughterhouse of blood staining the carpet in front, like some macabre welcome mat.

Because of his leg, Ted stood watching and listening at both ends of the hallway split, making sure nothing approached, while David and Jean Pierre hoisted one console after another and placed them into each hallway. One blockade was created on their side of Eloise's cabin, giving them almost the whole length from stern to an open area contiguous to the bridge. The other blockade was built in between 8000 and the next cabin, 8001.

David and Ted would shore it up a little better with tables and chairs from their luxury cabin destination, 8000. Until then, it was already a vast improvement. All they were looking to do was to fortify each sufficiently to slow down the parasitics enough to allow any one of them to escape back to the safety of either the bridge or the Queen's Suite.

Jean Pierre left them, not wanting to leave the bridge hatch open any longer than he had to. Plus, he wanted to get back on the radio and see if he could guide more of his passengers and crew to safety. They agreed whomever was on the outside would pound three times on the hatch or use the intercom button when they wanted in again.

David verbalized a suggestion that they use the mattresses from the cabin to block anyone's view, and to further buttress their blockades. They could then move those aside when someone who was not trying to kill them wanted in.

Jean Pierre nodded in agreement, thanked them and then shut the hatch, locking it in place.

Just after David and Ted stepped into the luxury cabin, Jean Pierre's voice sounded on Ted's radio, asking for an update from Deep.

Because they wanted to get the mattresses out onto the barricades quickly and they wanted to get back, as instructed, to watch for news updates the cabin's satellite TV, neither heard Deep's reply after Ted turned his radio's volume down.

If they did, they would have heard Deep say, "Sir, I can't seem to find any of the crazies. It's like they all disappeared."

34

More Bad News

They double-timed their gathering up each of the suite's two king-sized mattresses, pushing one up against each barricade. Once the suite's door closed, offering security, Ted and David dropped themselves into the lush couch in front of the suite's giant TV. Ted punched the remote's "On" button, filling the cabin with the staticky sounds of a television not receiving a signal, when they heard a loud click from the entrance. Both their heads snapped in that direction, and they sprang from their seats.

"Oh Christ, Officer," Ted gasped, "You gave us both heart attacks." He remained where he stood in front of the couch, a little unsteady on his one good ankle, and took in the officer standing just inside the suite's entrance.

David, in the swift motion of someone much younger, had hopped from his seat, grabbed his table-leg weapon and taken a couple of steps toward the door before Ted's words left his mouth.

It was Ágúst Helguson, from the bridge crew, standing just inside their cabin, looking almost embarrassed, as if he had interrupted something. But then Ted realized it wasn't embarrassment he was seeing; there was something not right about this man.

"How did you get inside? We locked the door," David bellowed over the TV static. He took another step toward the officer, while he repositioned his hands for a better grip on his weapon. Ted could see he was getting ready for a battle.

The officer held up his key card, in answer. It seemed like a casual *Through the door, you dummies* point, without actually saying this. He said nothing else, keeping his head down, sunglasses on, pointed at the floor.

The man looked pale, like he was suffering from a head cold, and Ted had to remind himself that this man had reddish eyes earlier. He was partially symptomatic with the Rage disease. Had he turned completely and become parasitic like the others? Ted frantically scanned the area around his feet for his own weapon. It wasn't there.

Then he remembered, in his exuberance to get to a seat and take a load off, he had forgotten he had left his club on the dining room table. He glared at it, at least half the distance to the potentially crazed officer. And he wasn't moving very fast right now. If this guy went crazy on them, he'd have nothing to defend himself or David—not that David needed much defending—except for the remote control he now cradled in his right hand.

The officer held up a thumb and forced a weak smile, lifting his head up slightly. Then he burst into the suite's bathroom, slamming the door behind him.

Ted glanced at David and David glared back before giving him a shrug of his shoulders and a smirk. Then they heard the officer heave and both nodded. They understood—the poor guy was just sick, not crazy. They were just learning about the Rage disease and how it worked in humans. Perhaps it simply made some of the infected sick, but didn't give them all the symptoms, including the aggressive part of the disease. He so wanted to know more and felt like their survival would depend on it. Finding out what was going on in the world would help. He wasn't sure what they should do next with the sick officer.

David lifted his head slightly, a half-nod. "Why don't you find a channel that works and I'll stand guard by the bathroom door, in case our officer comes out feeling a little charged up."

Ted nodded back. But rather than sitting down, he hustled over to the dining area table and snatched up his weapon. He heard David try to hold back a snicker unsuccessfully, as Ted lumbered back to his seat. He'd not let go of this until they were free of this threat, or he found a better weapon.

Ted glanced back once more to the bathroom door, behind him. David, whose club was now resting on a shoulder, busily inspected the bathroom door. Feeling satisfied, Ted returned his focus on the TV and the remote.

He remembered the first channel was always the ship's channel, and it was likely to show nothing, especially now without any content to broadcast, nor crew to operate it. The next few channels were cable channels and they had pre-recorded content: movies, television series, and some reality TV show called The Colony. Ted realized pretty quick there were far more satellite channels on this TV than the one in their cabin, even when they were fully operational. He continued his progression forward, pressing the channel-up button until he found a news channel. He let out a deep sigh when the bad news poured in, like a fire hydrant opened up during the summer time.

A big part of him—the unrealistic side—had still held out a small glimmer of hope that it wasn't as bad as his logical side knew it was. He kept telling himself that maybe it was isolated or somehow different outside of their ship.

It wasn't.

BBC World News showed video after video of cities damaged or destroyed: some beat to hell and barely standing, perhaps because of the tsunamis; some still burning, with uncontrollable fires; and some completely gone, as if they were leveled by a nuclear-bomb-like explosion. And then there were the bodies. Most of the videos showed them everywhere. All but one video chronicled the aftermath of what places looked like after the event, whatever it was, that caused the destruction. British reporters described what each saw or vignettes from survivors they'd interviewed.

But Ted wanted more about the infected.

The next channel was CNN. They had some of the same videos, and a few different, but showing the same level of destruction, all while a panel of guests argued the cause of this apocalypse. The consensus was climate change. Ted changed the channel.

On Fox News, the same video was played over and over again, on a loop, all while a talking head with psychology accolades after her name droned on. The video showed people running down a street in London, away from something. At first Ted didn't see it, but then after the third or fourth loop, he caught several of the red-eyed parasitics among the group; they weren't running away, but doing the chasing.

It was confirmation of what he already knew: this disease wasn't just local to their ship and what the media was calling Rage was turning animals and people into crazed killers.

It still wasn't enough. He wanted—no, needed—more examples, more information so they could figure out how to survive this.

He flipped up to the next channel, which was Sky News, hoping they had more videos about the crazies and more information about the infection.

"Any details on the chyrons or just sensationalism like the videos?" David asked, startling Ted, who turned to see he had wandered from the other side of the suite and was now sitting on the arm of a chair closest to the door. His shoulders were still pointed toward the bathroom, while his head was riveted to the TV.

Ted had been trying to read the chyrons while watching the videos too, which is why he'd first missed the parasitics in the video until it had looped back a couple of times. "Only that the mayor of London was killed by one of his aides, who had become parasitic from Rage. They were at first calling it a hate crime because of the mayor's religion, which was laughable..." He trailed off and added, "Really nothing that we don't already know. Anything more from our sick officer friend?"

"Nope. He's been quiet in there. I think he was embarrassed by his queasy stomach. But I'm still watching, just in case—Oh, look at that one." David pointed to the screen. His whole body was now trained at the TV.

It was a live news feed, coming from Paris, from one of their local correspondents. The camera was on her and a street below in the distance, crossing over the Seine. It looked familiar because Ted had been there several times. There was some sort of blockade down the middle of the bridge, made up of clusters of black. But before it could focus on the blockade, the camera swept past to a mass of movement beyond.

It was some sort of mob, which appeared to be moving toward the blockade.

Ted turned up the volume so that they both could hear it better.

"You can see police below us in their riot gear on the historic Pont Norte-Dame." The camera had refocused on the reporter's pretty face, and then it zoomed into the black clusters, which were obviously made up of police in riot gear, standing behind human-sized shields they were holding up. "A large group of Les Fous, which have swept the city, are headed to the Latin Quarter. The Gendarmerie are attempting to hold them back. You can see Les Fous now..."

"What the hell is lay faux?" David asked.

"It means crazy people in French," Ted responded, matter-of-factly.

Les Fous hit the blockade and were momentarily stopped. Then more piled into the line, some climbing over others, the blockade broke, and many of the military police fell, their batons flailing at their attackers.

"Oh dear," bellowed the French reporter. "They weren't able to stop Les Fous. The same thing happened in London earlier today."

Ted and David glowered at the screen as they watched the surreal images of infected Parisians pouring over La Pont, attacking everyone who moved, and even those who didn't. There were just too many of them as they then fanned into the Latin Quarter en masse.

David now was leaning against the back of the couch, mesmerized like Ted, when they heard a loud crash behind them. David spun around, almost hitting Ted's head with his club. Ted sprang off the couch, this time with his own club held high.

It was the front door they had heard.

It was still closed, though the bathroom door was wide open now, and Ágúst Helguson wasn't there. He must have just left.

David was already running for the door, Ted not far behind, as the TV continued to report on the mayhem in Paris.

David yanked open the door and burst through in one motion. And Ted caught up to the door, just before it crashed closed again.

David had stopped just beyond the entrance, first scanning starboard and then forward, doubtless checking out their two blockades. He hollered, much too loudly, "It's the starboard one." Ted could see it too. The officer had pushed aside the mattress and knocked over a console.

David dashed to the broken blockade, which was the only thing slowing down any crazies that might come at them from the starboard hallway.

Ted limped in the same direction, swinging his head forward, until he had passed that blockade. He could have sworn he'd heard footsteps running away.

"Still, you can't find any parasitics anywhere?" Jean Pierre asked again. It had been over half an hour since Deep had reported their conspicuous absence.

"No, sir. I'm telling you they're all gone. I still don't see any of them running around anywhere. It's like they left the ship."

"We should be so lucky… Okay, Deep. I need you to go back to checking each and every camera feed on the ship and cross off the places you can verify they're definitely not there. We'll do a physical search if we have to. But we must know where they are. Until then, this is for all personnel listening to my voice. Until we know the location of the parasitics, do not leave your position. Repeat, stay where you are."

Jean Pierre let go of the transmit button, considering what else he could say or do right now.

"Staff Captain?" It was Deep, once again. "Hold on." His normally even voice sounded harried.

"Sir... I see a group racing toward the bridge on the port side... I can't tell if they're human or parasitic."

David and Ted tugged hard at the king-sized mattress, so they could get through, all the while shooting quick glances down the hallway. There was no sign of the officer.

They moved the tilted-over console back into place. It had been moved aside by the one man, even though they struggled nudging it back into place between the wall and the other console. They then righted the mattress, setting it up more snugly on each side, so there was less access room. Finally, they breathed giant sighs of relief. That's when they heard the growing sounds of rapid footsteps. Lots of them.

"They're coming from the other side," David blurted, but didn't wait for Ted's acknowledgment; scooping up his club from the floor, he raced back to the port side blockade. Ted humphed, then attempted to move as fast as his damaged ankle would allow, pulling up to David a few moments later, behind this blockade's giant mattress. Ted peeked through a crack between it and the far port wall and saw at least a dozen people jogging toward them.

"I see at least a dozen people," Ted huffed. "Can't tell if they're parasitic-looking or not. Let's get back into the bridge: it looks like they can move heavy weights easier than we can." He backed up from the mattress a few quick stutter-steps, when David held up his hand, signaling for Ted to stop and wait.

A muffled thump sounded from the other side and the mattress shuddered and started to tumble toward them. Both men put their weight against it and pushed back, involuntarily grunting as they did. They weren't sure now if in fact this wasn't a bunch of parasitics. Both helplessly glanced at the distance from them to the cabin door, which looked much farther away than either remembered.

A woman called out from behind the mattress, "Is someone there?"

Ted's face, a mug of furious focus with sheets of perspiration skidding off, instantly turned into a giant grin. "TJ? Is that you?"

"You were expecting someone else?" she said in that same playful voice he knew so well. "Are you gonna let us in or do we need some sort of magic password?"

It was definitely TJ, acting as if nothing had happened.

35

Reunited

Ted tugged with one mighty grunt at the mattress, followed by ripping off the additional furniture pieces they'd just piled on top of the barricade. His mind impatiently reunited them, while his physical self caught up. And then his mind wandered. He could almost imagine none of this had happened. A crisp mental picture of TJ materialized. It was from the day of their wedding: her lips had an extra shade of rose-colored gloss, her cheeks shined from a healthy dose of tanning she had done earlier in their backyard, her eyes shined bright blue like the most beautiful sky he had ever seen...

He couldn't wait to see that face. And with each tug of the console to give her enough space to slide in with the others she must have rescued, he found himself hyperventilating, in anticipation of the moment.

He caught a glimpse of her feet and legs and his heart soared, and then somehow jumped several beats faster. For just the briefest of moments, Ted wondered if he was about to have a heart attack and collapse before he could get his arms around her.

The final tug, the space was now clear and Ted lifted his gaze. His eyes skipped past what she was wearing and bulleted to her face, fully expecting the same visage of his beautiful bride he'd been visualizing, only twenty years older.

What he saw struck him with a jolt. He sucked in his breath, tensed and stutter-stepped backwards, so in shock he nearly fell over.

His wife's beautiful blue eyes were now mostly red, like two open wounds; her skin was pale, like someone newly deceased; her lips thinner than he could remember, and lacking all color; and her face and body were covered in giant splotches of blood, as if she had just taken a bath in it.

This couldn't be his TJ.

Oh God, no! She's a parasitic.

Then her eyes met his, and she flashed the coy grin he knew so intimately.

It was her.

He exhaled all his tension.

He didn't know what happened to her or why. At this moment, he didn't give a damn. He needed her embrace. He needed her, no matter her condition.

She slid through the small opening they had made in the barricade and found herself wrapped in his arms. He squeezed her so tight, he almost expected something inside her to break.

She squeezed back, but let go quickly, tensing up as if something were seriously wrong. She pushed away from him, hard. And he looked back to find her strained, her face painfully drawn, as if something revolting hit her senses all at once. Was she in pain?

She regained some composure and said unemotionally, "There will be time for us later. Now, let's get the rest of these folks to safety."

Ted held his gaze on her for just a little longer, as she turned from him and focused her attention to the others who had followed her here. She was right. Whatever was going on with her, they could address that later. She was safe and here with him. They needed to get out of the hallway, which was now unprotected.

Ted watched and waited as others, one by one, made their way through the opening in the barricade. Some were injured, with makeshift bandages; the rest looked fine, though every single one of them looked like they carried a heavy load of fear on their backs.

"Yes," David said. "Let's get the rest of you safely into a cabin... Evie? Oh, thank God, you're safe."

Ted wasn't paying any attention to the joyous voices, nervous laughter, the happy sobbing, or the congratulatory hand-shaking. Instead, he found himself staring at his wife, who had taken a position against the stern wall of the hallway. Her face was cast down at her feet and her chest heaved rapidly—*was she out of breath, like him?* Not once did she look up at him. She was obsessing about something, but it was not something in the carpet where her gaze was cast, but something inside. Her whole demeanor and stance were foreign to him.

Ted senses were both overloaded and confused at the same time. He wanted to rush over to her, but she obviously didn't want that. And now, what had become of her? How did she survive? How did she contract the disease? And why didn't she display the other symptoms of the Rage disease?

"Are you okay?" he whispered in her direction, taking a couple of tentative steps closer.

David pounded three times on the bridge hatch, but Ted held his gaze on his wife.

She seemed to wait before acknowledging his question. His heart raced again, this time in fear. Finally, she raised her head up, a grin painted roughly onto her pale features that was meant to say, I'm fine. But Ted read it to mean something was very wrong with her. Her eyes were the exclamation point to this feeling.

The bridge hatch opened and friendly words were exchanged between the staff captain and someone else, but Ted remained riveted.

As her eyes burned into his, he remarked at how one of her irises was sort of pinkish, with a blue hue as if it hadn't completely turned. The other was a bright crimson, the color of blood. They both blazed bright. It was all so surreal.

"Really, I'm fine. Everyone else is in, come on," she said and breezed by him and into the luxury suite, where most everyone had entered, except for Niki Tesler of engineering and part of TJ's group, who joined Jessica on the bridge.

Ted followed TJ into the suite, shooting a quick glance at the already-fixed barricade, before the door closed behind him with a *thwack*.

He had no idea what he was about to walk into.

36

Mixed Emotions

Ted examined the faces of the more than a dozen passengers and crew. He knew there were many other survivors on the ship, but part of him wondered if these would ultimately be the only survivors.

Many he didn't recognize, but some he did. Wasano, the new head of security, was there, and so was Dr. Molly Simmons. Ted vaguely remembered seeing her arrive on the back of some brawny guy who he recognized now as Flavio; Ted could no longer see him as a waiter, after what he had witnessed and how he looked now. Also there were Boris and Penny. Evie stood beside them in the back of the suite, holding hands with David, who was beaming. And then it clicked: Ted remembered the joyous sound of a reunion. It was David and Evie's reunion.

Some sat, some stood, but most were wide-eyed and holding to a nervous quiet, while they listened to Jean Pierre speak with Wasano, Flavio and Molly about the captain, as well as what was going on on their ship.

Al, the ship's vet, was there too. And he appeared to be acting as their temporary doctor, examining the three injured folks' wounds.

Ted briefly watched this before refocusing on TJ. She was once again stoic, her back pushed up against a wall away from the others, head hanging, her gaze fixed at her feet. This time he noticed that she was wearing a swimmer's nose plug on her nose, a pink cord connected to each side and wrapped around her neck. The words rushed out of his mouth, "What's going on with you?"

"What do you mean?" she said, barely looking at him.

Ted just glared at her incredulously.

TJ gave a slight nod. "It's the only reason I survived the fall. I can't explain how it happened, though I'm pretty sure I know why..."

Ted folded his arms around his chest and tried to patiently listen to all his wife had to say, though his mind was darting in a thousand directions, filling up with thousands upon thousands of questions he wanted to ask her.

"It was that dog mauling. That's how I must have contracted the parasite, from that bite. I'd never had cats, and since the dog bite, you know I haven't spent much time around animals much. And you also know I don't eat my steaks raw, at least until now..." She paused again, like she was considering a new thought that hadn't occurred to her until this very moment.

"Yeah... So, I didn't tell you everything about that day. Mostly because I didn't want to remember it. But after I was mauled by that dog, I had to put the perp down—"

"—You told me that already," Ted cut in. This was going too slow. And he desperately needed to ask her some of his questions, if she wasn't going to cover them.

"I didn't tell you about the dog and its master's eyes. They both had red eyes! The target of our investigation had gone crazy. And like his dog, he had rushed me with the intent of killing me. That's why I shot him. This parasitic thing had been going on for a long time before today, Ted. It's just this current iteration with the volcanoes that's new."

He thought about this for a moment and then asked his question again, "So again I ask, how are you? What I mean is do you feel like you want to kill?"

TJ cast her rufescent gaze downward before looking back up again. It was obvious she didn't want to answer this question.

"Most of the time." Her brow furrowed, and her lips pouted, then quivered. "I go from calm one moment to nearly insane with rage the next, and I want to kill everyone who isn't like me..." Her eyes welled up.

"But not now?" He felt like he was breathing almost as heavily as his wife was right now.

Her eyes sparkled through her tears, like two rubies drowning in the deep end of a bright pool. "No, but I fear it will happen at any moment. And when it does, I feel sure I won't be able to regain control again, especially around you, or others."

Ted noticed movement and saw Al was standing nearby, listening intently. He was waiting his turn to say something.

Seeing now that they both acknowledged him, Al held out a thermometer and said, "With the dogs, when their temperature had dropped below 99 degrees, they were no longer enraged and aggressive. I've wondered about body temperatures and this disease after speaking with Chloe Barton, the ship's nurse, who said she picked up the thermometer of one of her patients, who had gone from calm to crazy, when it had dropped out of the patent's mouth. She told me it had read 99.5 degrees, a low fever. So I'm wondering, miss... Could I take your temperature?"

TJ drew the backs of her hands over her eyes to wipe away her tears. Then she straightened up against the wall. "Tell me this one hasn't been used on a dog." She flashed him a weak grin.

"No worries. Just sterilized and previously only touched by human mouths."

She accepted it onto her tongue and clamped her jaw down.

Ted thought she was probably glad to have accepted the thermometer, if only to not have to answer any more difficult questions at this moment. He then noticed Dr. Molly Simmons, the parasitologist he'd met after his talk, and the one who shared with him the fact about the thermophilic bacteria. She had made her way to them and was listening in on their conversation. Ted also noticed everyone else in that room was silent and staring at TJ.

"Hello, Mr. Bonaventure," Dr. Simmons said, looking much older than when he'd last seen her.

"Ted, please, Dr. Simmons."

"Molly is fine, as well. I suspect your wife's temperature is below 99 degrees now. But I also suspect when her temperature rises above this level, she'll feel those urges again to kill. I believe that's the T-Gondii working with the thermophilic bacteria. The thermophilic bacteria are attracted to mammals with a temperature of 99 degrees and above. Further, I believe the thermophilic bacteria cause a fever as well. And when the affected mammal is already infected with T-Gondii, it also wakes up the parasite, which as you know has already rewired the brain of its mammal-host. And that's when that mammal changes, and becomes symptomatic, and that's when the mammal appears to become what you think is crazy."

"What else are they, if not crazy?" asked Jean Pierre, who was now part of their little group surrounding TJ.

"This is all part of their new genetic makeup: to kill those who are a threat, and to do so without fear and the ability to suppress pain, so that it can do its job more efficiently.

And then of course, to eat," Molly answered, sounding detached, as if she were reading this from a textbook.

"That's enough," Al said, holding out his fingers to her. "Let's see what your temp is now."

TJ pulled the thermometer out of her mouth, glanced at it and then handed it to Al, who squinted to make sure he read it right, before announcing to all of them, "98.8."

TJ's eyes snapped back to Ted, sparkling and bright. If it weren't for the red irises, they appeared otherwise normal. They now possessed an aura of excitement. Yes, he knew this look to mean she'd just figured something out.

She turned her head to Molly and Al, and then to Jean Pierre, and then back to Ted. She smiled a chasm-wide grin.

"I know how to save our ship."

"You see," she projected her voice out so that everyone in the room could hear her clearly, though it wasn't needed because she was already the center of everyone's attention, "it's all about the body temperature. When the infected's body temperature is above 99 degrees, they become symptomatic and aggressive toward anyone and anything not infected, just like the two doctors said. But when the infected's temperature drops below 99 degrees, they lose much if not all of their aggression, even if they retain all of their other symptoms."

TJ paused, but not for effect. She wanted to make sure everyone was keeping up with her and she just didn't want to have to repeat herself again, if someone wasn't paying attention.

"So all we have to do is drop the temperature of each infected to below 99 degrees."

"How ve do that? Give every crazy cold drink?" Flavio asked. He had pulled alongside Ted and Molly.

"No Flavio, but if we could drop the air conditioning down low enough, that would drop their body temperatures below the 99-degree threshold."

"That's brilliant, my dear," said Molly. "Just like you did with the fire extinguisher in the engine room."

Ted frowned at TJ, like he wanted to ask her about this, but then turned to Jean Pierre. "Is the air conditioning working well enough to do this?"

Jean Pierre's features twisted and turned, revealing a flurry of mental gymnastics. When TJ had worked with him on the Eloise Carmichael investigation, she remembered that look. He had the answer, he just wanted to make sure it was correct.

"Oui—I mean, yes!" Jean Pierre exclaimed, his face now animated. "Yes. We still have some other issues. But depending on where the crazies were, we could throttle the air conditioning down."

Al asked, "Why can't you turn the air conditioning down on the whole ship?"

"Not recommended. It would take a lot of fuel, and we have a very limited supply. But if we needed to..." Jean Pierre turned to TJ, "How low a temperature would we need, and for how long?"

TJ shrugged. "Don't look at me; I just came up with the plan."

"Molly?" Ted begged.

"I was just thinking about this. Based on what Al told me about the dogs getting locked in the refrigerated storage room, which is at what temperature, Staff Captain, normally?"

"I believe it was four degrees, or rather, about 40 degrees Fahrenheit. But I'm not sure I can get the room temperature down to forty degrees with our systems, and definitely not for long."

"Forty would be better, but I'm thinking forty-five or even fifty degrees, for about an hour, should do it."

Jean Pierre paced to the conference table, pulled out his walkie and called into it. Although it appeared that he did this to make his conversation more private, TJ could hear the conversation clearly on Ted's radio, which must have been monitoring the same channel.

"Buzz and Jessica, this is Jean Pierre."

"Yes, sir," Buzz crackled back.

"I'm here, sir," Jessica responded.

"I need to know, without a doubt, if we can run the air conditioning in multiple areas of the ship and drop the temp to below ten degrees? This is a priority."

"Aye, sir," Buzz chirped back. "We'll get working on it immediately."

"Thanks. Deep, you got your ears on too?" Jean Pierre moved the walkie from his mouth to his ear.

"Still on watch, sir."

"Any sign of the parasitics?"

"Not a thing, sir."

"Fine, call me the moment you see something." Jean Pierre adjusted his volume up and clipped the radio to his belt and marched back to the group.

"What do you mean, any sign of the crazies?" Ted asked.

Jean Pierre glared at him and then his walkie, catching on that his conversation was overheard.

"Yes, JP. You said earlier, *depending on where the crazies were.*" TJ's hands were on her hips. "Do you not know where the parasitics are right now?"

"I didn't want to frighten everyone, but no, we don't know where they went. And I'm guessing for your plan to work, we need to find their location first, then make sure we get them to a secure area, then assuming the air conditioning works, then we drop the temp to around forty-five to fifty degrees for an hour. Then, we can regain control of our ship."

TJ pushed from the wall. "Sounds like a good plan to me."

37

Divide and Conquer

"So how are we supposed to find these things?" Wasano asked.

"Can't you smell them, Mrs. Villiams?" Flavio insisted.

All eyes turned back to her. It was only then that most of them noticed she was wearing a nose plug.

"Actually, I can't smell them any better than you can. But I can smell those who are not infected." She did not want to tell them anything more than this.

Molly perked up at this. "Okay, I'll bite... Ah, sorry dear. Tell me, what do we smell like?"

TJ looked down again at her feet. She could feel everyone's gaze and she knew she was being obvious in avoiding Molly's question. So she just blurted it out, not caring for a moment, until it came out. "Like the most wonderful food in the world."

"That's some screwy shit," someone in the back room blurted.

"Actually, no it's not," responded Molly. "In fact it makes perfect sense. There are many instances, like in the use of pheromones in insects, where smells are used for hunting."

"Oy," announced a large German, sitting on the couch Ted and David had been watching the television from, "why don't we let the Fräulein sniff out the ship while we sit here and wait."

Jean Pierre scowled at the man before returning his attention back to TJ. "It's not a bad point. Can we use that ability to seek out the crazies? You know, if you smell someone or a group of someones, then obviously they're not a parasitic."

She didn't want to be having this conversation, not in front of her husband. The simple answer was yes, she could detect them or rather not detect them, and therefore know they weren't in a location.

"Yes, I'm sure I can."

"Sir," Wasano cut in, "the ship is a little too large for one person to sniff every single room or cabin. We have a lot of people waiting for us to get them to safety. And they've already been waiting for hours."

"You're right, of course. We'll need to send more people."

"Sir," this time it was Flavio, "if any of these crazies smell people walking around, they could easily be overcome and hurt. Why don't we just kill every one of those crazies?" He glared at TJ. "No disrespect to you, Mrs. Villiams."

"No!" TJ's words leapt out. "No killing, unless it's to protect yourself. We treat these people like people who are sick—"

"—who want to fawking eat us," the German yelled out again from the safety of his chair.

"Enough discussion. We're going to break up into three groups: Flavio and Wasano, Paulo and Igor, TJ and me--"

"—I'm going with you," Ted belted out, like a cough. "I've been separated from my wife, whom I thought was dead. I'm not letting her out of my sight now."

"Sorry Ted, but no." Jean Pierre placed his hand on Ted's shoulder. "I'm afraid you're too slow and you'll make too much noise with your bad ankle. It's a risk to all of us, and especially to you. I need you to stay and coordinate with Deep on the bridge radio. And to work with Jessica and Niki on the air conditioning. In fact, since I won't be there, I'm going to instruct them to follow your lead on this."

Ted nodded, seeming to accept his fate quickly enough. At his heart, he was a logical man, and pragmatic. He knew it was the right thing to do, even though he hated it.

"I'll go." David stepped forward, but his wife immediately pulled him back.

"Oh no, you don't," Evie demanded. "You're staying with me this time."

David shrugged his shoulders and then mumbled something to her, and she smiled at him.

"Excuse me, Staff Captain," Molly interrupted, her voice animated. "I suggest you have Hans go with one of your groups."

Jean Pierre flashed a glare first at Molly and then at the German, who seemed just as shocked to be included. "I'm sorry Molly, but I don't get why?"

"Yeah. Why would you listen to that old Jew?" yelled Hans, who stood up and squared his shoulders toward the group that wanted to send him out into harm's way.

Molly smiled. "Because you're infected too. And so is your brother."

All eyes drilled into the two Germans. A couple of passengers sitting near them shot up and moved away. Franz just sank into the seat lower, pulling the blanket he had been wearing over his head.

Hans took several steps forward, like he was about to pick a fight. "My eyes look red to you?"

"No, you're not symptomatic. Not yet anyway. But I've seen how the parasitics react to you and your brother.

They're not interested in either of you, and you know this."

Hans acted like he was sucker-punched.

Everyone was so focused on Hans, no one noticed TJ had left her space against the wall and was now standing in front of Hans. She pulled off her nose plug and made a loud sniffing sound. Then she did the same with Franz, before walking back. "Yep, they're infected," she exclaimed.

"Fine! Yes, I know both of us are... infected." He said this like it hurt him. "And it sucks, by the way, because I no longer have an appetite for my favorite food."

"Okay then. If both you Litz boys go with our search parties, I'd be happy to ignore all of the illegal liquor and drugs you brought on board," Jean Pierre commanded.

"Like—like you're really worried about the rules now," Hans stuttered.

"No, I'm not. But at this point I'd be happy to dump you two overboard, for whatever reason I come up with."

Hans scowled at the staff captain, considering whether or not he meant it, and then let his head fall forward. "Fine, we'll go. Come on, Franz." He beckoned his brother to stand up.

Conversations erupted, like little wildfires: several expressed the same concern that an infected could be any one of them and that it was impossible to tell. While discussions were escalating, Jean Pierre grabbed the big German by the arm and pulled him to the group surrounding TJ. He instructed Franz to go with his guards, Igor and Paulo. Hans would be with Flavio and Wasano. He stated something about Wasano not taking any shit from the German and he would keep him in line.

Before exiting the cabin, Jean Pierre gave instructions for everyone to remain behind the cabin door. He asked David and Molly to assist Ted in the bridge and his two remaining officers to monitor the cabin and bridge doors, and just outside, in case anyone else showed up and wanted in.

Jean Pierre then requested his volunteers meet him outside the cabin, while he updated Jessica and Niki on the bridge with their plan.

Ted grabbed TJ's hand and cupped her face with his other hand.

"I'll be fine," she said, her voice soft and emotional.

"I just don't want to lose you again." He leaned in and kissed her.

She accepted, but immediately pulled back.

Even though she had her nose plug on, she could taste him. And she felt an evil urge rise up from the dark reaches of her psyche. She wanted to kiss him, but something even more that she dare not think about.

"Let me do what I can, so we can get through this crisis," she said. Pulling her hand from his, she stepped out the door.

38

Hiding Places

A ding announced their arrival on deck 8. The elevator doors slid open with a slow growl, or at least it sounded that way. Once open, a blast of light from the late-afternoon sun shot in and they had to shield their faces. Hans pressed his hands against his eyes, acting like he was suffering from a nasty headache. Then they heard the sound once more, only fainter.

"Did you hear that?" Hans whispered, shirking back into the elevator. "It sounded like one of those damned dogs. I hate dogs."

"You people have German Shepherds and you're scared of dogs?" Flavio humphed. He stepped out into the hallway, not even waiting for an answer. His fingers squeezed tight around the smaller end of the club—*more like a table leg*—that Ted had given him. It wasn't as hefty as his wrench, but since he'd lost that, it would have to do.

He turned back to see what was keeping the other two and noticed the acting security director roughly grabbing Hans' arm and giving him a couple of tugs until the German reluctantly exited the elevator and they both pulled up alongside Flavio.

Wasano let go and now had both his hands on his rifle, slung in front of him, at the ready. "Do you smell anything?" he whispered to Hans, in between him and Flavio.

Hans grimaced and shook his head vigorously. "Only lots of alcohol."

Flavio smelled it too. Anyone would. A friend of his family from Romania had a bootlegging operation and made their own vodka, which actually wasn't too bad, if he drank the stuff. One day, he was invited to visit so he could pick up several bottles as gifts for him and his friends, as thanks for what he had done fighting the Russians. Flavio remembered entering a giant room where his friend bottled the stuff… it had the same gagging smell as this one.

"Let's keep moving," Wasano whispered. "We have a lot of decks to cover."

"And I think we want to find them before sunset?" Flavio quipped. For the first time in memory, he was feeling a little anxious.

Wasano stared at the big man, perhaps picking up on his anxiety. "Why is that?"

"I was thinking… Vampires and other monsters; they always come out at night."

"Come on," Wasano huffed, taking the lead into the Crows Nest nightclub and bar.

Flavio had rarely been up here; there was no reason to. They didn't serve food, the people were noisy and obnoxious and everyone was drunk. He didn't drink, but even if he did, and he was a passenger, he wouldn't come up here. A bartender-friend of his, Vicki Smith from England, often worked up here and the Anchor Bar, where they did serve food, and he would hear stories from her about some of the shenanigans that went on at the Crows Nest late at night. By the smell of this place, if the ship had not been overrun by crazy animals and crazy people, he would have thought they were walking into the aftermath of a giant party. "Wow, alcohol smell very strong here," he whispered, mostly to himself.

"I think I smell something," Hans said.

They halted mid-step. "Wait," Wasano breathed. "You smell us, not crazies. So that means you smell more of us?"

"Yes, I think so, but—"

There was a loud thump behind them.

The three swung around toward the noise: Wasano sighted his rifle, finger hovering just off the trigger guard; Flavio lifted his club up into the air, ready to strike; Hans turned his shoulders the other way, as he readied himself to run away.

"Hold on, mate," a female voice huffed. She and an officer were standing behind the large semi-circle bar, holding up full bottles of premium vodka, as if they were ready to use them as weapons for their own battle. "Flavio?" She lowered her bottle.

"You were going to hit friend with hundred euro bottle of Grey Goose?" Flavio huffed.

"Wa-wa-we thought you were one of the zombies," stammered the officer, who lowered his own bottle-weapon.

"Or the zombie-dogs," Vicki said with a smile. She always smiled, even when she was having a crappy day. "Hey, you didn't see them when you came in, did you?"

"No, but we heard a lot of growling," said Hans.

"I think they're gone now." Flavio then sniffed the air, making a show of it. "Vicki, they not have your perfume in gift store?"

"Ha, Flavio! You don't like my eau de Hennessy?" She made a show of extending her head and exposing her neck, ready for nasal inspection.

"Wa-wa-we—well actually, Vicki,—came up with the idea when we heard the zombies could smell us," said the young officer, who acted like he had had one too many cups of coffee.

Vicki shrugged her shoulders. "Tosh. When we heard on the radio about them smelling us, I thought maybe they wouldn't be able to if we dowsed ourselves in some pongy alcohol. Guess we were jammy, because a few of them came in here and left. And then the zombie-dogs—those things creep me out—they came in and scratched at the door with all the people, and then left."

Flavio's eyes were drawn to some movement on the other side of the nightclub room. It was Wasano, clearing the place out further to make sure it was safe. That was the other point of their mission: clear out and secure areas of the ship, for survivors to gather.

Wasano stopped beside a bloody corpse up against a wall. He leaned over, checked the pulse and then continued toward the bathrooms.

Flavio returned his gaze to Vicki. "What people?"

"Oh, there was a large group of people that came here, after the zombies started attacking."

"Why do you keep calling them zombies?" Hans asked, seemingly annoyed by the term.

"I'm a big *Sean of the Dead* fan—sure would love a cricket bat right about now. Plus, they seem kind of like zombies, only the fast kind."

"But they're not dead," Hans continued his needling, definitely annoyed.

"I know, but—"

"Vicki," Flavio interrupted, more irritated at the uselessness of this banter, "where are the people?"

"Oh yes, of course, they're over there, in the loo." She pointed in that direction.

Wasano picked up one of the broken bottles of liquor littering the entry into the ladies' room and then knocked on the door. It cracked open and a mascara-streaked face peeked through the crack.

"It's safe, miss," Wasano said. And then to the officer behind the bar, "Second Officer Rolland, please lock the doors to this place so that no unfriendlies come in.

The young officer snapped to attention. "Ye-ye-yes, sir." He shuffled around the edge of the bar, on the side near the entry, while fumbling with the keys in one hand, but reluctant to let go of the bottle-weapon with his other. After a few moments, he locked the doors.

Vicky leaned over the bar and whispered, "He's all collywobbles."

Flavio didn't know what that meant, but it seemed to fit the nervous officer.

Wasano had knocked on the men's room door, also announcing to its inhabitants that it was safe. Slowly, passengers and crew exited the restrooms, carefully stepping over the broken glass around the doorway.

"Sorry for that," Vicki called out to them, and then back to Flavio she explained, "After we doused ourselves in the Hennessy, I realized the zombies could smell all the people in the bathrooms. So we heaved several bottles at the doors, hoping they would break and throw off their scents. Seemed to work, but the noise attracted them into the bar. That was my bad."

"No apologies, Ms. Smith," Wasano said, slinging his weapon around to his back. "You may have saved all these people's lives."

"Maybe you should warn others on radio about the dogs and the alcohol. And that we have another safe place now." Flavio held out his hand and laid it on top of Vicki's. "You did good."

"Why, thank you." She curtsied.

Jean Pierre turned the volume to his walkie down to its lowest setting and clipped it to his belt before whispering to TJ, "We now have a safe place up on deck 12 forward, in the Crows Nest. And two of our crew found out that alcohol covers human scents, so..." He stopped short. She could see his mind completing the sentence, *so infecteds like you can't smell us.* He was obviously nervous about her transformation and his own role in their mission.

"Looking for an excuse to get a drink?" The words just fell out of TJ's mouth. She was surprised the humor still came so easily, even in her present state. But she didn't want this. She needed to focus so that her mind didn't wander off onto other, more troubling subjects.

A small tremor erupted inside her.

"Ha! You know I don't drink," Jean Pierre whispered. His eyes wandered again to her, and then shot back out in front of him, appearing to search side to side. No doubt scanning for the parasitics she may have missed, even though that was not his purpose for being here.

She didn't reply. Her focus was on the task at hand, which was difficult enough. But then another humorous thought sprang to mind, like the forgotten image of an old friend. "And don't think you can get out of being my guinea pig. We need your—what did you call it?—Yes, your manly scent..."

She was losing her train of thought again. *Skip the damned humor and focus,* she told herself.

Another shiver shook her.

"I know," Jean Pierre said off hand, not really paying attention to his words. His eyes once again glued to her.

When she caught him, he abruptly blurted, "You're really cold, aren't you? Never mind, I can see that." He snapped his gaze to his feet, his cheeks flaring a rosy tint.

Any other time, a comment like that would have brought her utter embarrassment and she would have reacted by covering herself. *But it was only JP.* He's not even attracted to women, she reminded herself. More so, she no longer felt weighed down by the chains of vanity any longer. Part of her changes.

Yeah, she was cold. No, she was *damned* cold. And no wonder, all she wore at that moment was her compression shorts and a sopping-wet sleeveless T that clung to her every curve. It was her own suggestion to pour the bar tub of ice water over her head to cool herself down. Gone were her socks, shoes, and the sleeved shirt she had been wearing over everything before her dousing.

Much more concerning to her than the revealing nature of her ensemble was keeping her core temperature down. Knowing that she might have to do battle again at any moment, she was afraid of her body temperature popping up above the 99-degree-threshold Molly had informed them about. This was especially true after finding out that she had only been a couple tenths of a degree south of this mark when Al had taken her temp.

When she was doing battle in the hot engine room earlier, she must have gotten too hot because she could feel herself losing all control as she beat on the other dementeds. A part of her wondered if she completely surrendered to this beast inside of her, if that was it. Perhaps she'd no longer be human; she'd be one-hundred-percent "crazy," like all the other dementeds. A beast carrying out marching orders by the parasites that battled for control inside of her.

"I'm very sorry, Theresa Jean, that I made that comment. It was rude." Jean Pierre interrupted her mental meanderings.

"It's all right. I am really cold right now, but that's better than the alternative. Let's get th through this."

They had been searching the stern of the ship, from deck 10 down, starting with the At Sea Spa. When they had entered the spa's lower level, they had found several survivors in one of the spa's Zen Rooms. Jean Pierre had done the honors of talking to them, not wanting TJ to frighten them with her scary-red eyes and pale complexion.

Within a few minutes, the spa was cleared, and they decided that it too was a good sanctuary for survivors on the aft end of the ship. When they found other stragglers who were exposed, they would send them there. Jean Pierre had also made this announcement on his radio, just before Wasano made his, so that Ted and Deep, on the radio, could inform those in unprotected areas both aft and forward where to go.

Still absolutely no sign of any of the dementeds.

Next, they would go into the Solarium, where they expected to find more find survivors still hunkered down, per reports from Deep and his eyes in the sky.

Just before stepping out of the Spa, TJ huffed, "Hang on." Then she spun on bare heels and doubled back, popping into one of the Zen Rooms they had just cleared.

A moment later she exited the room, wearing reflective wrap-around sunglasses. She'd remembered seeing these, obviously left behind by a passenger. Her reddish eyes were now covered—hopefully making her less scary to survivors. Plus, she could better see under the bright lights of the ship's hallways and the glass enclosure of the Solarium. Bright light was hard to take now.

"Okay, I'm ready to meet my public." She flashed a smile and pushed through the glass door.

They continued running, even though they were so tired. And so hungry. Since their release from captivity, their unstoppable hunger was not only for food, but for the need to bite and tear and rip and kill.

The pack could smell all of them, and almost all at once. This just fueled their ravenous desire for more.

They dashed down one stairwell after another, following the strongest scent they'd smelled in a while.

The mini-poodle, whose amber-colored coat was now a dark red, led the way as the pack's alpha dog.

At the deck 8 landing, all the dogs halted their progression. Some just stood and some spun around in circles. All thrust their snouts into the air at once, sniffing for the scent again.

It was the scent of their next kill.

They had it now. It was very close to them.

Max, the German Shepherd, woofed his acknowledgment that he knew where the scent was coming from. The little poodle, Monsieur, did as well, only its bark was more of a shrill screech. The two dogs bolted first, and the others followed. They were on the scent's trail.

They raced toward the port-side hallway of deck 8, toward the bridge, where now all could smell something glorious: people-food.

39

The Attack

The attack would be quick but not painless. And by the time any of them realized what had happened, another one of their surviving group would die.

A few minutes before the attack occurred, David and Molly had hunkered over the large map table, on the port-side of the bridge, arguing their options in animated bursts. Although listening in and sometimes offering a comment, Ted was mostly busy on the radio, helping to coordinate with Deep to direct survivors who were not yet in a safe place to the two newly designated sanctuaries on the ship. They had split up the different frequencies used by the different departments of the crew and spread the word up and down the spectrum, mostly warning survivors to stay where they were until they could make sure the parasitics were incapacitated.

The discussion turned to what to do about the parasitics if they couldn't find them right away. The three search teams had been gone for an hour now, laboriously going through each room and crevasse on the ship, and there were many to search. But there were still no reports of parasitics, as if they all disappeared. Ted listened to the back and forth, but then stood up and stated his case.

He had already advocated for immediately turning on all air conditioners and setting them to their lowest settings throughout the ship. As much as he was worried for the other survivors, his primary concern was for his wife and the three teams out there, who were putting themselves in harm's way.

"If the temps were dropping, would the parasitics not at least be more likely to become lethargic? It may not drop their core temperatures to below ninety-nine degrees, but at least it should help. We don't know if they're hiding out somewhere, specifically waiting for unsuspecting survivors to come by, at which time they'd attack. Turning on all air conditioners to their lowest setting makes the most sense. But we must do it now."

Jessica and Niki had been busily working together on the two functioning consoles, all in an attempt to regain the remainder of the helm controls. When Niki heard Ted's interjection, she turned to him and the group, casting a stern gaze in their direction.

Niki had similar smooth Icelandic features and a striking physical presence as her counterpart, Jessica. That's where the comparisons ended. Niki was almost guy-like. Her checks were more muscular, her biceps more pronounced, and her blond hair was accented by splashes of purple. Jessica, whose natural beauty seemed temporarily masked by lines of worry and an unwavering focus to her duties, had much more of a warm radiance. Even in their turbulent situation, Jessica would occasionally flash a smile, which was more of her normal persona. Niki, on the other hand, appeared to be one-hundred-percent business, lacking all warmth, her mannerisms almost robotic.

Niki's features twisted to almost a pucker, which she held for a moment before releasing. It was like Niki wanted to say something she knew she shouldn't and held back at the last minute. It was obvious she wanted to unload her fury and contempt upon Ted for speaking impetuously. But she restrained herself and became robotic once again.

"The staff captain told me to follow your direction, if he was off comms like he is now. Because you're not a member of this crew, you wouldn't know that if I were to turn on the air conditioners, I'd have to first cycle on both engines, and with it our propellers. This is because we don't have the control to separate the two. This means First Officer Mínervudóttir would have to plot a course so we don't run into another island. Knowing all of this now, are you giving us an order… sir?" Niki's scorn was unmistakable.

Ted was taken aback by both her obvious dislike to have been told to follow his orders, but also because he didn't realize his statement, on the bridge, was akin to giving an order. "Ahh," he turned to look at the others, who just stared back at him, offering no help for his conundrum. "If it wouldn't be too much trouble, Ms. Niki—sorry, I forgot your last name."

"It's First Officer Tesler, sir," she barked.

"Oh, like in the great Nikola Tesla, except a…"

"A woman?" she said, her voice inflecting upward. "Yes, my parents had a sense of humor. I don't."

"That's obvious," quipped David under his breath.

Molly giggled, immediately trying to repress it, but like a sneeze in a crowded elevator, some of it came out.

Niki tossed a scowl in Molly and David's direction before continuing. "My biggest concern about turning the air down below sixty is that it might burn out the compressors." She quickly stepped over to the map table and impatiently waited for Ted to follow. "You see, here." She repeatedly stabbed the table with her forefinger around deck 9, mid-ship, while Ted did all he could to repress his grunting with each of his steps to the table.

"This large section here where we don't have a sealed area. This further burdens our compressors. That means we'll never get our temperatures low enough, even though our systems will fight to do so, until they fail completely."

She paused and mumbled something under her breath, while air-pointing at each deck. She silently mouthed something else, like she was mentally calculating numbers. "I can return us to zone cooling in most other areas, and get us down to maybe sixty-five degrees Fahrenheit"—she enunciated this loudly—"within half an hour. Then I suggest we back off each area that's been cleared by our three teams. This should give us more capacity to lower the temperatures even further."

Niki folded her arms across her chest and waited for what Ted guessed was the order to move forward with her suggestion.

"Sounds like an *excellent* suggestion, First Officer Tesler. Ah, make it so." He didn't know what the normal ship command protocol was for a request to execute an order, and the only anecdote he could come up with was from *Star Trek*.

With that, she pivoted on a heel and marched back to her console. She mouthed a few words to Jessica, and then rapidly tapped on her keyboard.

They all turned their gazes to their feet when they felt the rumble below, as if they could see through the floor to confirm the engines had started. Then, like they'd been given a nudge, they were pushed forward, and then to their port side. Ted watched a small island off their port-side slip past their bridge windows, slowly at first and then more rapidly with each passing moment. They were now moving, in a circle.

"Thanks, First Officer," Ted said.

She acted as if she hadn't heard him.

Ted returned his focus to the group. "So, unless they're all in one enclosed location, how are we going to get them into—"

The radio blared, "Bridge, we're under attack."

The two remaining officers in their group were following the staff captain's orders: each monitored a blockade, so that if any other survivors showed up, they could easily let them in. It was what they added to his orders that led to someone's death.

Not having a key card to the luxury suite, and not wanting to be stuck outside if one or both of them had to rush in, they inducted Boris into doorman service, and tasked him with holding open the cabin door. And being there if they needed their quick retreat.

"I have almost two hundred cruise days with this company, and you want to make me a blooming doorman?" he complained. But they ignored his complaint.

Boris wasn't about to indulge these tossers, no matter what they commanded. *What were they going to do to a guest?* he reasoned. Besides, they had ample barricades to keep the nutters back. And unless they were stupid, they could easily retreat without his assistance. So while each officer was staring through cracks in their barricades, Boris snatched one of the cabin's life-vests and wedged it under the door to keep it open.

He returned to a soft arm chair to continue watching BBC on the telly. The fact that their now deceased captain had lied to their ship about not getting satellite wasn't that much of a bother to him. He was just glad they were getting the news, no matter how ghastly it was.

Penny couldn't take the telly's drumbeat about death and destruction. She preferred escape in fantasy stories over anything scary from the news, or the movies. She wouldn't go with him to watch action-thriller pictures; he always had to call his mates. So while Boris was immersing himself in the news, she grabbed her new chum Evie, and they retreated into the master bedroom to lie down on the two sofas.

Al, the doctor, who was really a vet, bothered him once more to check on his wounds, which were itchy, but fine. Then Al excused himself to check on the ladies. That's when Boris heard a commotion outside the cabin.

Holding the volume button, Boris waited for it to slowly cycle from 28 down to 5. He turned his head toward the door to see if he could tell what was going on. He certainly wasn't going to get up out of his seat, if he didn't have to.

One of the two officers burst into the cabin, ripped open the door to the loo, dashed in, and slammed the door behind him.

The volume was low enough now that Boris could hear someone yelling outside the cabin, "Bridge, we're under attack."

That's when it went balls-up.

Boris bolted upward, his knee instantly buckling and shooting ice picks of pain throughout his body. With only one good leg to support all of him, he toppled in the other direction. His size and gravity worked against him, and he tumbled back onto the chair. And then over it.

When he came to rest, once more on the floor, head pointed to the ceiling, feet shooting straight up into the air, propped up against the overturned chair, he heard the only sounds which now completely terrified him.

"No," he whined, flipping his gaze to the open cabin door.

From his sideways view, just like he'd experienced earlier in the cruise, he watched with horror as the same band of loony dogs, led by the same little devil-poodle, raced through the door and headed directly for him.

He closed his eyes and waited for more pain.

Al was much more at ease looking after his animal boarders than nursing humans: his animal patients did what he asked and were rarely fussy, whereas his human patients were impossible, with only one exception.

Boris complained loudly every time Al attempted to check on him. This was fine because his wounds were superficial. His wife, Penny, whined every time he checked on her, but she had an anxious stomach and excused herself once again, dashing back into the luxury suite's bathroom. Evie was his third patent and the easiest to deal with, but there was little he could do with her. She'd cut her foot badly on some broken glass in their escape to this part of the ship.

Evie never so much as winced when Al bandaged her, even though he could see by her expression that it was painful. Al did the best he could with the supplies at hand. But her cut was deep and would require stitches when or if they could get out of this mess. All he could do was tell her to avoid moving and keep her leg elevated, which she did without complaint.

While waiting for Penny, he started again to wonder about his dogs: he didn't know where they were; if they'd hurt anyone; and if they'd find them before they did. Ever since their last escape, he'd been a nervous wreck not knowing. But he was also exhausted and since he had to wait, he took up a chair near Evie, on the other side of the bedroom. Then he closed his eyes.

He wasn't sure how long he nodded off, but some noise startled him awake. There was a click across the room and he watched Penny lumber out of the bathroom door, and walk his way. Her features were ashen: she was obviously sick. As he watched her lumber toward him, part of him started to wonder if she was infected. If she was, what could he do? They probably needed to isolate those who were infected, but hadn't yet shown signs. That sure wouldn't go over well. Another reason why he preferred dogs.

Al was about to instruct his patient to lie down when he heard a loud clatter outside the cabin. Then he heard their barks.

It was his dogs.

Seeing their bedroom door was open, and Penny was closer to the back slider, Al yelled to Evie to take Penny outside. Now!

Al dashed the other way, toward the bedroom door.

Penny scrutinized Al, in slow motion when he passed her. But when she heard the dogs, she became immediately animated, and raced for the back slider. Evie was already working on the latch.

At the bedroom entrance, Al first caught Boris, upended in a seat, on the floor. Then he saw the dogs bound through the cabin entrance. Boris would have no chance of getting away. So Al yelled and flapped his arms to attract their attention, knowing movement and noise would do the trick.

The lead dog—*that awful little poodle called Monsieur-*—took the bait first, turned the corner and leapt through the door, right at Al. He turned on his hips and batted the pup away from him with his right hand, and the dog tumbled halfway toward the slider.

It recovered way too fast.

The little dog, who was now almost completely red and brown, must have caught the women's scent—they were still not outside yet—and dashed in their direction. The slider was open, but based on Penny's slow speed, he knew they wouldn't make it in time. Then all the dogs would get them and the two other passengers outside, who were staring through the windows wide-eyed. He couldn't let more people get hurt from his animals.

He ignored the other dogs, which he knew were no more than two seconds away, and catapulted himself toward the poodle, who was getting traction on the blue and white carpeting. Last time he sprang for the poodle, he was too slow. This time he was quick enough.

He reached for and snagged one of the little poodle's hind legs, and clasped onto it with all his strength, not worried about hurting the animal. But just then a giant weight hit him in the small of his back, knocking the wind out of him. He knew this was Max, the big German Shepherd.

Then a trumpet-sound of loud screeches and growls rang in his ears, right when he felt his neck explode. But he ignored this.

Al even ignored the poodle, who whipped around and bit him multiple times and then struggled against his unyielding grasp, shrieking from anger.

Al was focused on one thing: the ladies. When he finally saw they'd successfully exited the room and slammed the slider home, he let go of the vicious dog and accepted his fate. He turned his gaze to the poodle, right when it dove at his face; its little fangs found his eyes.

"It's dogs!" Deep hollered breathlessly on the other end of the radio. "Someone attacked in hallway. Now in eight-zero-zero-zero."

Ted reached down below the workstation where he was sitting, snatched the small footrest he'd been using, and pushed up from his seat. He hobbled to the bridge hatch, David already there clutching his table-leg club.

David snapped a curious glance at Ted's clutched foot-rest.

"I gave my table leg to Flavio. Come on. Let's go."

David drew open the hatch and they slipped into the hall.

Ted scanned forward and then to the starboard side, along the long hallway, toward Eloise's cabin and that blockade. One of the ship's officers, was curled up in a little ball on the floor, whimpering. That must be the one Deep said was attacked.

"He's just scared," David whispered.

"So am—" Ted bit his tongue when he heard the growling and other unspeakable sounds coming from the Queen Suite.

They tiptoed, into the suite and saw Boris pulling himself up off the floor, using an overturned chair. His face looked tortured and paler than normal.

David caught movement outside on the balcony, and started in that direction. Ted limped over toward the bedroom, where the ghastly noises of dogs fighting and chewing were as loud as ever.

He caught a glimpse of a body on the floor and the dogs going at it, when one of the dogs turned in Ted's direction.

Then a loud bang on the other side of the room distracted the dog, who turned toward the noise. That's when Ted moved faster than he thought he could. He darted three steps forward into the bedroom, hurled his foot-rest at the far wall and reached inside the bedroom.

He grabbed the door handle as his foot-rest clanged off the wall, adding to the racket inside. Without even looking—he didn't dare—he yanked so hard on the door, it slammed shut and sent him to the floor.

One or more of the dogs immediately banged loudly on the other side.

When he caught David escorting his wife and the others back into the cabin, Ted laid his head down. He was tired.

40

Deep Freeze

"Look, they're already settling down," David exclaimed, his head pressed up against the glass, hands cupped around his face so he could see.

"I know." Molly didn't need to look: she knew this would happen once they directed the cooling to that enclosed bedroom. Mostly she didn't want to look: her stomach turned cartwheels every time she thought of the dead vet, all ripped apart. He was a nice young man she'd just been speaking with earlier. Just picturing his face sapped her of her remaining energy. Her back slid a little against the slider, the rest of her weight balanced on her cane. She even started to go wobbly, like she might fall over, and there were no chairs out here to sit down on. They had used them for the blockade.

"Are you all right, Dr. Simmons?" David asked, his firm hand grasping her arm at just the right time. "Let's go in and sit for a moment."

She wanted to say, "Yes that's what I need, because I'm a tired old lady." All she could manage was, "Yes."

She remembered being led inside the luxury suite to a chair, although moments were starting to blur.

An open bottled water appeared on a table in front of her, as did David and Ted. They were all sitting at the dining room table now.

She snatched the bottle with a shaky hand and took a large gulp.

She heard her name mentioned a few times, but didn't hear the context. And then a question, directed at her. She looked up.

David repeated his question. "Can we help you into the other room to lie down for a while?"

She felt better now, though chilly. A little uncontrolled shudder erupted inside of her.

"I'm fine now, David. Thank you. I just had to sit a spell. Please keep talking though. Hearing your voices helps."

Ted had popped up out of the chair while she'd said this and put a man's jacket around her shoulders, before he sat down again in front of her and beside David.

"Thank you, dear. Please stop making a fuss over me. I'm feeling so much better, just sitting and talking."

She looked down for her cane and saw that it was resting against her chair. One of the boys must have put it there.

"That's the Rod of Asclepius, the doctor's symbol, isn't it?" Ted asked, smartly trying to get her mental faculties regrounded on terra firma.

She picked up her carved cane and held it up so both of them could see it close. It was a gift from her son. Her mind wondered what happened to him with all of this craziness happening. He was a Doctor without Borders, now somewhere in Africa. And the cane was something hand-carved by a local African artisan. She hoped he survived this thing. A wave of sadness overwhelmed her then, when she knew there was a good chance he did not.

So much death right now.

"I've always wondered what the two snakes crawling up a pole had to do with being a doctor." It was David, who was also trying to bring her back from now an emotional cliff.

"Well..." She wiped a tear from her cheek, and then gazed at both men and then finally the cane. She knew this story well. "Some say that these are not snakes, but Guinea worms." She looked up again to see Ted had a slight grin—he obviously knew this story, but wanted her to tell it.

"You see there's a parasite called a Guinea worm, a fascinating two-foot-long creature that escapes their host by punching through an ulcerous blister on the infected's skin, over the course of a few days." She was feeling better already.

"You couldn't yank it out at one go-round, since the parasite would snap in two and the remnant inside the body would die and cause a fatal infection. So the thousand-year-old traditional treatment was to wrap it around a small stick, and then slowly turn the stick, winding it around the stick, until you were able to pull out the parasitic worm and kill it. So you see, these aren't snakes, but parasitic worms."

That's when it hit her. She quickly turned in her chair and gazed at the outside. It was getting dark. She turned back to the men.

"I think we don't have any more time. We need to recall the three teams and get them back before it's dark."

"Why?"

"Because parasitics love the night, and I have a feeling that ours will too."

Jean Pierre held the door closed and waited. TJ was on the other side but had been gone for much longer than she had been previously. Usually she'd just stick her head in, sniff and say whether or not the area was clear.

Although at this point he wasn't sure if the longer time was good or bad.

Just previously to this, they'd found their first parasitic, but that was inside a cabin, on deck 7. It was then they decided to skip the cabins for now, and just focus on the public spaces. The cabins were secure, either keeping the parasitics inside or protecting the non-infected from any parasitics that might try to attack from outside. So they would make sure the "outside" was clear first. Then they'd work on the individual cabins.

Ted and the others had come up with a plan to air-condition the uncleared areas and the cabins and with each area cleared, they'd turn off the air. It was getting cooler inside, but it was not cool enough. They had to clear out more of the ship before turning the air on at max, or risk burning out their compressors.

Jean Pierre examined the colored printout of the deck plans, with his own markings, and saw they still had six more decks to go, including this one. At this rate, they'd be at this all night, even without the one-by-one cabin checks.

There was a triple-tap on the other side of the door. It was TJ.

He unlocked the door and pulled it open, and she slid out, still wearing her slinky outfit.

Her face told him the answer to the question he always asked. There were no parasitics there, or non-infected. He marked an "X" over Giovanni's, their premium Italian restaurant. That left one final place in the stern of deck 6. The Wayfarer Lounge.

TJ was already headed there, marching ahead of him. She had quickened her pace.

She was an amazing woman, especially now, with everything going on.

If she were not married, he would have been interested.

He stopped this line of thinking. This is what got him into trouble years ago. It's why he told everyone he was gay. And why he pretended to live that life. The company was tolerant of everyone's lifestyle, but it was a big no-no to fraternize with the crew, and most especially the passengers. And women all loved the uniform. So he thought it was just easier to tell everyone he was gay. From that moment forward, women treated him different than the other male officers, thinking he was no longer a threat. The fact was, he loved women. And he especially loved driven women like Theresa Jean.

He noticed she was out of sight, so he double-timed it until he saw her again. She was there at the Wayfarer Lounge entrance, back to him, focused on something in a dark corner of the floor.

Jean Pierre was about to say something when she held up a hand to silence him. It was then he noticed she wasn't trying to focus on the floor, but something else. She beckoned him forward.

When he was beside her, she leaned over to him and whispered. "I think they're here. Please go back there." She pointed to some place diagonally across the hall. "I'm going in, but prepare to run back to that last restaurant."

He nodded, and stepped backward quietly, not moving his eyes from the dark opening of the lounge. He couldn't see in, but he thought he could hear something now. Some guttural sound. And while he was thinking of it, he caught a whiff of the most horrible smell. *Like a slaughterhouse.*

Once TJ saw he was at the place she had suggested, she turned and walked inside.

It felt like she was gone for an eternity, but he knew it was only a few short moments. She appeared out of the shadows, looking calm but focused. She reached to one side of the hallway and gave a short tug at one of the two double doors. Then she tugged at the other. Both began their slow swing inward, guided by her, until both were closed. She held both of the handles, her biceps and shoulders tensing.

She turned her head toward him, threw a scowl and mouthed the words, "Come here." She wanted him to lock the door.

There was a thump on the other side of the door. And then another.

He jogged over, his right hand in his pocket, feeling for the keys. Like the other main public spaces, this door required an old fashioned metal key. The restaurants were on one electronic master key, and the lounges and theater were on another.

There was another deep thump on the door, followed by several more.

He had the keys out and then fumbled with the first, which he knew wasn't the right one because of its shape. It was one of the four longer ones—he couldn't remember which one it was.

"Would you mind hurrying? They're there, and they're waking up now."

"Merde!" he mumbled, his hand shaking.

He slipped in one and turned.

Wrong key.

Almost in response, the doors thundered; their vibrations caused more tremors in him.

He slammed in the next key and turned.

Nope!

"Please hurry," she said. Her shoulders were hunched and she was digging her heels into the carpet. The doors moved back and forward.

They were pulling from the other side.

The next key slid in and it turned slightly, but no further.

The doors rattled hard. And TJ grunted. He could tell she couldn't hold it much longer.

Then he remembered this door's lock was backwards. It was the only one in the ship like this. He slammed the last key back in again, but this time he turned it the other way, just as the doors were being pulled inward. The lock started to engage, but stopped short. With the two doors opening and now at an angle, there was no way to fully engage.

He grabbed her wrist and the handle with his free hand. "One more tug," he said and they both pulled, while he put pressure with his other hand on the key.

The doors gave in their favor, just a little. It was all they needed.

Finally, it clicked home.

TJ let go of the door and they both fell backwards onto the carpet, breathing heavily.

"Oh merde. That was close." He huffed. "How many are there?"

She didn't answer right away. Her chest rose and fell rapidly like a sleek ship in rough seas. Finally, she gave him a grin. "All of them."

Jean Pierre detached his radio from his belt, put it to his lips and whispered, "We have found the parasitics. Repeat, we found all of the parasitics. They are in the Wayfarer Lounge. Repeat, commence Operation Deep Freeze on just the Wayfarer Lounge.

He put the radio down on his lap and smiled at Theresa Jean. "Merci!"

DAY TEN

I AM UTTERLY EXHAUSTED.

THE PLAN, OR WHAT WE CALLED OPERATION DEEP FREEZE, WENT OFF WITHOUT A HITCH... WELL, MOSTLY.

WE WERE ABLE TO FIND MOST OF THE HIDING PARASITICS—THAT'S THE WORD MOLLY GOT US TO USE WHEN DESCRIBING THE FULLY SYMPTOMATIC INFECTED, AT LEAST THOSE WHO APPEARED TO BE COMPLETELY CONTROLLED BY THE T-GONDII PARASITE.

WE WERE INCREDIBLY LUCKY: MOST OF THEM WERE IN ONE LARGE LOUNGE THAT WE WERE ABLE TO LOCK UP. WE GOT TO THEM JUST BEFORE THEY WERE GOING OUT TO HUNT. THEY WERE JUST WAKING UP WHEN TJ FOUND THEM.

THE REMAINING PARASITICS WE ROUNDED UP CABIN BY CABIN, KNOCKING THEM OUT AND THEN TRANSPORTING THEM TO THE WAYFARER LOUNGE WITH THE OTHERS.

AND WE'VE BEEN ABLE TO KEEP THEM THERE THESE PAST FIVE DAYS. AND AS LONG AS THE AIR-CONDITIONING HOLDS UP, WE CAN KEEP THEM UNDER CONTROL.

BUT EVEN COUNTING OUR MANY BLESSINGS, OUR LOSSES WERE STAGGERING.

BARELY FIVE HUNDRED GUESTS AND CREW SURVIVED, MANY OF THEM INJURED, SOME SERIOUSLY. THE REST

ARE EITHER PARASITIC OR DEAD. OUR BEST COUNT OF THE DEAD WAS OVER THREE HUNDRED AND FIFTY. IT'S MIND-NUMBING TO EVEN THINK ABOUT. WE'LL HAVE TIME FOR THAT TOMORROW MORNING, WHEN WE HOLD THE BURIAL AT SEA AND MEMORIAL SERVICE.

AND YET IT COULD HAVE EASILY GONE THE OTHER WAY.

WE ARE AT LEAST ALIVE AND WE HAVE CONTROL OF THE SHIP AGAIN. MOST IMPORTANT, MY WIFE IS ALIVE, EVEN THOUGH SHE IS PARTIALLY SYMPTOMATIC FROM THE PARASITE.

SHE CONTINUES TO CHANGE: GETTING STRONGER, SEEING AND HEARING BETTER THAN EVER BEFORE—SHE COULD BARELY SEE PAST HER FEET BEFORE ALL OF THIS. BUT OTHER THINGS HAVE CHANGED IN HER AS WELL, MANY NOT GOOD.

SHE'S DIFFERENT IN WAYS I CAN'T POSSIBLY EXPLAIN. IT'S AS IF A PART OF HER PERSONALITY HAS LEFT HER, EVEN THOUGH SHE SAYS SHE HAS THE SAME FEELINGS SHE DID BEFORE.

YET BECAUSE OF WORRIES ABOUT MY SAFETY, WE SLEEP IN SEPARATE CABINS.

AND SO, EVEN THOUGH I LONG FOR HER, WE SPEND ONE MORE NIGHT APART.

I DO NOT KNOW WHAT THE FUTURE HOLDS FOR TJ AND ME, FOR OUR SHIP, AND CERTAINLY NOT FOR OUR WORLD. SO WE WILL TAKE IT ONE DAY AT A TIME. GOODNIGHT.

41

The New Normal

He scratched around the bandage covering a large portion of his forearm. The bite wound itched like crazy now, which was a far cry better than how it felt a few days earlier.

Nurse Chloe had told him that bite wounds would hurt more than any other cut or wound he'd sustained before, because of the amount of skin surface broken and possible nerve damage.

Pain was not part of his worry. Of course, it hurt. But he'd felt much worse from many previous injuries, including a bullet to the brain, which still caused him migraines. What Flavio feared more than anything, was what would happen after the pain went away.

Would he become infected, and if he did, would he turn into one of those damned *parasitics*, as Dr. Molly called them?

No matter how much the nurse tried to reassure him that he was most likely not infected, he became sure that it was just inevitable.

With each flash of anger or each moment he wanted to slap someone for being stupid—this happened daily—he'd stop himself and wait for some sort of change to begin. But it never came.

And when he'd see Mrs. Williams, during their daily campaign to root out any other parasitics hiding in the ship's shadows, he'd pull her aside and ask her to smell him. It sounded strange when the request came out of his mouth, but he saw what Hans could do and knew she could do this as well.

He didn't dare ask Hans for the sniff-test, because Hans was feeling all high and mighty about his status as one of the few people on the ship who could recognize the difference between an infected and a non-infected. He didn't want to add to that man's ego. And he just didn't like him. Mrs. Williams was more discreet, and like him, less emotional about such a request.

Yet each time she would grant him a sniff, she'd shake her head, telling him, No, you're not infected. But her reassurances didn't assuage his anxiety about becoming one of them.

He glanced up and scanned the crowd attending the service and saw Mrs. Williams standing back in the far corner of the open forecastle. Her arms were folded around her chest, nose-plug clipped to her nose—*too many non-infecteds for her to smell*—and her normal-looking sunglasses covered up her abnormal eyes.

Mr. Williams stood nearby, but they almost didn't seem together.

"And now we take a few moments of silence to honor our friends, our family, and our crew members we lost in the attack."

Flavio pulled his gaze away from Mrs. Williams and visually addressed his staff captain, who had just lowered his own head. Everyone else did as well. He searched the faces of his fellow crew members and passengers, feeling the weight of the pain of their losses.

Vicki, who stood beside him, also lowered her head. She reached up with both of her hands and grabbed one of his, squeezing it tight. Tears slid down her cheek, serenading her quivering chest. She was a big crier.

She was one tough lady, but the death of the captain and her close friend Zeka were very difficult for her to take. This was hard on all of them: they all lost someone they knew or cared about.

Everyone did but him.

Flavio had been purposely detached from most people. It was the thought of losing people he cared about that drove his personality. It was much easier not to care. And ever since he'd lost much of his family to a war, he had made the decision to just turn off his feelings for other people.

He had always smiled and was cordial to the passengers and crew, when it was appropriate. But he rarely asked anyone anything personal. The less he knew about people personally, the simpler it was to remain detached. This detachment worked well for a long time. Then Vicki came into his life.

Vicki Smith from England was the first woman in a long time that he gave a damn about. And it was obvious that she liked him...

What are you thinking, Flavio? he scolded himself.

There was no time, especially now, for relationships.

He told himself to let go of her hand, but he couldn't. She needed someone's hand to hold onto. And if not his, whose would it be?

A light bell-chime rang out from the ship's loudspeakers.

All their heads rose. Vicki released his hand and then wiped more tears away, smudging her thick mascara even more. *She looked so sad.*

The bell-sound rang again.

She flashed a smile at him. It was a facade. She was genuinely hurting inside. And because of this, he started to hurt as well. She returned her gaze to the staff captain, who was finishing up the service.

"Almighty God, we commit the remains of our brothers and sisters to the deep, for their eternal sleep. Protect their immortal souls. Amen."

Dozens of crew and passengers followed the staff captain to the port-side rail of the forecastle. Each held boxes of various sizes, which contained the remains of one or more family members, friends or crew. Once at the rail, each dumped the cremated remains over. Like clouds of chalk, billows of gray rained down onto the frothy waters below, and then disappeared, as if they never existed before this.

Meanwhile, the bell rang every five seconds.

Vicky startled him by wrapping her arms around his trunk. "This is so bloody hard," she sobbed.

Flavio hesitated, and then reciprocated, squeezing her back. It felt good to give comfort to someone... Someone he cared about.

He held her tight against him, while her body trembled in his arms, not even caring if she spotted his uniform with her mascara.

Out of the corner of his eye, he caught a glimpse of someone running. It was Mrs. Williams. She pushed through the exit, with Mr. Williams chasing after her.

Not everyone attended the burial at sea services. A few of the passengers still didn't seem to understand that their luxury cruise had permanently ended days ago.

Josef Rauff was emblematic of this mindset. Each day, while many of his fellow passengers chipped in to help the crew, he chose to lounge in his own ignorance, bathing in the blissful sun's rays. And at least until four days ago, he had drowned himself in generous helpings of the ship's alcohol. That was until the staff captain cut him and everyone else off.

And what right did he have to do this, when they paid big money to go on this cruise? And that wasn't the only thing now lacking on their ship.

Normal services were now nonexistent. Restaurants were closed, there were no shows playing at the theater, their Internet and satellite TV didn't work, and finding someone to serve them even a soda was impossible.

"Where the hell are the servants?" he croaked to no one in particular.

Apocalypse or no apocalypse, the crew's job was to wait on him and his fellow passengers. It was what he paid for. Yet the service now was inferior even to those big cruise lines serving the masses.

"Dammit!" Josef pounded his lounger's armrest, generating tsunamis in the flab of his belly. "I want some damned service."

A shadow appeared in front of him, blocking his sun. So he shot a scowl of hatred at the silhouette.

"Get out of the way," he spat. "If you're not here to get me a drink, I don't want what you're selling, *Grunzschwein*."

"Hey, dude," said the young American, his high pitched voice thick with scorn. "You know people died?" He pointed forward, in the direction of the burial at sea service he'd just attended. "And most of the crew is out there—"

"Get out of here, you idiot. Before I..." Josef shot his fist in the air to finish his sentence.

"German prick," quipped the American, who turned to walk away.

Josef snapped. He bounded out of his lounger, tripping over an empty table next to him. He tumbled, but remained vertical just long enough to tackle the American's legs. Josef bellowed his anger, in a combination of screams and growls.

Other passengers, having been attentively watching Josef and the American's interaction, assumed it wouldn't go too much further. That was until they saw the big German tackle the other man. Most still remained in their seats, but a couple of men popped up to intervene, arriving just as the German was yelling something inarticulate which sounded like obscenities.

The situation changed dramatically when they tried to separate the two men.

Each Good Samaritan held onto a shoulder of the German, while the American slithered his legs out of the man's grasp. But then the German turned to the first man, hyper-extended his neck and then sank his teeth into the man's hand. Both yelled and attempted to release themselves from the German.

"Oh my God," yelled the American, now gawking a few inches away, "he's one of them."

Josef responded by growling, red and foamy spittle, glaring reddish eyes of malevolence at each of the frantic witnesses, before setting his sights back on the man he'd just bitten.

Most every passenger, at first casually watching the show, fled the sun deck. They ran break-neck for the exits, fearing a repeat of what happened here five days ago.

The American man, who'd tried to calm the German down before getting accosted, had had enough of this. He snatched a small table, kicked over from their scuffle. And while the parasitic German tried to lunge at the man he'd bitten, the American drove the table hard into the attacker's skull, subduing him.

The other passengers and a couple of crew, seeing the parasitic man was now unconscious, ran over to help out.

They would drag the man to the elevator and place him into an ice box they'd set up just for this type of incident. There he'd remain until he calmed down. Then he would be separated and placed in with the rest of the parasitic population on deck 6.

"The infected are not like any of us. We must remember that," said the very British-sounding animal behaviorist. "They're very much like animals, driven by instinctual needs: hunting, food, sex..." "Did you say sex?" a male voice cut in. "Why yes, of course," responded the British woman. "The Pyschotics have a strong sex drive, and we must—"

"—useful?"

Ted slid the headphones from his ears and glanced up. "Sorry?"

"I asked if you've found anything useful?" Jean Pierre strode through the door of their newly created communications room, formerly the master bedroom of 8000's luxury suite.

Ted laid the bulky headphones on the desk, pulled his blue Cubs hat off his head, and massaged his temples. He waited for Jean Pierre to settle into one of the hard chairs set up by the door, knowing their conversation would be a long one.

After running his fingers through his hair, Ted put his hat back on. "David left just a few minutes ago to have lunch with Evie. So I'll report what he found first." He turned about ninety degrees in his chair to address his captain.

"He only found one working television broadcast today. It's RTP from Ponta Delgada. But it's a taped talk show, being replayed over and over again. And it was in Spanish, which of course neither of us speak. More troubling, as of today, none of the satellite channels are working: even the BBC is off the air now." Ted paused to let that point sink in. It was a shock to David and him as well.

Since they were both asked to check on the radio and TV broadcasts, and Buzz had set up the suite's master bedroom as their communications center—he said this was because of the ease to connect to outside antennas—they'd been listening and searching for updates as to what was going on in the world outside of their ship.

Listening to radio broadcasts was not necessarily Ted's forte, nor was watching TV for David. But both wanted to contribute. And it helped Ted gather more data about the parasites' progression outside of their ship, so that he and Molly could help the acting captain decide on their next steps. And as Jean Pierre explained it, David and he were now considered trusted members of his bridge crew.

"Keep in mind, this ship is given a package of satellite broadcasts from a third-party company that Regal European subscribes to. So it's entirely possible that there are many broadcasts out there and we just don't know about them, because only our package has gone down. Buzz will be rigging up a new antenna system for us and he says he'll be able to hack some of the satellite TV systems out there. But it won't be for another day or two, since you've got him doing so many equally important tasks to get the ship systems back up."

Jean Pierre nodded to all of this, and then leaned forward. "So what about the radio?"

"Well, that's another story altogether. I've listened to hours of various commercial broadcasts and some ham radio as well." Ted stretched over his desk and grabbed a yellow pad, with scribbles all over its pages. He sat back in the chair and starting with the first page, he flipped through the pages quickly until he stopped about twenty pages in.

"Okay, best I can gather, reports of parasitic attacks have sprung up on every continent. It's pretty much the same story everywhere, only different gradations of chaos. The worst are London and Paris, both of which are mostly black now."

"Black? You mean as in nothing?"

"Correct. No commercial broadcasts whatsoever. Only intermittent shortwave broadcasts from there. Parasitic animals and humans control these two cities, roaming the streets freely."

Jean Pierre fell back into his chair. "I guess we should count our blessings then."

Ted had thought the same thing. They were in an environment they could better control. "Correct. Although there are places out in the Western US, including near our home in Arizona, where the Rage disease hasn't really taken hold. Only sporadic reports of animal attacks. But I expect that to change fairly soon." Ted tossed the yellow pad back onto the desk. "It's pretty much a shit-storm everywhere else."

"So we're completely on our own," Jean Pierre stated rhetorically.

"I'm afraid parasitics in control of our towns and cities is the new normal for the world." Ted examined the man who had assumed command of their ship, and therefore their lives. He appreciated the man's pragmatic processing of everything. And he felt lucky to be included in their tight circle to help him craft future decisions. And it was nice being one of the few in the know.

Realizing he forgot something, Ted popped forward in the chair. "Sorry, I forgot to mention one other broadcast you should know about." He snatched the pad back and moved to a page that was marked by a paper-clip.

"Here it is. Every couple of hours, with the last one about an hour ago, there's a shortwave broadcast in both Spanish and English from *L-Ha-D-Core-Vo*?" He said it phonetically. "I know I'm saying it wrong." He turned the pad around so that Jean Pierre could see it written carefully in his block-styled lettering.

"Ilha De Corvo. Yes, it's the northernmost island in the Azores archipelago."

"Makes sense. They're saying that they have fuel for any ship that needs it and that they'll exchange fuel for any supplies, especially food. But here's the weird thing." Ted looked back up to Jean Pierre. "They say they don't have the Rage disease on their island."

"Have you spoken to them?"

"No. I didn't want to presume. And who knows if it's not just BS."

Jean Pierre's radio chirped at him and he answered it in one motion.

"Sir, this is Mr. Agarwal. We have another report of an attack on the sun deck, with a passenger turning parasitic. He's in the cold room right now, with the other one."

"Thanks, Mr. Agarwal." He clipped the radio back onto his belt.

"Damn, that's three cases in the last thirty-six hours, right?"

Jean Pierre nodded. "That's actually why I wanted to speak with you. I have some ideas on how we should manage the passengers and crew going forward. I hope you don't mind, but I've asked Dr. Simmons to join us. I need feedback from both of you before I announce new rules to everyone at tonight's meeting."

"That sounds good, Captain. It will give us a chance to share our idea about what to do about the parasitics."

42

Empty

It was a full house, with standing room only ten minutes before the doors closed. Every passenger and all but maybe the dozen or so skeleton crew who had to man the ship's critical systems were there. The only thing they were told on the intercom or from the door-to-door messages delivered by crew was that the meeting was mandatory. Short of being deathly ill, in the infirmary or one of the parasitic population, literally every person on their ship was required to be at the Tell Tale Theatre at 19:00. Ted was quite sure no one, aside from a few select bridge crew, had any idea how much their lives were about to change.

On stage, a line of seats facing the audience were occupied by their acting captain, Jean Pierre; security director, Wasano; first officer of navigation, Jessica; acting engineering director, Niki; acting medical director, Chloe; and special envoy to the captain, Molly. Ted—he didn't think he had a title yet—sat at the end, beside Molly. They all remained in their seats, silent, just waiting for the meeting to start.

Ted leaned forward in his chair and stared at his wife. She was hiding in the fold of a giant stage curtain, in a dark corner of the stage. She wore her now normal uniform: running outfit, nose-clip and sunglasses. Her breathing was more rapid than even normal. But with her changes, that could be nothing. It was the tension in her neck, head turning toward each cough or word spoken, and the stiffness in her posture which told him that she was distressed.

It was a complete role reversal. Before all of this, it was he who would have been hyperventilating with such a large crowd only a few steps away. Now it was his wife that couldn't stand to be around people.

She slid farther into the curtain's protection, no longer visible to him or anyone else.

Jean Pierre rose from his seat and proceeded to the lectern. Ted's watch, synchronized with the captain's, read 19:00.01.

"Good evening. For those of you who don't know me, I am Jean Pierre Haddock, acting captain of your ship, the *Regal European Intrepid*." He paused for a moment and then continued.

"The people behind me are the current members of my wardroom. That means, they speak for me. They, along with several other members of my crew and a few passengers, were the reasons why we are all still here today, alive and having this meeting. When you see them, you should thank them for their selfless commitment and for their sacrifices."

He didn't intend to pause for more than a moment before moving directly into the main reasons for their meeting. He needed to get through the part that would be most difficult for most of this audience to hear. And even more difficult for them to accept.

But several of the audience stood up unexpectedly and cheered loudly. Then every one of the nearly five hundred people inside joined in and cheered for their good fortune and the people who got them here. He allowed it, because they probably needed it.

He waited impatiently for the applause to ebb. When it didn't, after two solid minutes, he raised his hands, palms out, and said, "Thank you... Thank you. Please, hold your applause."

Finally, they stopped and everyone who had a seat, sat. And other than a few murmurs and coughs, it was quiet again.

"I would ask you to hold onto your applause and your comments until the end of our presentation. We have much to cover.

"The purpose of this meeting is to give you an update on what is happening aboard our ship, the status of the world around us, and our plans going forward.

"First, because I know many of you have concerns about the Rage disease, I've asked Mr. Ted Williams to speak to you and help you to understand better what it means to each of us on this ship." Jean Pierre turned to face Ted.

Ted rose and walked up to the lectern, his head still pointed in TJ's direction. She still wasn't visible.

Some of the crowd started to mumble questioning comments, obviously not making the connection between the man they knew as TD Bonaventure and the name Ted Williams. A few started to clap.

Jean Pierre, who stood just aside and behind the lectern, took a step forward and leaned into the microphone, "Again, I'd ask you to please hold your comments and applause until after the formal part of this meeting has concluded."

Ted nodded and mouthed "Thank you" to him, before bellying up to the lectern. He wore the same suit he wore during the formal night and his public toast. His hair was tightly combed and perfectly in place. Gone was his handlebar mustache and the grin he often wore when he spoke in front of people. Even four nights ago, when he was tasked with speaking on behalf of their now deceased captain, at this very same theater, he at least tried to mix some humor into his talk. He was dead serious tonight.

"Thank you," he said in his normal American voice, no longer pretending to have any sort of a British accent. "As the acting captain said, my actual name is Ted Williams. Many of you may know me by my pen name. But I'm not speaking to you as an author or entertainer, but as a member of the Intrepid crew. With the assistance of Dr. Molly Simmons—our resident parasitologist and other recent addition to this committee—the captain wanted me to explain what has been occurring on-board and outside this ship, as it relates to the Rage disease."

While speaking, Ted had been addressing four imaginary points of his audience—something he learned from a speech coach when speaking to large groups—so that it appeared as if he was personally addressing each person in the audience, even though he couldn't see any of their faces. When he glanced to his right and down, he caught a glimpse in his periphery of TJ, still standing just inside the folds of the theater's curtains. She was visible because she was now trying to see Ted, and she acknowledged his gaze with a small glint of a smile... and tears. He quickly flashed back a slight grin and then returned his serious focus to his audience.

She was so sad.

He took a deep breath, recollected his thoughts to make sure he would cover all of the points Jean Pierre had wanted, and then continued. "We have all experienced the so-called Rage disease firsthand, and the effects of the parasite known as *T-Gondii.* What you probably don't know is that everyone who has become symptomatic, and appeared to have gone crazy, was already infected before they boarded this ship. They did not contract this parasite from a bite, or from something they ate on the ship, or even breathing in the air. Again, everyone who was already infected picked up this parasite before they stepped on board. They just didn't know it.

"The disease transformed most of the infected into what we are calling parasitic; in other words, someone controlled by the parasite. This parasite was benign to most people, before a small bacteria, spread by volcanic clouds all over the world, woke up the parasite and caused so many of our fellow passengers and crew to become parasitic and thus seemingly crazy."

This is where Ted diverted somewhat from the truth, at Jean Pierre's insistence. "The good news is that we don't expect any more flare-ups of the disease. Pretty much everyone who was going to contract the disease and become symptomatic has already... become symptomatic. That is showing signs of the crazy behavior."

In truth, Molly explained to the captain's wardroom that they could expect as much as an additional 20% or more of their ship to, at some point in time, become symptomatic. There was just no way for them to tell for sure, without doing a blood test for each person on the ship. And they needed equipment they didn't have for this. Those who were either slightly symptomatic or who didn't pass TJ's smell test were going to be separated from the non-infected. But that would be addressed individually with each person another day.

"I will be happy to answer all of your questions afterwards. So please hold them until then. I return you to the captain. Thank you."

Ted abruptly turned and walked back to his chair. And before the audience could react and begin to disrupt his delivery of this meeting with their questions that they were supposed to hold for the end, Jean Pierre took over.

"Thank you, Mr. Williams. Again, I would ask you to hold all questions and comments until the end of this talk.

"Next, we have a short, five-minute video presentation."

Jean Pierre also abruptly turned from the podium and returned to his seat, just as the lights were dimmed on the stage. The curtains drew back, revealing a large rectangular screen that hung just above the heads of each of the wardroom members, all of whom remained almost motionless in their stage seats. They wouldn't be able to see the video, even if they turned to look at it, because they were too close. Not that any of them needed to see it, as each had previewed it at least once.

A blast of light exploded onto the screen and Ted's *TD Bonaventure* voice erupted from the speakers, narrating scenes from a real-life apocalypse they weren't going to want to hear. Using video clips that Ted, David and Deep had grabbed from previously available satellite broadcasts, TD Bonaventure described a world that had permanently changed in just ten days. All major cities around the world had already fallen or were about to fall to the parasitic animals and people. Normal services were gone: TV and Internet were down, as far as they knew; no planes were flying or trains moving; stores had been emptied, as food and other supplies had stopped being delivered; all communications other than rudimentary radio transmissions were down, including with their head office or any potential ports; and finally, medical services were difficult to find at best because most people were hiding, dead, or had become parasitic.

"For all of these reasons, the crew of the *Intrepid* have decided to remain at sea indefinitely... Or until we can find a safe place to port.

We will continue to work tirelessly to keep you safe, and to survive, even if our families and friends in the outside world do not."

Ted's crude mind kicked in, thinking, We should have played the Rolling Stones' "*You can't Always Get What you Wan*t" at the end.

The movie stopped, the spotlights were brought back up and the stage curtains slowly closed. Jean Pierre rose once again, just as a member of their security team breezed over to Wasano and whispered into his ear. Jean Pierre watched this, while pretending that it wasn't distracting, as he stepped up to the lectern.

Already, there was a loud groundswell of conversations which had burst out around the theater. Many in the audience were sobbing from the video.

"Friends." He held up his hands again to quiet the crowd. "Friends, I know this information is difficult to digest. It was for each of us as well. But it is a fact that the world we presently occupy has completely changed. The good news is that this ship is our safe haven. And until we've identified a safe place to port, this will be our home, for a while."

He knew he should have stopped for a moment or two and let them take a breath. But he thought while they were shell-shocked, it was best if he'd plow through with the rest. They had a lot of time together to process all of this, and it would not happen in one night.

"Because the world around us has changed so much, and so that we can be assured of survival, we all must make changes on this ship. As your acting captain, the one who is in charge of your welfare as long as you're on board, I am instituting some new rules."

He turned because of a loud conversation behind him was taking attention away from him. He glared at his acting security director who was just thanking the guard he was speaking with, and signaled Jean Pierre that he needed to now speak to him. Jean Pierre returned his attention to his audience.

"In a moment, you will each be given a set of rules of conduct, which will help you to understand what will be expected of you during your extended time on board the Intrepid.

"Here are the most important changes... As of today, you are no longer considered guests of this ship; each of you is now a member of my crew. And as a member of my crew, you will at some point be assigned tasks to do. Additionally, because we do not know when or if we will ever get supplies again, our food will be strictly rationed. All the other restaurants will remain closed, and we will all eat out of the same dining room."

He let this sink in, and then continued more slowly. "There will be no misconduct or breaking of any rules. You will not hoard your food or any other of the ship's supplies. Anyone who does not wish to abide by my rules, and make no mistake, these are my rules, will be dropped off on one of the islands, with none of the protections you now enjoy."

Wasano cleared his throat loudly. Jean Pierre cocked his head back and acknowledged that he saw that Wasano was standing and furiously signaling him.

Jean Pierre held one hand out to tell him to wait, and then turned back to his microphone.

"We are now passing out the list of rules and in a moment, we will take questions. Please excuse me."

Jean Pierre stepped away from the lectern, Wasano meeting him part-way.

Although Wasano tried to speak in hushed tones, the theater became incredibly loud, so Wasano spoke louder than he probably should have to be heard. Everyone on stage heard at least his side of their conversation.

"Our fuel tanks are almost empty," he told the acting captain.

"How much time?" Jean Pierre asked.

"At most... five hours."

43

Alone

TJ pulled the door closed behind her and sobbed into her palms. She felt utterly alone.

She found her bed, in a cabin separated by what felt like miles from her husband, when it was only a few decks.

She was absolutely exhausted, having not slept for many days now, even though her new body demanded sleep, and lots of it now. She literally could sleep for a week and it still wouldn't be enough.

As she stared at the ceiling in the dark—she could make out every detail—she longed for her husband and for his touch.

She pulled the necklace out of the folds of her running shorts. The clasp broke and it was the only way she could prevent losing it, and yet keep it close to her. Her fingers ran over each of its intricate curves and angles, knowing its shape and look so intimately now.

She considered the reasons behind Ted buying this: he had thought of her as a warrior, because she had always insisted she was a warrior, taking the job of a warrior, until her fears took that away from her. Now she was afraid of nothing. Almost.

She wished she could go back to being that fearful person.

Her previous fear of animals was a distant concept. The only fears she held were not being able to be with people, without wanting to hurt them. And most of all, she was terrified that she'd never be with her husband again.

She tried to tuck these fears back into the dark recesses of her mind. Before all of this, she was really good at repressing her fears, or at least hiding them so she didn't have to deal with them. So she would try to do this now.

She focused on his face tonight. He looked so handsome, with his perfectly shaved face. Even his mustache was gone. She grinned to the darkness at this.

TJ kissed the necklace, and then placed it above her heart, until finally she drifted off.

Ted let the door to his empty cabin slam shut, and all at once, he felt like he would collapse from fatigue. He'd been working for endless hours on the video project, the monitoring, the endless wardroom discussions, the confabs with Molly and Chloe. But, it was that image of his wife, with tears streaming down her cheeks, that sucked every last bit of energy from him.

When the meeting concluded, he tried to find his wife, but the endless questions poured out and Jean Pierre asked him and the others stay and answer them for an hour. So he did.

After an hour or so, he did what Jean Pierre asked and told the audience that they were concluding the meeting, because the acting captain couldn't be here to attend to a problem on the bridge. So they would have to reconvene again soon. And fellow crew members would be in touch with each of them soon.

They concluded and the wardroom members broke free and met up with Jean Pierre and Niki, who also left early.

That was when they heard the details of the problem. Their fuel problem was real, though not quite as bad as they'd first heard: Niki was able to change the efficiency of some of their systems to buy more time. They also turned off all air conditioning throughout the ship, except in the Wayfarer lounge where all the parasitics were still being held. Even with that, they had maybe a day and a half of fuel left.

It seemed fortuitous that Ted had found the group who had fuel for trade. They made contact and were set to meet in the morning. If all went well, they'd avert one more disaster.

And what a disaster it would be: if they ran out of fuel, not only wouldn't they be able to go anywhere, but their parasitic problem would come back. And even though they had them locked behind doors, there was no way those doors would hold back the strength of two or three of them, much less a few hundred.

Ted looked over at the empty space where TJ should be lying beside him. She'd separated herself from him, out of fear of what she might do. And he was pretty sure that's what she was crying about tonight. His own tears welled up as he patted her side. "I miss you, darling," he whispered.

That's it; I can't sleep, he thought.

He was wired for sound, though his body was exhausted. He couldn't sleep now, even though his body demanded it.

He often found peace and the ability to sleep when he wrote. So he grabbed his Mont Blanc box and pulled out the pen she had given him for their anniversary. Right when this whole thing started... It was on Day Five, the day I lost her...

A couple of tears crept out, and he furiously wiped them away.

Ted pulled out his journal, and reread his last notation. He examined his pen, with "T.D. Bonaventure" embossed on its shaft.

He clicked off the pen cap and slipped it onto the back of the pen.

Another tear burst out and was immediately wiped away.

He paused for a moment, thought about it, and began to write.

The Journal of TD Bonaventure
DAY FIVE cont...

What's Next?

The final chapter of the trilogy
SYMPTOMATIC: MADNESS Chronicles III

Go to:

http://mlbanner.com/madness3

Did you like PARASITIC?

In case you weren't aware, I'm an independent writer who relies on ratings and reviews to help get the word out about my books. This is why reviews are so important to me and why I truly need your help. If you enjoyed *PARASITIC*, please let others know, by leaving even a short review.
Thank you!

Please
leave a review here:

http://www.mlbanner.com/madness-review2

FREE BOOKS

Sign up for ML Banner's *Apocalyptic Updates* (VIP Readers list) and get a free copy of one of my best-selling books, just for joining.

In addition, you'll have access to our VIP Reader's Library, with at least four additional freebies.

Simply go here:

http://mlbanner.com/free

(give us an email address to get your free book)

Who is ML Banner?

Michael "ML" Banner is an award winning, USA Today Bestselling author of Apocalyptic Thrillers

Michael writes what he loves to read: apocalyptic thrillers, which thrust regular people into extraordinary circumstances, where their actions may determine not only their own fate, but that of the world. His work is traditionally published and self-published.

Often his thrillers are set in far-flung places, as Michael uses his experiences from visiting other countries—some multiple times—over the years. The picture was from a transatlantic cruise that became the foreground of his award-winning *MADNESS Series*.

When not writing his next book, you might find Michael (and his wife) traveling abroad or reading a Kindle, with his toes in the water (name of his publishing company), of a beach on the Sea of Cortez (Mexico).

Want more from M.L. Banner?

MLBanner.com

Receive FREE books & *Apocalyptic Updates* - A monthly publication highlighting discounted books, cool science/discoveries, new releases, reviews, and more

Connect with M.L. Banner

Keep in contact – I would love to hear from you!

Email: michael@mlbanner.com
Facebook: facebook.com/authormlbanner
Twitter: @ml_banner

Books by M.L. Banner

For a complete list of Michael's current and upcoming books: MLBanner.com/new-projects/

ASHFALL APOCALYPSE

Ashfall Apocalypse (01)
A world-wide apocalypse has just begun.

Leticia's Soliloquy (An Ashfall Apocalypse Short)
(Exclusively available from a link at book #1 end)

Collapse (02)
As temps plummet, a new foe seeks revenge.

Compton's Epoch (An Ashfall Apocalypse Short)
Compton reveals what makes him tick.
(Exclusively available from a link at book #2 end)

Perdition (03)
Sometimes the best plan is to run. But where?

MADNESS CHRONICLES

MADNESS (01)
A parasitic infection causes mammals to attack.

PARASITIC (02)
The parasitic infection doesn't just affect animals.

SYMPTOMATIC (03)
When your loved one becomes symptomatic, what do you do?

The Final Outbreak (Books 1 - 3)
The end is coming. It's closer than you think. And it's real.

HIGHWAY SERIES

True Enemy (Short)
An unlikely hero finds his true enemy.
(USA Today Bestselling short only on mlbanner.com)

Highway (01)
A terrorist attack forces siblings onto a highway,
and an impossible journey home.

Endurance (02)
Enduring what's next might cost them everything.

Resistance (03)
Coming Soon

STONE AGE SERIES

Stone Age (01)
The next big solar event separates family and friends, and begins a new Stone Age.

Desolation (02)
To survive the coming desolation will require new friendships.

Max's Epoch (Stone Age Short)
Max wasn't born a prepper, he was forged into one. (This short is exclusively available on MLBanner.com)

Hell's Requiem (03)
One man struggles to survive and find his way to a scientific sanctuary.

Time Slip (Stand Alone)
The time slip was his accident; can he use it to save the one he loves?

Cicada (04)
Cicada's scientific community... the world's only hope, or its end?

Made in the USA
Columbia, SC
22 May 2024